Short Stories

Volume One

Neal James

PNEUMA SPRINGS PUBLISHING UK

First Published in 2009 by:
Pneuma Springs Publishing

Short Stories - Volume One
Copyright © 2009   Neal James
ISBN: 978-1-905809-60-8

This is a work of fiction. Names, characters, places and incidents are either products of the author's imagination or are used fictitiously. Any resemblance to actual events or locales or persons, living or dead, save those clearly in the public domain, is purely coincidental.

Pneuma Springs Publishing
A Subsidiary of Pneuma Springs Ltd.
7 Groveherst Road, Dartford Kent, DA1 5JD.
E: admin@pneumasprings.co.uk
W: www.pneumasprings.co.uk

A catalogue record for this book is available from the British Library.

Published in the United Kingdom. All rights reserved under International Copyright Law. Contents and/or cover may not be reproduced in whole or in part without the express written consent of the publisher.

Short Stories

Volume One

Dedication

Gavin Jones   1922 – 2001
More of an inspiration than he could ever have known.

ACKNOWLEDGEMENTS

Thanks to Lisa and Rob for their time in proof reading the final drafts, and to my wife Lynn for listening through the months of preparation.

Appreciation also extends to Sally and Kevin Hindson for their understanding and patience.

I am once again indebted to the members of the Storiesville Writers' Community, without whose constant and consistent critique these stories would have remained in manuscript form.

Once more I extend my thanks to Vivian Akinpelu and the team of Pneuma Springs Publishing. Their advice and expertise over the past nine months has been an invaluable guide in the minefield of commercial writing.

CONTENTS

A Deal of Trouble
It all seemed too good to be true, and for Mike it certainly did turn out that way, especially when his crippled leg mended.

Paws For Breath
Did Ollie have a pedigree? Well, let's just put it this way, if he could talk he wouldn't have spoken to either of us.

Battle Royal
How many more times would they have to confront each other before the conflict finally came to an end?

Flight of Fancy
George's novel way of pensioning himself off holds a surprise for the one person who should have known him best.

Chance of a Lifetime
Like cat and dog they were, but Julia finally gave her brother Jack his come-uppance in life's lottery.

Tell Laura I Love Her
Terry and Laura met at a disco. He was shy and reserved and she brought him out of himself. All the more heartbreaking when they finally realised the true nature of their relationship.

A Golden Opportunity
Rosemary had struggled on since the death of her husband, but her son's chance discovery provided them with a way out of their drudgery.

Bull in a China Shop
Terry's clumsiness had always held him back, but now he had Sandra as his girlfriend; would he be able to shake it off?

Dear Mom
Travelling can be a real pain sometimes, and when you've got stacks to do your mom is your best friend.

Finders Keepers
A deserted station, a thick fog and now where on earth was his wife? James Taylor was lost but he knew exactly where he was.

Loose Ends
They seemed to be the ideal couple, but ambition got in the way, and attempt an at reconciliation came very late in the day.

The Best Summer
A family story set in an age long gone, when times and pleasures were far simpler, but when troubles were still the same.

Hit and Run
David had no idea how he'd driven on to the motorway, nor why he was travelling so fast, but the blood on his forehead told him that it couldn't be a good sign.

Falling
Falling doesn't kill you; falling is easy - it's the impact at the end that's fatal.

Out of the Frying Pan
Burt Travers was the company hatchet man and Mark was his next target. Fortune gave the victim a way out but it didn't always favour the brave.

A Shot in the Dark
He had always taken care with planning, but coming up against an opponent as meticulous as himself was not what Sharpe had anticipated.

At Your Command
You would have thought that a set of rules handed down by the boss would be easy enough to follow. Not for this man.

And Did These Feet
Simon's hitherto humdrum life is about to take an unexpected turn when he meets a very unfortunate pedestrian.

The Cracker
Just when you think there's nothing left to achieve, a perfect opportunity for padding out your retirement pops up.

A Sporting Chance
When you're down and out, looking a gift horse in the mouth is not advisable. Colin didn't know what he was grabbing, but he grabbed it anyway.

Sticking the Knife In
She had to go, there was nothing else for it. But which 'she' would it be?

Race Against Time
Barry shouldn't have gone to the match up north, they lost 5-0 anyway; but then he never would have met Danielle would he?

Tommy
Tommy Watkinson was back, but what did he want, why now, and what was he doing talking to Dave's son Paul?

A Shot Too Far
Maninga was holding all of the cards, and was about to deal Sharpe a hand that he would rather not have played.

Bitter Sweet
When her mum was diagnosed with terminal cancer, Liz thought that she was going to be alone. That was until she found the photograph.

Foot in the Door
Never step beyond what you know. The rewards were too great for David to ignore. Ironic that he was completely innocent of the job they nailed him for.

Facing the Demon
Brian Powell's life lay in tatters until he met Charlotte - she gave him a reason to survive.

The Visitors
Ray didn't want to save humanity, it was far too big a job for someone like him, but the old couple who came calling did not agree.

Spring Eternal
Stuck in the middle of nowhere, and in the house of a host who seemed to be just that little bit too helpful. Rob was stepping blindly into the spider's web.

Boxed In
An almost perfect insurance scam comes disastrously unstuck in the most unexpected way.

Reggie's Revenge
A classic example of the mouse biting the cats.

Marks on the Wall
Dennis Marks knows that the death of Susan North was an inside job, but proving it was going to be quite a different matter.

Killing Me Softly
Gary was a hell-raiser heading steeply down life's hill. Jane put the brakes on him and turned his life around, but fate had other ideas.

Secret Life
Dennis Marks' investigation into the death of Thomas Weston is anything but a run of the mill homicide.

Identifying Marks
The second instalment in Dennis Marks' search for the truth about Thomas Weston.

Footsteps in the Darkness
The culmination of Marks' investigation into the circumstances of his grandfather's death.

A Deal of Trouble

Mike knew as soon as he'd made the tackle that something was terribly wrong. He'd heard the 'snap' but there was a momentary delay until the agonising pain hit him, and when he looked down at his mangled right leg he realised that his football career was over. He was 20 years old, and one of the best players in the club's academy with a great future in prospect – all that was gone now. Three years down the line he was part way through an accountancy qualification in a job that he hated, but at least the pay wasn't too bad. He'd been out for a drink with friends one evening and was walking home when this guy stepped out of the shadows and blocked his way. At first he thought it was an attempted mugging and set himself to counter an attack with his walking stick, but none came.

"You can play again." the figure said. Mike couldn't make out his features and started to get an uneasy feeling.

"What?"

"You want to play again, don't you?"

"Well, yes……..but………"

"OK, how much do you want to play?"

"I'd sell my soul to make it in the League, it's always been my dream."

"Done, I'll be in touch."

He stepped back into the shadows and disappeared into the night. Mike stood for a while trying to make sense of what he had just seen, but then went home and thought no more about it. The following morning when he got up he found that he was able to stand unaided, and that walking was no longer a problem. He had his breakfast, phoned in sick and took a football out to the park instead. He started very carefully with some gentle jogging at first, but soon realised that the leg was as good as new. The nets around the goalposts had been left out, so he tried a variety of shots from different angles. Not only could he hit the target every time, but was now able to dip and swerve the ball – he couldn't do that before.

He managed to get a game in the local Sunday League team run by his older brother at the weekend and ran the midfield, setting up a host of chances for the forwards. The team won 7-0 and he scored twice. As he was coming off at the end, Mike was approached by a scout for one of the local league teams, and was invited for a trial the following week. The club was languishing in the lower divisions but there was no hesitation in accepting the offer – this could be his big chance.

The trial went very well and the club offered a twelve month contract subject to him becoming match fit. Over the next six weeks, and following a strict regime of diet and training, Mike was back to his level of fitness before the accident. They put him in the reserves at first, but it quickly became apparent that he was far too good and he made his first team debut against Port Vale on November 17th. The day couldn't have gone better and a 3-0 victory was followed by rave reviews in the local papers. The team hit the top of the league at the end of February but had to settle for a play-off place for promotion. By the end of the season he had scored 19 goals from midfield out of a team total of 82. They hadn't lost a single game since he joined.

The post-season matches saw victory against Swansea in a two leg semi final, giving them a trip to Wembley where they would play Oldham. Mike was untouchable and the opposition didn't know how to deal with him. This was the showcase for newly found skills, and his free kicks from around the penalty area caused havoc in the Oldham defence. The game was over by half time with the team leading 4-0, and they ran out winners 6-2. The post-match celebrations were all about him and even the extended climb up to the new royal box for medals presented no problem. He wasn't tired and hadn't even broken sweat.

It wasn't until he was coming back down the steps that he noticed the figure. It appeared anonymously in black amidst a bright spring afternoon, and no-one else seemed to notice. Mike shivered and a cold feeling permeated his whole body. He stepped past the guy, vaguely recognising him, but heard him speak as he did so.

"Well done, Mike."

He looked round but the figure had gone, and he wondered if he had imagined the whole thing. It took the shine off the day and he couldn't summon up the enthusiasm for the lap of honour, but the manager made him go anyway. Mike couldn't hear the cheering and the chanting of his name, and several team mates took exception to his aloofness. The figure appeared again at a post-season city centre tour the following week and again no-one else seemed to notice him, but Mike could hear a voice calling his name from the side of the street.

"I gave it, and I can take it away," it said. "I'll be coming for you, Mike – a deal is a deal."

He panicked and recalled the conversation after his night out earlier in the year. What had he said? 'I'd sell my soul to make it in the League'. What was this guy? Had he come for Mike's soul? Surely not – things like that just didn't happen. He tried to shake the experience off, but it knocked his confidence and friends noticed a change in his manner. Mike went through the summer break without seeing the apparition again but it reappeared on the first day of the new season in a home game against Coventry. He was terrible – his passing was off target, his positioning was all over the place and he even missed a penalty. A 0-0 draw was enough to keep the fans off his back for the day, but whether it would last long he didn't know. The figure was in the crowd as the team came off, and beckoned to him. He walked over, drawn to it and unable to resist.

"It won't be long Mike, a deal's a deal."

"No, I'm not ready," he whispered, afraid that someone might hear. "It's too soon."

He recovered his composure and his form returned to normal. The team did well and the season closed with the team once more at Wembley in a play-off final, and a pulsating game against Sheffield United saw them promoted after a 3-2 win, with Mike scoring the opening goal direct from a free kick. The climb to the royal box didn't bring any memories until he had collected his medal and was turning to go down the steps. The dark figure stepped forward from the crowd, and for the first time Mike saw his face. He had never seen anything so hideous before, and as a bony hand reached out towards him he stepped back involuntarily. Arms reached out to try to catch him as he went over the rail, but he slipped through them like a bar of soap. The fall was over thirty feet and Mike was aware of twisting and turning in the air as he tried to grab hold of anything to slow down the rate of descent.

He hit the bedroom floor with a dull thud, and awoke bathed in sweat. His mother was at the door knocking to see if he was alright and he groggily told her he was OK, explaining that he probably had one too many the night before. So it was all a dream, and an immense feeling of relief swept over him – perhaps working in an office was not so bad after all. Having showered and dressed, he headed downstairs for breakfast. Looking at the clock he realised that he had overslept, and that the bus would be gone if he didn't hurry. Grabbing a piece of toast, he picked up his briefcase and hurried out of the door. The bus was just pulling up at the stop when Mike turned the corner of the street, and he had to run to catch it.

He had sat down in the empty upper section of the bus and was reading his newspaper, when he realised to his annoyance that in the rush to get out he had forgotten his walking stick. An uneasy feeling crept over him as he became aware that he had run for the bus, and moreover that he had caught it without the slightest effort. Mike suddenly knew that he was no longer alone and, turning around with a sense of foreboding, his gaze was met by the same face from his Wembley dream.

"It's time, Mike, it's time……………."

PAWS FOR BREATH

We had moved into our first house in 1976, and it was during this period that we first experienced the 'pleasures' of living with a member of the feline fraternity. His name was Ollie, a Burmese Blue and he belonged to some friends who were going to visit family in Australia. It was to be a very enlightening five weeks.

Ollie needed somewhere to crash for the duration, and I had suggested that we might be interested. We had no idea what a Burmese Blue was, as I had considered all cats to be out of the same mould but finished in a variety of colours. Ollie was the bee's knees. Tom and Barbara brought all his bits and pieces over on the Friday evening prior to their departure, and Ollie was freed from the confines of his carrying case to inspect the house. He put his glasses on (bifocals of course), took out his notebook and gold-plated Parker and, starting with the downstairs back sitting room, commenced his inspection like some feline estate agent. We followed him around the house at a respectful distance (you don't like to cramp the style of a professional, do you?), looking anxiously for some sign of approval, but he was giving nothing away.

Ollie was an aristocrat. 'Ollie' wasn't his proper name of course, it was short for Lord Oliver of Some-thing-or-other of Somewhere-abouts, and he had a pedigree as long as the M1. Being Burmese, his ancestors probably got caught up in the conflicts at the time of Genghis Khan, were captured and served the warlord loyally for many years. This would have been rewarded in due course by freedom, and the family's emigration to the new world in Europe, where they eventually settled down in the Normandy region of France.

After a number of generations working their way up the French nobility league table, they finally made it into the premiership via a play-off final against Famille D'Orleans United, which had gone to penalties after extra time. This caught the eye of a minor noble by the name of William of

Normandy, and they were invited to the away fixture against Hastings Athletic managed by Harold Godwinson, for the European Cup. The rest, of course is history. An overwhelming victory in 1066 was marred only by home supporters throwing rock cakes at the victorious team. This wouldn't have been so bad except for the fact that they were actually made from rocks.

Thus Ollie's family had made it into the big time, and he never let us forget it. Having said that, we were awarded four paw prints (the maximum is five), he said his discreet farewells to Barbara, ignored Tom and curled up on the settee for a kip. That was when the fun started.

He wasn't much of an outdoor cat, and tended to stay within the confines of the house or back garden. What he did require at all times was full and unrestricted access to the entire property, and this was made clear to us from the first evening when we shut up shop for the night. Having tidied up, lights were turned off, doors were locked and we went to bed leaving him shut in the downstairs back sitting room with fresh water, food and all his bits and pieces. He howled, long and loud. Pillows were useless. It was the kind of howl which would have penetrated the finest double glazing. We gave up after half an hour. He joined us and slept at the bottom of our bed, happy in the knowledge that we understood clearly how the land lay. You had to keep your toes tucked in though, as they tended to be regarded as toys, and his claws were very sharp. His period with us was full of incident as we were going through a program of renovating the property; Ollie found himself in his element.

Whilst we had all the floorboards up and the house was a building site, we decided to rewire. My father-in-law provided the know-how but the labouring was all down to me. Ollie came into his own here. He acted as project manager, reporting directly to my wife, and his supervisory skills were legendary. Every piece of ring main and lighting cable had to be inspected prior to installation, and he didn't even need to work from drawings.

Those who have ever laid new ring main cable will know what an awkward piece of work it can be. Unless you get it flat to the wall and all the kinks removed, you have the devil of a job pinning it to the brickwork. Well, this drum of cable was the granddaddy of the lot. It refused to lie down, turned in its sleep, kicked off the clips already in place and generally acted as if it owned the place. We got it right in the end, but when you are feeding the stuff between floors it comes into its own, since you can't see whether or not it has twisted itself or, worse still, snagged on the nearest convenient protuberance. Ollie was no help at all here. No doubt he thought that he was making a significantly positive contribution to the project, but when you are trying to pull ring main through a wall for a spur socket in the next room, the last thing you expect is a cat sitting on the far side pulling back on the other end.

We couldn't understand why the cable was stuck, each time it was given a tug something snagged. A look into the kitchen revealed nothing but a cat going through its ablutions, and we gave it another go, but the result was the same. It wasn't until this pantomime had gone through several scenes that we decided Ollie might be involved. I returned to the front room, but instead of trying the cable, walked immediately back into the kitchen to find him with the other end of the cable in his mouth ready for the next round of the tug-o-war. Cats don't usually wear pants, but Ollie got caught with his well and truly down that day.

His five week stay with us coincided with most of the major structural work in the downstairs rooms, and what he lacked in practical skills he made up for as resident comedian. The plastering on the walls in the back sitting room left a lot to be desired, so we decided to wallboard them instead. These boards come in sheets measuring 8' x 4' and are the most stupid building materials ever invented. They have absolutely no idea how to behave and spend all their time flopping around looking for somewhere inconvenient to fall. You can only handle one of them at a time due to their size, and cutting them with anything else but a Stanley knife is not recommended. At first they scared the life out of Ollie because they turned up wherever he wanted to be, but once they were flat on the floor he could sit on them and give them a good talking to, safe in the knowledge that all they could do was listen with that annoyed look on their faces that you only normally get with naughty children.

Cutting each board resulted in a spiral of waste material shooting off to one side of the knife, and Ollie decided that this was his opportunity to get his own back by attacking this random piece. He constantly got in my way, coming close to the knife blade on more than one occasion. Finally, after appearing under my armpit for the umpteenth time, I gave him a firm push to move him out of danger. He lost his footing on the board's shiny surface and spun gracefully, with legs splayed, down to the other end of the sheet. At that end, my wife turned him quickly round and shoved him back to where I sat waiting. Back he came again rotating gently as he desperately tried to regain his balance. He finally managed to engineer a dismount off the side of the wallboard, and staggered off to regain the small part of his dignity which we had not stolen from him.

Funny, but he kept very much out of the way after that, preferring to watch from afar atop the tallest piece of furniture he could find. He'd still offer advice and the occasional sarcastic comment but we ignored him, leaving him to sulk in silence. It's a good job he was only with us for the five weeks – I don't know how we'd have coped for much longer.

They say that curiosity killed the cat, and with this individual it was a wonder that he had any of his nine lives to take home with him. You couldn't leave any door open or the lid off anything whilst he was around, and Lynn found this out the hard way one weekend. With both of us out at work during the week, the bulk of our washing was done on a Saturday morning and it was on one of these days that Ollie went missing. When you're babysitting a pedigree cat the last thing you want to happen is that he gets lost, and we were starting to get very worried when he hadn't turned up by lunchtime, particularly since his stomach was one of the prime movers in his life.

We hadn't noticed the whining at first, and when the normal noise emanating from a Burmese is comparable to a pneumatic drill with a cold, we ignored it for a while. It's like the squeak in your car which you ignore because it doesn't seem to mean anything – eventually you get fed up and try to find out what it is. We scoured the downstairs, never thinking to check inside the washing basket, but there he sat looking up in such a pathetic manner. He had clearly jumped in, settled down amongst some towels and fallen asleep. It was only when his digestive system registered a lack of input since breakfast that he woke up. He didn't do it again though.

The loft was worse because I couldn't reach him. He shinned up the step ladder, climbed over my shoulder as I was coming down, and disappeared into the gloom. We hadn't got a light fitted up there at that time, so all I had was a torch. The semi where we lived was not completely separated from next door, and Ollie scampered through the gap for a good look around. He wouldn't come down and without floor boards I didn't fancy chasing him all over someone else's property, so we had to leave him up there until he decided that the game was over. When he did actually grace us with his presence again he was so distraught that he'd been left up there all alone, that he felt the need to superglue himself to one of us for the rest of the day. Although he was only with us for a short period of time, we did miss him when he went home, and if we hadn't been so heavily involved in working on the house, we may not have waited so long to have cats of our own.

BATTLE ROYAL

*I*t was becoming less and less clear if there would ever be any resolution to the conflict, and sitting down to attempt a diplomatic solution had proved fruitless on many occasions in the past. It was as if there was some suicidal determination to stand and fight to the last man, and it just seemed to be a complete waste of time and resources, not to say manpower. The struggle had been going on for ages now and there didn't seem to be any end in sight. Both sides had made advances and been forced into retreat on a number of occasions, only to regroup and try again. There had been casualties of course, but no more than could have been reasonably foreseen at the start of the conflict, and several of the encounters had resulted in a situation of stalemate after which both sides had withdrawn to lick their wounds and reassess their situations.

The King was in a dilemma, and his tactics were becoming a little worn and predictable. Perhaps there was a spy in his camp, reporting back to the other side on all matters relating to the dispute between them and battle plans for the next round of the campaign. He could only hope that his opposite number was suffering the same logistical problems, and there was no doubt that the sides were evenly matched. There was never any problem with resources and both rarely had any difficulties with recruitment – there were always those willing to throw themselves into the carnage. Why was there this constant conflict of good against evil? Why was it all so black and white? The battle lines had been drawn long ago in the mists of time, and it was one of those situations where you would be hard pressed to find someone who knew the exact reasons for the dispute in the first place, as nothing had ever been written down. It was now a matter of honour passed down unreasoningly from father to son, and no quarter could be given notwithstanding the code of chivalry which existed at the time. He needed advice and sought out the local bishop.

The bishop had returned to his palace after observing the latest set of skirmishes. He was reluctant to get involved in the cut and thrust of the matter, but as the King's advisor on matters secular and political he was inevitably drawn into the fight, and whilst he wanted no part of any bloodshed his loyalty to the crown was absolute. They talked for many hours and the King felt in no better position following their discussion; he decided to sleep on the matter.

The Queen had already dined when he returned to the royal apartments that evening, and was sitting in the great hall with her entourage. She worried to see him in such an unsettled state and asked if there was anything that she could help him with. He had read of Queens like Boudica in the past, who had led her troops into battle in such a bellicose manner that she became the scourge of the nation, but could not see how his wife could fulfil a similar role and so politely declined the offer. They sat for a while discussing matters of state and possible solutions to the current impasse, but no firm tactical changes emerged, and he kissed her goodnight and went to bed.

The following day he summoned his knights and reviewed the previous day's events to see if any possibilities emerged for ending the war in his favour. One or two gaps in the battle plan emerged, and after reviewing reports from the previous day he came up with a few tactical changes. Hopefully these would rectify any errors which were apparent that afternoon. He had to be careful to keep them to himself in the light of his suspicions of a spy in the camp, and returned to the bishop later that day to go over plans for the next meeting with the other side.

The cleric was impressed and upbeat about the proposed alterations, and suggested in addition that the knights be used as a shock force once the infantry had been engaged, perhaps coming in as a flanking manoeuvre using a setting sun at their backs as a surprise tactic. The King had not considered this, thanked the bishop for his advice and returned to the castle to summon the knights for a council of war. He also told them to polish up their armour in the hope that reflection from a low sun would confuse the enemy.

He refrained from finalising his battle timing until the last possible moment to prevent word leaking out to the enemy, and did not assemble his forces until late in the afternoon. The infantry were formed up in line and marched out on to the battlefield in front of the knights. The bishop made his appearance along with one of his fellow clerics who had come along to observe the conflict – both bore arms just in case they were needed. It appeared to the King that these battles always started in the same way, and it seemed to be his turn to move first this time. He was very careful not to rush into the conflict in any precipitate manner, and received a very curt reminder from the other side to make his move. The infantrymen were brought to attention and marched forwards in their traditional manner, mere pawns in a much greater plan that they probably didn't understand. Their entire future rested upon victory in the conflict, and the fall of the King would be disaster for all of them.

Theirs was not a role which allowed for backward movement once they had engaged the enemy, and they were amongst the first of any casualties every time, but they clearly understood this and none of them complained. The encounter dragged on during the evening and into the following day with the usual minor successes and failures, except this time the King thought he had seen a chink in the formation of the opposition. Sending out two knights in an early morning probing skirmish he harried the opposing King and his infantry in an attempt to isolate him in his castle. The raid was repulsed, but not until reinforcements had been brought in from the other side of the battlefield, and this exposed the whole of the left flank to a lightning movement involving the bishop, who had seen his opportunity for glory and, surprisingly, the Queen, who had donned a suit of armour and led the attacking force.

The Knights quickly withdrew from their attack on the castle and cut a swathe across the field through the line of now slow-moving infantry in support of the onslaught. With the pawns in the struggle falling like ninepins and now out of the way, the area was clear for a final push for victory across the entire rank and file of the opposition lines. It was a catastrophe for the enemy formation, and although the other King regrouped his now rapidly diminishing forces, he saw his own Queen captured whilst retreating to their castle for protection. She went down fighting amongst a sea of infantry bent on destruction, and in a late charge to the end of the battlefield his knights were cut off and isolated. He stood alone in the face of approaching enemy forces but was not about to surrender or resign himself to the inevitable. With only a couple of knights still at his disposal a rousing final confrontation was fought, and through the use of consummate skill he was able to fend off wave after wave of attacks, and although it did seem briefly that he would survive another day, in the end it was all too much for him and the final act was delivered with a cry of jubilation.

"Checkmate! Beat you, beat you, beat you dad!"

"Ok, Ok it's only a game of chess. Keep your hair on."

"Shall we play again? Come on, I can do it again………..please."

There was no doubt about it, he was getting better each time. Goodness knows what he'd be like when he reached the age of ten. Perhaps buying him that chess book by Leonard Barden was not such as good idea after all; maybe reading it himself would have been a better idea.

FLIGHT OF FANCY

He should have known that there was something in the air from the moment that his toothbrush did a suicide dive into the laundry basket. Looking back now, the signs had been there for a while and he had been just too blind and wrapped up in his work to see them.

George had worked at the bank for nearly twenty years, and had risen through the ranks by a combination of sheer hard work and a flair for information technology. He had been instrumental in setting up all of the financial systems and the computer networking throughout the country. Now they had sidelined him into an area which they felt best suited his abilities. What that had meant in practice, was that his new boss' son needed a job, and George had become the target. The lad had come through university, had a degree and clearly knew his stuff - of that there was no doubt - but George had the bank's name etched into him – it was his reason for getting up in the morning.

Approaching fifty, he found his options for alternative employment becoming limited, and he suspected that after a suitable period he would be quietly 'pensioned off'. He was normally a placid man and his employer was probably relying upon this fact in his redeployment. Well he wasn't about to go without a fanfare. He knew the bank's control systems inside out and that they relied upon the integrity and loyalty of the staff to minimise any risk. That had worked very well before his previous boss had been 'retired' in favour of the current incumbent. This guy was one of life's delegators and loathe to dirty his hands with mundane tasks. Getting a scam past him shouldn't present too much of a problem.

George decided that he would use the old building society account which his parents had set up for him whilst he was a child. It was untraceable, and as long as the amounts transferred into it were not large enough to draw any attention, it would be very unlikely that it could be discovered. He calculated that a small amount of less than £10,000 could be siphoned off on a daily basis without anyone becoming suspicious, bearing in mind the millions traded every day. They had given him the 180 days notice required by his contract of employment of any changes relating to his duties, and careful planning over the next six months could net him something in the region of £1,000,000. This gave him the time to set up an intermediate account at an offshore bank to handle a regular movement of funds in preparation for his departure.

No-one had removed any of his security clearances; all of his passwords to the financial systems had been left in place. He had access to his boss's files as the man was too stupid to realise that George had watched him at his keyboard enough times to work out the only password he used. Setting up the funds transfer hadn't been a problem, and as all the banking reconciliations fell under his control he would have no difficulty in concealing the operation by use of the overnight credit transfer system. Nevertheless, he spent an anxious period whilst the first batch of transactions were processed, expecting at any moment that he would be ordered to the boardroom under escort. It didn't happen, and things just carried on as normal – at the end of the first week his building society account balance had risen by £49,568.19.

He would have to ensure that he made no changes to his daily routines which were likely to draw attention to him. Of course all the staff were very sympathetic to his situation, and there were even murmurings of a letter to head office in condemnation of the action taken by the new boss. George was very quick to discourage anything of the sort, saying that he didn't wish to be the instigator of any trouble and that they should all look out for themselves instead of fighting his hopeless cause. This fitted in perfectly with his mild-mannered character; it was vital that he remain anonymous.

Now that the process had been put in place and was working correctly, it was time to plan an escape route. With a figure of around a million pounds at his disposal, he could emigrate to some South American country with no extradition ties to the UK and merely disappear. He had kept his passport up to date, and language would not be a problem as he had studied Spanish to "A" level and had a flair for foreign studies at school. He would merely prepare for departure at short notice with hand luggage only – anything else could be bought once he arrived at his destination. His flight tickets would be purchased one week in advance, and he would merely not turn up for work on the appropriate day – it would be assumed that he was unwell, and who could blame him in the circumstances?

The scheme had been running for around ten weeks when the internal auditors arrived. George was nearly caught off guard and hadn't expected them so soon after their previous visit. They said it was just down to a number of senior staff changes throughout the bank, and that the check would be cursory at best due to a full system review having taken place some six months earlier. They were scheduled to be on site for one week only, but there was always the chance that their materiality routines and random data samples would pick up one or more of his transfers. His head told him that this wasn't likely bearing in mind the vast number of transactions going through the system on a daily basis, but his heart was running at overdrive and he could be in danger of blowing the whole scam.

This seemed to be the longest week of his life. He had to remain calm, be at his desk at all the correct times, smile his usual smile when asked for any information by the audit team, and generally go through the kind of hell he wouldn't even have wished on his new boss. At the end of the visit his meeting with the team manager lasted the customary half hour, resulted in a clean report and after the usual shaking of hands and exchange of pleasantries, departure with the parting 'See you next time'. George smiled, escorted him to the door and thought 'No you won't mate'.

This galvanized him into action, and a quick check on the building society account revealed a balance of £499,689.25 He now felt that he would be safe after the auditors had filed the report, a draft of which he had already seen, but he would need to be cautious around the boss' son who would be taking over his duties within the next couple of weeks. That would still leave him a reasonable amount of time during the handover period to ensure that the transfers were still going through as normal, but after that he would be left to concentrate upon the final timing of his exit route.

George now needed to make sure that the money in the building society would be accessible without any questions being asked, so the time came to organise an automated transfer to the offshore bank account which he had set up at the outset. These banks didn't ask too many questions if all the paperwork looked in order, and a mandate signed by him would merely be honoured at the building society end without further recourse. He would simply clear the new account when he arrived in South America, and then disappear.

Time ticked on to the end of his six month period, and he estimated that the final figure would be in the region of £1,200,000 – a final gesture of defiance of £300,000 on the last day appealed to his sense of humour, and by the time that anyone noticed he would be half a world away and untouchable with £1.5 million and a new life. The level of confidence took him by surprise - the old saying of the worm turning came to mind, and he was sorely tempted to deliver a personal message to his boss but he needed the cushion of a time delay to effect his escape, and any show of bravado now would just draw attention to him.

The morning of departure arrived, and it was with a real sense of regret that he stood in the hall of his house with the taxi waiting outside and looked around him for the last time. He had all his travel documentation and a confirmation from the offshore bank that all the funds had been received. All the bills had been paid, and there was no likelihood of anyone from work tracing him, as he had removed all items of personal property from his office the previous week after everyone else had left for the day. The drive to the airport was uneventful, and in no time at all he had boarded his flight and was on his way. Once in the air he breathed a huge sigh of relief and ordered a scotch from the air hostess. She asked him if he needed anything further, but he just shook his head and smiled as he wondered what his wife was going to think when she came home to find him gone.

CHANCE OF A LIFETIME

*T*hey just didn't get on. It just seemed to be that way with brothers and sisters. From early childhood there were always arguments between them, and usually when either mum or dad stepped in it would result in one of them being either forced to apologise or lose some privilege or other. It was worse now. Since the car crash which deprived them of their parents, Julia's brother Jack had seemed to make it his aim in life to cause as many problems as possible for her. He had always been a spendthrift, and when dad left control of the family printing business to her, she threw herself into the job with a passion.

A university degree in English together with five years spent under her father's expert tuition in the ways of the printing world had given her a sound basis for moving the Derby firm onwards, and she had succeeded remarkably well in a short time. This went down like a dose of the flu with Jack. Despite her father's attempts to bring them both into the business, he had done nothing himself to earn any share of the company's success. Mum and dad had made financial provision for him in their wills, but after the fatal accident which ended their lives, Jack had blown his portion in a very short time.

He had made several increasingly strident demands for money, and she had helped him along at first, but now, after a drunken escapade last weekend which saw him spend a night in police cells, Julia had reached the end of her tether. It was time for him to be taught a lesson. The problem was in selecting the best method of bringing him to his senses. Some weeks had passed without a viable idea presenting itself, but as she sat in front of the TV one Saturday evening, the lottery draw came on. She sat up from the usual lounging position she adopted, and the grain of a plan germinated in her brain.

What if she recorded the program from one week, bought the winning numbers from that week for the next draw, and played the tape the following Saturday whilst he was in the room? It would be easy to persuade him to buy a ticket – he'd wasted plenty of money gambling before. If she chose a week with only one winner it would appear that he'd hit the jackpot. Weeks went by without a success, but sure enough, late one Saturday evening the winning numbers were announced, with one lucky ticket holder scooping a rollover of £7.8 million. This was it. Julia rewound the tape and replayed it to make sure that it had recorded OK. Now all that remained was to get him to buy the ticket.

Bearing in mind his chronic cash shortage, this was quite simple – she even persuaded him into letting her pick the numbers! The next bit wasn't so easy however. She had to make sure that he stayed in on the following Saturday (his birthday) so that he watched her tape of the draw rather than the live one from the correct week. She hated his mates, they were a bunch of drunken kids, but a free party was just what would attract them, whilst keeping Jack at home. Now she could pull it off. All it needed was some food and drink shopping at the local Tesco and all would be ready.

It all went very well. Of course Julia would have to invite some of her friends or it would look suspicious, and she could always tip them the wink as to the real purpose – Jack wasn't exactly the flavour of the month with any of the local female population. When Saturday came, she had to hide her nervousness very carefully. Busying herself with preparations helped – he was useless in the kitchen anyway.

The party was remarkably restrained, with all guests behaving so responsibly, that she had begun to feel a little guilty about the trick she was about to play. That changed when she overheard him complaining to his mates about how he had been swindled out of his fair share of the family inheritance, and how he intended to find a way to reclaim what was rightfully his. Julia had already made sure that the tape was in the VCR, so all she had to do was to set it running at the correct time and switch the TV on – everyone would assume that the programme they were watching was live. It worked like a charm. Jack picked up the lottery ticket from behind the clock on the fire surround, and watched as the balls went down from the hopper into the catch-tray below. His hand started to shake after the third one dropped, and you could have cut the atmosphere with a knife as the rest dutifully took their places.

There was complete silence in the room as the final ball fell. Jack stood transfixed as they were sorted on-screen into ascending order, and he heard the sequence announced out loud. He looked from ticket to screen and screen to ticket, tracing the numbers with his finger until he was sure of what he had heard. The explosion of noise was startling, even for Julia. She was quite unprepared for the level of the celebration involving Jack and his mates, and now had to face the dilemma of how to break the news to him in a way guaranteed to cause maximum embarrassment. Making an excuse to leave the room to replenish the now dwindling stocks of beer, she retired to the kitchen followed by a couple of her own friends.

A brief consultation resulted in the conclusion that it would have a greater impact if she were to leave him to dig himself deeper into a self-congratulatory hole, before breaking the news and revealing the scam she had pulled across him. Accordingly, the party carried on into the small hours of the morning until the last of the guests had been persuaded to go home, leaving her no chance at that time to expose the ruse she had played.

The following day saw no sign of Jack until mid afternoon, when he emerged from his bedroom still celebrating his good fortune. He took great pains to gloat over the win, going into great detail as to how he would use the money and labouring the point that none of it would be coming her way. He was obviously off out to renew his celebrations with his mates. There was, quite clearly, no point in revealing the trick to him at this point. It was early evening before he returned home, and some time later before Julia considered him sober enough to understand the nature of the joke which had been played on him, and even then she had to explain twice how she had been able to fool him into believing what he had seen with his own eyes. Once he had seen a replay of the tape the reality of the situation hit him.

He had been made to look a complete idiot not only in front of his mates, which was bad enough, but also in the presence of Julia's friends who regarded him as something of a throw-back to the Neanderthals. He was livid. He ranted and raved at her – violence was not his style, so she knew she was physically safe. Finally, finding the ticket he tore it into shreds and threw it into the fire before storming out of the room.

She was still preening herself over the success of the joke some days later, when she picked up a copy of the local paper. The headline stopped her short. "LOCAL WINNER OF LOTTERY NETS £4.1 MILLION", but the full implications of the article didn't dawn on her at first. She read on with an increasing sense of foreboding.

It appeared that a single ticket purchased in the Derby area had scooped the top prize. The numbers were listed, and Julia's heart froze as they had a very familiar ring to them. She hurried home, found the tape which she had played on the Saturday evening, and sat watching in horror as the same set of numbers rolled out once again. Unconvinced, she rang the paper for confirmation. "No", they said, "There was no mistake, the same set of numbers had appeared on successive week-end draws, was she making a claim?" Julia replied quietly that she was not, how could she when the ticket lay in ashes in the fireplace where Jack had thrown them?

TELL LAURA I LOVE HER

*F*ive o'clock – great, and it was Friday too – even better. The whole weekend ahead without the drudgery of returning to work until Monday, and that seemed a long way off right now. Terry Mason liked his weekend out with the lads. Tonight would involve an evening on the town, a few beers, something to eat and maybe a disco or a night club. Saturday afternoon was reserved for football, and this week they'd hired a minibus for an away fixture. Sunday was his, and he spent the whole day watching TV and reading. He was 27 and alone since his mum died five years previously. His father had walked out when he was just nine years old.

Terry wasn't what you might call one for the ladies, preferring to remain in the background enjoying the company while his mates did most of the talking, but if someone interesting came along he was not too shy to engage in conversation, and there had been a number of girls in the past with whom he had struck up brief, if inconclusive, relationships. Last week however had been different, and this was the reason for his particular interest in the current weekend.

He had met Laura Davis at Tip Top, a disco in town, the previous Saturday when they had bumped into a group of girls out for a similar evening. The two of them had hit it off almost immediately, and there seemed to be a chemistry between them spurred on by a combination of interests which they shared. Both groups had arranged to meet again this weekend, and Terry hurried back to his flat to get ready for the evening. No need to go over the top; if she liked him last week there was no point in doing anything different, so he needed to be casual without giving the impression of disinterest – he was treading a fine line and it would be a shame to spoil it.

He needn't have worried. As soon as they met she greeted him with a smile that lit up the room, and much to the annoyance of his mates they spent the entire evening sitting in a corner talking. She seemed perfect company, and the more he learned about her the better he felt. The end of the evening came all too soon, and as they parted all his uncertainties returned. Should he kiss her goodnight or merely wave and say 'See you again?' He didn't want to ruin a potentially good relationship by moving forward too quickly, but Laura solved the problem with a brief peck on his cheek and a 'Call me' before she left in a taxi with her friends. Terry did call her, several times during the following week when he could fit it in with his work schedule. The more they talked the closer they seemed to grow, and their relationship developed and blossomed like a delicate flower in a greenhouse. He couldn't imagine being in a situation without her any more, and began to drift apart from his weekend friends as they spent more and more time in each other's company.

It was about three months later that the first hint of a problem reared its head, and Terry found himself completely at a loss as to what to do. They had spent their entire weekend together, as seemed to be the pattern now, and had become so at ease in each other's company that a number of their friends had remarked that, to all intents and purposes, they had the appearance of a married couple. Laura had noticed a reticence in his behaviour and tried to coax him into talking about it, but he dismissed her concerns, and when they parted company on the Sunday it was in a somewhat sombre mood.

If he took their relationship to the next level and asked her to marry him, would she be scared away? He couldn't bear the thought of that, and yet if he did nothing she might consider that he was losing interest and simply leave him and look for someone else. They had been close to sleeping together on a number of occasions but Terry had this old-fashioned idea of saving it for the wedding day, and Laura didn't seem to be too concerned about it, so they let it pass.

With no parents to use as sounding boards, Terry did what had always done in situations like this – went to see his Aunty Pat. She was his mum's older sister and had been married twice, so he treated her as expert in all things romantic and matrimonial; she had been his rock on more than one occasion. She was delighted to see him, and he timed the visit for a weekend when Laura was off on a course related to her work.

Pat and Harold had lived in a cottage in a small village outside Dorking for the last twenty years. They had no children of their own, and had 'adopted' him after his mum died. Harold was just like a father to him and everything was so easy in their company. After the usual greetings and news had been exchanged he explained his dilemma over a bottle of Cabernet Sauvignon to his attentive 'parents'. They listened carefully to all that he said, and at the end told him to sit down with Laura, open his heart to her and take the consequences. If there was no emotional or economic reason for holding back, the decision would be a simple one – they either loved each other or they didn't.

Of course Terry had known the answer all along, but it was still good to hear it from someone else, particularly those whom he held most dear. It set his mind at rest for the remainder of the weekend, and they had the most wonderful time. At the end of Sunday lunch at the local pub he had decided to make his approach to Laura and ask her to be his wife.

He arrived home at around eleven on Sunday evening, too late to call her right now, and he spent a very anxious and sleepless night. He rang her the following morning but was told by a work colleague that she was busy and that she would call him back. When the afternoon passed without a call he was disappointed and rang her again. This time he was informed that she had already gone home for the day. Terry looked at his watch – it was 3.15pm; he wondered why she would have left so early, and without at least speaking to him first.

He rang her home number after work but got only her answering machine. He left a message asking her to get in touch, but by the end of the evening was still waiting and was now becoming anxious. He went round to her flat only to find it in darkness, and calls to her mobile had been diverted to voicemail. Terry was becoming very worried and rang Jill, her closest friend. Jill's voice seemed oddly strained, and all that she would say was that Laura was unhappy about something but couldn't speak to him right now. It was clear that she was there, but this didn't seem to be the time to make an issue out of it.

"Tell Laura I love her", he said.

The next day he was waiting outside her place of work when she came out of the car park, and she stopped dead in her tracks. He walked up to her slowly – this was not the place for a showdown. She was very pale and clearly unprepared for seeing him. Their conversation was strained and awkward, but she made her excuses at work and led him over to the coffee shop a little way down the street. He started to explain how his feelings for her had developed over the weekend, and that he had something very important to ask her. She held up her hand to stop him saying anything more, guessing what was about to come. From out of her purse Laura produced a photograph and placed it in front of him.

Terry frowned, and looked back up at her, questioningly.

"What's this?" he asked.

"Give me the locket, the one you always wear around your neck." She held out her hand, and he dropped it into her fingers. Laura started to shake as she prised open the clasp. She let out a gasp and dropped it on the table.

"What? What is it?" He asked, his voice becoming more insistent.

"I wasn't sure until now, but look at the two pictures; it's the same woman."

"And?"

"I've been trying to trace my dad ever since I was old enough to realise what happened to me. He took that photograph." She jabbed at the snap on the table and Terry's face froze in horror at the realisation of what she was about to say.

"Don't you see, Terry? The children at her side – it's you and me. Look at the picture in your locket. It's mum. We're brother and sister. We can never see each other again."

A GOLDEN OPPORTUNITY

*W*hen you are a little boy of ten with no brothers or sisters, living in a cottage in the middle of nowhere and with just your mum for company, life can be very boring. There was Patch, his dog, of course and they went just about everywhere together, including school. He was allowed to take him along for security due to the long walk there and back (5 miles each way) because you just never knew who was likely to be around in the bleak Cornish countryside, especially in winter when the early mornings and late afternoons were dark.

William Daddow and his mother Rosemary had very little spare money, and kept a variety of animals and birds to eke out their food supply. All other items had to be home grown, and there was a patch of land behind the cottage where she grew all the vegetables and fruit that they needed. His father, George, had been killed in an accident at the tin mine five years earlier, and Rosemary had taken in sewing and knitting for a textile retailer in Penzance in an attempt to make ends meet.

William spent much of his spare time, after helping around the house, out on the cliff tops with Patch. They would run and play, or just lie in the grass staring out to sea. He wondered what it would be like to be a sailor, braving the elements across the world to bring home riches from around the globe. He dreamed of captaining his own boat, and making a fortune so that his mother would no longer have to work the long hours she did to put food on their table.

It was after school had finished, and he had completed what jobs Rosemary had given him, that he lay with his head right on the edge of the cliffs and saw the ship on the horizon. It was getting dark but he could just make out its shape by the lights hanging fore and aft. Maybe it had arrived back home from the Far East and was laden with valuable cargo ready for unloading. It was strange then, that it appeared to drop anchor instead of heading for one of the Cornish ports. Stranger still half an hour later when a boat was lowered into the water amid the gathering gloom and headed for shore.

There were six men aboard, and in complete silence, with only storm lanterns to light the way, they unloaded a number of items and carried them into one of the caves which nature had cut into the foot of the cliffs. The operation lasted only fifteen minutes and they had taken what looked like a small chest back to the ship with them.

What could this be? He had heard of smugglers from some of the old men in the village where he went to school, and their tales were filled with blood curdling accounts of huge men, with swords and daggers, who would cut your throat as soon as look at you. William wasn't scared, you learned not to be when you were growing up on your own, but his pulse quickened as he made his way down one of the many rocky paths which led to the beach below. It was getting dark very quickly now so he didn't have much time to spare, and the path back up to the top could be dangerous without a lamp.

William had a good idea which cave had been used and found it almost immediately. There were twenty or thirty barrels and they smelled strong and sweet. Whistling for Patch, he made his way back to the top of the cliff and headed off for home. He was late for supper and Rosemary had been out looking for him, but when he told her what he had seen she sat him down and made him repeat everything word for word.

She explained that the barrels probably contained brandy, smuggled across the Channel from France, and that the chest could have contained payment for the delivery. All this activity was illegal of course, and if caught the men would face severe punishment. If the money could be intercepted before the next delivery had been taken and the customs post in Penzance alerted, then the two of them could get away in the confusion which would surround the arrest. They would need to monitor the next few shipments to ensure that they themselves did not get caught up in the aftermath of the events.

William and Patch duly spent all their spare evenings up on the cliff top looking out for the return of the smugglers' ship, but it wasn't until after sunset on the seventh day that he saw a sail appearing over the horizon. He kept low in the grass at the edge of the cliff to avoid detection, and waited. The ship dropped anchor as before and lowered the rowing boat on to the incoming tide. Hardly daring to breathe, William watched as the men went about their business and left once more. When they had gone he scrambled down to the cave to see what they had left; as before there were at least thirty small barrels.

Rosemary kept him away from school the following day. He needed to watch for any activity on the beach from the same spot on the cliff top, so that they would have some idea as to how much time they would have to intercept the money. He stayed up there all day, but it wasn't until dusk that he heard someone approaching along the cliff top road. Two men in a small cart drove along the dirt track. The horse's hooves had been muffled with cloth to prevent them being detected, and if he hadn't been lying in wait William wouldn't have heard them.

With two dark lanterns the men made their way down the cliff pathway and were back in little over ten minutes with four barrels each, strung with ropes and hung about their shoulders. Four trips later and they were done. The last trip saw them take two bags down to the cave, and this must have contained payment for the barrels. William had used his father's pocket watch to time the whole operation – it had taken less than half an hour from start to finish. Five more minutes and they had disappeared from sight, and it was as if nothing at all had happened. When he told his mother what had taken place, she set him up for one more observation the following week. The ship was right on schedule, the cart appeared at the same hour the following day, and all the timings matched exactly.

Rosemary now knew what to do. An anonymous letter to the Revenue Men would ensure that the smugglers got a warm welcome, but she would have to make sure that the two of them were well clear by that time. She was due to travel into Penzance with her latest batch of sewing and could ride with the local mail carrier – this would give her the chance to drop a letter into the day's deliveries without arousing the suspicion of the village postmaster.

All was set, and when William reported the arrival of the next delivery they set out for the cliff top the following evening. They didn't have long to wait, and the cart arrived on schedule. As soon as the two men descended to the beach Rosemary and her son ran to the cart. They found the cash bags immediately, but were startled by loud voices and gunfire from the beach. Running as fast as they could they made their way home, hid the bags beneath the floorboards in the workshop and closed the house up for the night.

It was a week later that they learned about the capture not only of the men in the cart, but also of the entire crew of the smugglers' ship, which had been intercepted by the Royal Navy whilst trying to return across the Channel. There was no mention of any money, but it was another three weeks before Rosemary summoned up the courage to remove it from beneath the floor boards. What she discovered almost took away her breath

– she had never seen so many gold sovereigns in her life before.

It was a further two weeks before Mr Potts, the village schoolmaster, paid Rosemary a visit. William had been absent from school and this was most unlike the boy, but when he arrived at the cottage it was to find no one there. Enquiries in the neighbourhood revealed nothing – they had simply vanished leaving the house unlocked, the remains of a fire in the grate and the mouldy remnants of a meal on the kitchen table. A search of the area, including the cliff tops, revealed nothing and after six months the whole matter was forgotten.

In a small township outside of Boston, Massachusetts a middle aged woman was sweeping the front porch of a typical New England house. She paused and stared at the changing colours of the trees surrounding the settlement. No one had questioned their appearance in the town, or their reasons for travelling the width of the Atlantic in search of a new life. Since changing their names to Dunston, Rosemary and William's previous existence in England had become untraceable. They had rid themselves of the hard life in Cornwall, and with the proceeds of the failed smuggling attempt safely deposited at the local bank, their futures were now assured. She smiled to herself, turned and went back into the house.

BULL IN A CHINA SHOP

Terry Bull, the teasing he had been forced to endure over the years as a result of that name had made him wish he could have been a girl, but then what if he had been christened Theresa? It would still have been truncated to Teri and he would have been in no better position. He didn't think he was accident prone or anything like that, it's just that things seemed to happen to him or to other people when he was around.

Even when he was small he would fall into the only puddle in the street, usually in his Sunday best clothes. It was as if some cosmic banana skin was constantly waiting around the corner for him. He clearly remembered one day in the park at the age of about six or seven when he jumped from one of the swings, as they all did, to see who could land furthest away. His leap took him to one side instead of straight ahead and he collided with Collette from down the street. As if this in itself wasn't bad enough, he knocked her ice cream cornet out of her hand and it flew through the air in a perfect arc to land squarely on the head of a passing toddler.

Faced with two scowling and rapidly approaching mothers he beat a hasty retreat, fell over Mrs Davis's spaniel and landed in a holly bush. Explaining this when he got home was not going to be easy, but what guarantee would he have that he would get there without further accident?

All the other children in the neighbourhood gave him a wide berth, and he was allocated far more respect than Daniel, the local bully. At least with Dan you had a fair chance of avoiding injury if you knew what to look out for – he was noted for his bad temper. With poor Terry there was no early warning system, and no way of avoiding a minor catastrophe if you happened to be around when Lady Luck turned up and was having a bad day herself.

There were very few of the children of his age who were prepared to risk being in his company and for those who were, parents usually stepped in and either shooed him away or fetched their own indoors. In the end his loneliness was alleviated when they had to move house after his dad got a promotion at work. The new job was over a hundred miles north from their current home, and although nothing specific was said to him by either parent, it was clear that this was the chance to make a clean start. You could feel the relief in the neighbourhood when the removal van pulled off and turned the corner at the end of the street.

The doctor had always said that he was just going through a phase of hyperactivity and that it would pass in time, but he was eleven when they moved, and he wondered how long these periods lasted. Anyway, a new neighbourhood and new school would give him the chance he craved, and he wasn't about to let it slip through his fingers. He worked out that if he stayed indoors and did his school work instead of going out to play, there would be less chance of him causing the kind of problems which had dogged his earlier life. At school he became known as a swot although this wasn't said in any malicious way, and a number of his classmates sought him out rather than the teacher if they had problems with homework.

As he progressed through secondary school Terry's grades improved with each assessment, and he was selected for 'fast tracking' on a number of his GCSEs. He revelled in the work and forgot all about his accidental past, even venturing outdoors more and more as his former problems seemed to have deserted him. Success at examinations became second nature, and by the time he had completed "A" levels his results gave him an embarrassment of choices at some of the best universities.

It was time to decide upon a career and to select the best college for the attainment of his goals. He picked out a course in maths and science offered by Warwick University, and was accepted immediately. He had read on a number of occasions that there was a chronic shortage of mathematicians and scientists, so these areas would be most likely to provide him with a well paid occupation. It was at Warwick that he met Sandra.

She was reading maths and engineering, and their courses intersected frequently but not often enough to force them together all of the time. As a result, a comfortable friendship started to grow between them, and in his innocence this was all that he considered it to be. It wasn't until one of his other friends made a casual remark about the amount of time they were spending together that Terry became a little nervous about it.

It was as if some radio signal had been sent out like a Morse coded SOS. Almost immediately the old clumsiness returned, and accidents seemed to wait for him around every corner. It started almost inconspicuously with the dropping of books and knocking over chairs in the college library. This latter fact got him several annoyed looks from other students and a warning from the librarian to take more care. It got worse when he was actually in Sandra's company, and drinks inexplicably leapt out of his hand. These would usually end up all over him, but there were times when innocent bystanders became the victims of his clumsiness.

He was banned from the union bar after one evening, when his glass collecting duties ended with large scale breakages and a clearing of the premises whilst the mess was swept up. It was as though all his childhood nightmares were returning. Once again he went back to the strategy which had served him so well at school. Shutting himself away with only Sandra for company, they both pushed on with their studies, and apart from lectures were rarely seen on campus. Friends would call round to the flat which they were now sharing and seemed to be safe from injury whilst on his territory, but the outside world appeared to be a different matter.

Like a magic trick, things seemed to calm down again and all his nervousness (and this is what it seemed to be) vanished. Cautiously he ventured out in public, and as the weeks passed he became confident once more that the problem had gone away. Their courses were propelling both of them quickly towards chosen career paths, and success in final exams was virtually assured. If they were to pursue a life together, it was important that they find employment in an area which would allow them to live within easy distance from work.

This presented no problem at all when their results came out. First class honours degrees for both gained them employment at a large local engineering concern with subsidiaries all over Europe. The future suddenly looked very bright indeed, and Terry could hardly conceal his excitement. They visited both sets of parents and broke the news of their engagement (or rather what would be an engagement once the ring had been bought), and on the following Saturday took a tour of all the jewellery shops in town.

It didn't take Sandra long to find the ring which she liked, and although the price was a little more than they had bargained for, Terry didn't bat an eyelid as he reached into his pocket for the money. How his finger got caught in the lining he didn't know, but a tug released it and all the pocket contents. His arm flew backwards and knocked over a display cabinet containing fine bone china, causing all its bulbs to explode like gunfire. Customers fled from the shop in fright, and out in the street, police appeared as if from nowhere.

In a matter of moments he was restrained whilst the shopkeeper explained that it had been nothing more than an accident, and not the attempted robbery which customers had mistakenly believed. After a brief period of taking statements and ensuring that the premises were secure, the police turned to leave. One of them stopped and turned around.

"Terry, isn't it?"

"Yes, but.........."

"It's me Daniel Parker, we were at junior school together. You were a right disaster in those days. Not much has changed then, has it?"

Terry looked at him, puzzled.

"Terry Bull...........terrible.............Bull in a china shop.............get it?"

DEAR MOM

Tuesday, 5th June

Dear Mom
How unfair is this? I get done out of my birthright by that cow Hera, dad can't do anything about it because he'd already opened his big mouth about the succession and Eurystheus gets the job, and now I'm up for murder because I let myself get all worked up about it. I tell you if this is justice, I'm a monkey's uncle.

Hercules

Wednesday, 6th June

Dear Mom
I don't believe this. They said they were letting me off as long as I went to see the Oracle at Delphi. Have you seen the cost of travel? It's miles away – I think I might walk. Anyway Theseus says he'll come with me for company so at least I'll have someone to talk to. I've got a really bad feeling about this though.

Hercules

Friday, 8th June

Dear Mom
Absolutely unbelievable! That dingbat, the Oracle, has given me and ASBO with ten jobs attached to it, and if that wasn't bad enough the guy setting them is, you've guessed it, Eurystheus. Like he's my number one best buddy, man I hate that guy! Apparently I've got to go to some place called Nemea and kill a cat – seems a bit cruel to me, but a job's a job. Catch you later.

Hercules

Tuesday 12th June

Dear Mom
Cat? It was a bloody great lion. I nearly pooed my pants. The thing had a skin like rhino hide and none of my weapons worked. I was so scared when it came at me that all I could do was stick out my arm and hope for the best. The stupid brute choked on my fist (all that working out finally paid off) and the next thing I knew was that it was twitching away on the ground. That was so close, but I still needed the skin and I couldn't cut it. I was getting really teed off when this bit of stuff appeared (said her name was Athena) and told me to use the thing's claws. It worked – one down and nine to go. That's one in the eye for Eurystheus.

Hercules

Thursday 14th June

Dear Mom
As I've been such a good boy, they gave me the rest of the list to study up on, and yesterday's star prize was the Lernaean Hydra. I'd seen pictures of this one. It had seven heads and the kind of breath you wouldn't want after a night on the curry. Called Iolaus on his mobile and he came over to help. He got this idea of burning the stump of each head as I cut them off to prevent re-growth and it worked. I'm getting the hang of this – now for the Ceryneian Hind, whatever that is.

Hercules

Saturday 16th June

Dear Mom
Nobody said anything about working weekends! This thing is a damn deer and they can really shift. I've got to catch it and bring it back for Eurystheus to put in his zoo. Not sure how long this is going to take.

Hercules

Friday 13th June

Dear Mom
Sorry it's been so long since the last letter, but it's taken me a year to track this thing down and nail it. If it hadn't stopped for a drink I don't know what I'd have done. You wouldn't believe the places I've been, and I only managed to catch it by laming it first. Had to carry it back all the way and they weigh a ton – still, good thing I'm a big boy isn't it? I've got the

Erymanthian Boar next, so I'll write you when I recover from that.

Hercules

Friday 20th June

Dear Mom
Another 'go and catch me one' – this'll be the death of me. According to this guy Chiron, I've got to drive the boar into the snow and catch it when it can't go any further – good job I brought my Wellingtons along! Actually this wasn't as bad as I thought it would be, and the best bit is that when I brought it back to you-know-who, he was so scared that he jumped into his chamber pot. That one really rocked! I'll let you know how I'm getting on when I find my list – must have put it down someplace.

Hercules

Monday 23rd June

Dear Mom
Found it. It was in one of my Wellingtons all the time. Good job I've got them because cleaning out the Augean Stables was one hell of a job in a single day. I'm sure no-one had ever been near these cattle, because the stuff was nearly up to the rafters and it stank to high heaven. Augeus, the owner, said that I couldn't have any help from anyone. Thinks he's clever that one, but I fixed him. I changed the course of two local rivers and let the water do the work. Boy was he mad – reneged on our agreement though and refused to pay, so I iced him. Had to really didn't I? Got to take some birds out next – should be great that, I'm looking forward to a night out.

Hercules

Wednesday 25th June

Dear Mom
Wrong kind of birds - I was so upset. What am I going to do with the new suit now? These birds are man-eaters, and I really MEAN man-eaters, with brass claws and sharp metallic feathers. To top it off, if they dump on you, you die of toxic poisoning. They were living in a forest and I couldn't see a thing, so I had to scare them out into the daylight. After that it was like a turkey shoot – I should have got a soft toy for the marksmanship, but you can't have everything can you?

Hercules

Saturday 29th June

Dear Mom
Got to go to Crete (wherever that is) to bring this bull back to Athens, and I'm not sure where I put my passport. Boat leaves in two hours so I'll rush this off to you now. Lots of love and don't fret about me.
                                                                                                    Hercules

Sunday 7th July

Dear Mom
Tracked the owner down and he was glad to see the back of the bull as it had been wreaking havoc in the local china shops, and the traders were threatening to sue if he didn't get it sorted. I'd been working out a little on the boat over here, so in the end it was no contest and was all over in the first round. See you very soon.
                                                                                                    Hercules

Friday 12th July

Dear Mom
Now I'm a horse thief! As if that wasn't bad enough I had to take them off a giant called Diomedes, and just what is it with Eurystheus and these man-eating creatures? I had to fight him for the livestock but while we were busy, the damn things ate Abderus, a dear friend of mine. I mean can you believe that? I tell you I wasn't best pleased so I fed Diomedes to them as well (killed him first, anything else would have been cruel). Apparently eating calms them down, and I managed to tape up their mouths and bring them home. Hope they do something nasty to Eurystheus.
                                                                                                    Hercules

Wednesday 17th July

Dear Mom
I'm so embarrassed about this one. Had to go to this chick called Hippolyta and steal her underclothes. I didn't realise, but she was one of those Amazon women with the big…………..everythings. Anyway she took a real shine to me and we were getting along just fine, when all of a sudden her pals come crashing in looking for a fight. Unfortunately in the confusion I accidentally killed her, so I thought 'what the hell', picked up the girdle and legged it.

Shame really, I thought we could have had a good thing going there. Next up I am going to be a cattle rancher!

Hercules

Saturday 20th July

Dear Mom
This one was a real bummer. Had to cross this desert in a place called Libya and the heat got to me a little. Funny the things you do when you're not yourself, and apparently I shot an arrow at the sun to teach it a lesson. This God dude Helios gave me a big gold cup for winning the archery competition, and I used it as a boat to get to the ranch in Erythia. Must have tripped over a black cat somewhere on the way because bad luck met me on the beach in the shape of a dog with two heads (got to stop taking those little yellow pills). Anyway, hit him with my club and it was goodnight Vienna, and just to show no hard feelings I dealt with his master, Eurytion, in the same way. Rounded up the herd, saddled me a horse, got me a guitar and we all set out for home. Now Eurystheus can stick it where the sun don't shine.

Rawhide Hercules (yee hah!)

Wednesday 24th July

Dear Mom
Now I'm really cross! Apparently I've cheated, and according to dipstick Eurystheus I've got to do two more jobs because somebody helped me on a couple of the other ones. You'll never guess what the first one is................I've got to go scrumping, and I haven't done that since third grade (skinned my knees that day as well). There's a group of nymphs called the Hesperides, and they have the mother and father of all orchards with a tree growing golden apples, and these are the things I've got to pinch. Get the oven ready and I'll bring some normal ones home for pies.

Hercules

Friday 26th July

Dear Mom
Saw Atlas doing not much of anything, so I conned him into nicking the apples for me while I held the heavens for him for a bit. Cheeky beggar came back and said he'd bring the apples back home for me and that I could keep the heavens as he'd read them all. I told him 'No deal' but he wasn't having

it, so I said 'OK' as long as he held them for me while I took a leak. Stupid fool agreed and I legged it before he realised what had happened. He wasn't very pleased – think I'll cross him off my Christmas card list now.

Hercules

Monday 27th July

Dear Mom

Found my calling in life – Dog Warden! Another one of Donkey-Breath's multi-headed creations. 'Go and get me Cerberus', he said, and gives me a piece of paper with an address on it in the Hades area of town. The dude himself was at home when I called, so I passed myself off as a dog walker. Damn fool went and got the lead and even gave me a bag of treats for the mutt so he would behave. Well I had to master this brute pretty early, and he must have gotten news of what happened with the Hydra because we became pretty good buddies. Well I got another laugh at Eurystheus' expense because one bark from my new buddy and the guy jumps into a storage jar. Boy, was I tempted to seal it. So now that I've done, the ASBO has been lifted. Put the kettle on, I'm coming home and I'm parched!

Hercules

Finders Keepers

At last, back home. The rail journey up from London had been the worst he could ever remember. Stop and start all the way with one delay following another, and precious little of anything edible in the buffet car. Three and a half hours to travel 200 miles on what was supposed to be a high speed railway, after a business meeting which seemed to go on forever. Never mind, he'd already phoned his wife Jane to tell her of the delay until 7.30pm, and she would be waiting in the car for him. They would soon be off home for supper and a relaxing evening in front of the TV.

James Michael Taylor was not one of life's high flyers, feeling content to be one of the cogs in the corporate machine, and happy to draw a monthly salary for a fairly routine set of regular tasks. He and Jane would always have liked a little more in the way of life's comforts, but they were by no means hard up and now that the children were off their hands there was money at the end of the month these days instead of the other way round. At 54, he had 'only' eleven years left to retirement, and today was his birthday – Friday 27th October 2006.

He had noticed the weather closing in on his journey north, but the fog had thickened and as he stood watching the train pull out of the station, visibility was down to about fifty yards. Looking around the now darkened and deserted platform, he wondered why he'd been the only passenger to alight from the carriage. At first James wondered if he had got off the train at the wrong stop, because the station buildings seemed 'wrong' but then again oddly familiar. It wasn't until his approach to the exit that he saw the name plate 'Bardon Hill' – definitely the correct place, but equally definitely the wrong surroundings.

A cold, uneasy feeling crept through his body as James realised that he was standing on the platform of the station closed by Dr Beeching in 1967, and demolished the following year. No, this couldn't be right, but as the fog started to lift, the immediate area became clearer and to his amazement the double glazing warehouse on his right had disappeared to be replaced by the Roxy Cinema which had closed its doors for the final time in 1963. He now knew where he was, the only question remaining was WHEN. He needed to find a shop, and if memory served him right, there used to be a newsagent on the corner of North Street and Station Road. James looked at his watch – it was 7.35pm, just five minutes after the time he should have been meeting Jane.

There it was, 'Suttons General Store' with the usual crop of advertising boards outside the door. A newspaper would do, along with a fresh pack of cigarettes. The door bell tinkled as he entered, and an oldish man whom he assumed to be Mr Sutton senior came through from the back room, smiled and asked if he could be of help. James asked for a paper and twenty Rothmans Filter Tips. The man looked at him as if he was mad.

"What?"

"Twenty Rothmans please."

"We've got Park Drive, Kensitas and Senior Service – take your pick."

James picked the Senior Service, poked around amongst the change in his pocket, selected a couple of ten pence pieces (the equivalent of four shillings then) and passed them over, hoping that the shopkeeper wouldn't spot them through his thick glasses. Mr Sutton picked up the coins and looked at them with a furrowed brow. He glanced back at James.

"What's this?" he asked.

"Pardon?"

"This" he said, holding the coins up in front of James's face.

"Oh, sorry."

"Daft beggar, you've given me too much. What price are fags where you come from then?"

He handed back one of the ten pence pieces together with the change from the other. James mentally heaved a sigh of relief. Mr Sutton just smiled and slowly shook his head. Looking at the clock at the back of the shop, the younger man nodded.

"That clock, is it right?"

"It certainly is." Said Sutton, taking his own pocket watch from his waistcoat and glancing at it as if in confirmation. "I check it every night with the radio."

Still shaken, James left the shop and looked at the top of the newspaper – the date was Friday 27th of May 1949, just 3 years after the final ending of hostilities in World War II. How was he going to get back to 2006? Would Jane be at the station waiting for him and wondering where he had got to after the train departed? Where on Earth was he going to go for help? He had to think clearly and fast. Stafford Street – of course! His grandparents would be living there with his aunts, and it was only a five minute walk away. There was no time to lose, and at least it would give him an opportunity to think while he worked out what his next move was going to be.

This would need some care. He could pass himself off as a relative, because his dad had told him stories of life at Stafford Street and also at the previous house on Green Lane. His grandfather was regarded locally as something of a 'free thinker' and had bookcases full of literature on what would, in later years, be regarded by some as science fiction. Still, it didn't make him feel any easier as he walked up the path and knocked on the old black and white panelled front door. A stunning blonde woman in her late twenties opened it, and it was all he could do to prevent himself wrapping his arms around her. This was his Aunt Jean and if he had a favourite, she was it.

"I'm sorry to bother you", he said, "but could I speak to Joseph Taylor, please?"

He was asked to wait for a moment, and after a brief conversation inside, a man in his late sixties appeared at the door. James had only ever seen photographs of his grandfather before, and it was now rather disconcerting to meet the man face to face. He had an air of dignity about him but life had clearly taken its toll. James explained that he was a relative and that he was trying to trace Michael Taylor, as he had something to give to him. If this conversation had taken place in 2006 the door would probably have been shut in his face, but back in 1949 people were inclined to be more trusting towards strangers after the upheaval of the war and the displacement of large numbers of the civilian population.

He was invited inside and offered refreshments when he explained that he had come all the way from London. The house was exactly as he remembered it as he had been growing up, and he felt oddly out of place amongst these familiar, and yet strange surroundings. He recognised the old long clock on the wall, except it wasn't so old – the time was 7.55pm. Joseph gave him a slip of paper with an address on it, and told him that Michael had been married for seven years and was living there with his wife, Joan. James heaved a silent sigh of relief as he realised that he had not yet been born – what would have happened if he had bumped into himself he didn't know. Gratefully accepting the cup of tea offered to him, and smiling as he saw the piano in the corner, he whispered a silent 'hello' to an old friend from future years. Joseph noticed his glance.

"It's a good instrument. Do you play?"

"Not for many years; in fact, since I was eighteen music hasn't held any attraction for me, but would you mind if I tried?"

"Not at all. There's some music in the stool."

James spent a further half hour reacquainting himself with the Bechstein, and found all the old rhythms coming back to him. He hadn't noticed, but by this time an audience consisting of his grandmother and three aunts had gathered at the doorway, and were listening in rapt silence. Embarrassment forced him to stop, and despite protestations from all in the room, he finished his second cup of tea and prepared to leave. It was now 9.00pm and an hour had flown by; it would take him a further 30 minutes to get to his father's address.

James fended off Joseph's probing questions as to his connection to the family, and thanking him for the hospitality set out for the address given to him. It was a walk of just over a mile, and gave him time to think on the way. The main priority was getting back home in the correct year, but the seeds of a plan were germinating fast in his brain. This was 1949 and he was the possessor of a considerable amount of information not available to anyone in this time; James wondered about the possibility of persuading his dad to gamble.

Michael Taylor had never, to the best of his son's knowledge, been a betting man apart from the usual weekly flutter on the football pools. Of course, that was it. James couldn't possibly predict enough draws to enable his dad to hit the jackpot with Littlewoods or any of the other operators, but he did know the names of the FA Cup winning teams from 1950 onwards, and he was sure that he could remember the winners of the Grand National from about the early sixties – including Foinavon, the outsider which came in at 100/1 in 1967.

He stopped at the top of Dunsfield Hill and sat down on the bench there under a street lamp. Taking a piece of paper out of his wallet and the pen from his top pocket, he wrote the information down, ready to hand over to his father. Now for another creepy encounter – he walked across the recreation ground which linked Dunsfield to the Goodman Estate where his parents lived. Once more he knocked at a very familiar door and it was opened by his dad. James explained that he had travelled from London, and had some important information which must never be divulged to anyone else. They went into the back parlour where the list was produced and instructions given for its use. Michael, unlike his father, was suspicious and asked what the catch was.

"No catch, just keep it secret and put any winnings into a building society. Keep the book somewhere safe, like under a loose board on the stairs, and don't tell anyone where it is."

Michael looked at him with a furrowed brow, but took the piece of paper and after giving it a cursory glance, put it in his pocket. Well, only time would tell now, and he really must be going. He made his excuses, saying that he had a train to catch, and left. At the bottom of the street he turned around for one more look, and saw his dad standing under the street lamp at the bottom of the front garden watching him – it was now 10.00pm. Moments later he was through the jitty and on to the recreation ground once more. Hurrying back down Dunsfield Hill he made his way back to the station only to find it closed for the night.

James had reasoned that as the station had 'brought' him to 1949, maybe catching a train there would take him back to 2006. It seemed the only chance he would have, but there was still the need for somewhere to sleep for the night, and he remembered the Midland Hotel near the canal basin. He would have enough for the train fare from the change given to him at Suttons, but had no other funds about his person. A decision was made to face that problem when it arose. The place was cheap and cheerful and he could get a meal – it seemed ages since he had eaten. He explained to the manager about his financial embarrassment, and the man decided that James's watch would suffice as full payment – people were still inclined to barter in those days when money was in short supply. The accommodation was comfortable, and shortly after dinner he retired to bed and was sound asleep. A knock at the door the following morning confirmed that it had not all been a dream, and he descended to a full breakfast, the size of which he had not seen for many a year.

The station master was just arriving as he approached the ticket office, and James accepted the offer of a cup of tea while he waited for the early morning train. Getting into the first carriage, he allowed himself the luxury of one last look (he hoped) at the long gone station buildings. He decided to get off at the next stop and simply travel back down the line, but looking out of the window he noticed that a dense fog had started to form and the sky had become very dark. The train halted at the next stop, and as with last time James was the only passenger to depart. It wasn't until the carriages had cleared the platform that he recognised where he was – back at the modern station at 7.35pm and presumably in 2006. He stood for a moment as the fog cleared and was shaken from his reverie by the hooting of a car horn. Turning around he was relieved to see Jane waving at him from the car park, a big smile on her face.

He tried to explain to her what had happened, and asked if she had been worried that he hadn't been on the platform the previous day. She gave him the kind of look to which he had become accustomed over the last 24 hours, and asked him what day he thought it was. There had been no loss in time whilst he had 'been' in 1949 and to all intents and purposes nothing unusual had happened. Nevertheless when he saw an entry in the properties section of the local paper some weeks later, his interest resurfaced.

His parents' old home on the Goodman Estate was up for sale. They had died, in this reality, a few years earlier, and the council had sold the property to a private purchaser. This person had now moved on, leaving the house vacant and in the hands of a local estate agent. A telephone call got James the keys to the house and an uninterrupted viewing. This was the chance to see if his dad had carried out the scheme which had been suggested, and taking a few tools along in a carrier bag, he set off.

There was no-one about when he arrived towards lunchtime, and letting himself in James made for the stairs. Thinking back to his childhood he now remembered that the stair riser next to the top had always seemed to be loose, and that his dad had never got around to fixing it. Taking a screwdriver out of the bag James levered it to one side to find a brown envelope behind it. With trembling hands he opened it and a building society deposit book fell out. He took a deep breath, turned to the last page and sat back in amazement. The date of the last deposit was listed as 1971 and the balance stood at £756,653.74 – this was the inheritance, and since there were no other children, it was all his. It wasn't until James' head had cleared and his eyes refocused that the little red stamp at the bottom of the page became apparent.

Account Closed – 26th May 1972

There was a neatly folded piece of notepaper on the stair, and this had clearly fallen out of the book when James had opened it. He unfolded it and immediately recognised his mother's handwriting. The message to his father was brief and to the point.

29 May 1972

Dear Mike,

Thanks for the gift. I'll make sure that I find a good use for it after all the years I've spent penny-pinching with you. Don't bother looking for me, I'll be long gone by the time you read this.

Joan

    He had to smile. In his original 'life', mum and dad had stayed together, but evidently the actions taken in 1949 had changed the course of their family history. Goodness only knows what his 'new' mum had done with the money.

LOOSE ENDS

Steve and Tracey had known each other since they were five years old. Her family had moved in next door to Steve's when Tracey's parents moved to the Midlands after her dad's job was relocated from the South East. They started school on the same day, sat next to each other in the same class, and went home together when one of either set of parents collected them at the playground gates. It wasn't really surprising then that they grew to become close friends.

They weren't inseparable, and each had their own set of school friends and activities, but outside of that environment they invariably spent much of their spare time together. They had similar interests, ate the same kind of food, and spent increasingly longer periods of time at each other's house. As they progressed through the education system, their academic records showed very similar levels of achievement and on one occasion both sets of parents were invited to a meeting with the headmaster to discuss the possibility that they had been cheating at one of their exams.

The allegation proved groundless, and the matter was quietly forgotten, but for a while Steve and Tracey were kept apart outside of school. This caused both children severe distress and both sets of parents relented, allowing the friendship to develop once more although now under much tighter supervision. As they progressed through school their grades maintained the early high levels, and public examinations at both GSCE and 'A' Level revealed exceptional performances, resulting in top grades in all subjects taken.

Both of them knew that there would eventually come a time when academic choices would force them in different directions, both physically and from a career point of view. Tracey had been awarded a place at veterinary college, while Steve's abilities in the area of information technology gained him access to the top university college in that field. They still spent all their free time in each other's company, and despite a number of other opportunities for relationships, kept to a promise they had made to each other at the start of their first undergraduate year.

Seven years later, with Tracey now a highly qualified veterinary surgeon specialising in small animals, and Steve at the top of his profession and working for a major player in IT system development, they took stock of their situation. They both believed that marriage and a family life was the obvious way forward, and Tracey was prepared for the inevitable career break at some point when children came along. What neither of them anticipated was the phone call Steve received from a high profile recruitment agency head hunting within the IT field.

His name had come to their attention as one of the top ten in his field, and they had been retained by the largest software developer in the world to recruit and hire the best young talent available. He was offered the chance to develop a career in the US, working at the client's head office in Seattle for a six figure salary plus benefits. He was stunned. The agency said that they would need an answer within a week, and gave him a direct line to the recruiter dealing specifically with the matter.

Steve's excitement at the opportunity dissolved immediately he explained the situation to Tracey. They would both have to live in the States for the foreseeable future, and although finding another job for her would not be a problem, it would mean pulling up roots which had been steadily growing for over twenty years. It was only now that Steve realised the strength of Tracey's family ties. She told him quite clearly that she could not possibly go.

Steve was angry, and accused her of denying him the career opportunity. She called him selfish and greedy, and asked if he had given one single thought to her wishes. They argued long into the evening and finished without any agreement whatsoever. The following day Steve discussed the offer with his mum and dad, and whilst they were pleased for him, both were very concerned at the rift which had appeared between the two young people. As the deadline day approached for his answer to the recruitment agency, Steve became more and more determined to go for the initial screening, and made the appointment without even mentioning it.

He had to travel to Birmingham for the meeting, and explained his absence to Tracey by telling her that his employer had scheduled a brainstorming session for a new operating system planned for release within the next eighteen months. It required an early start and he wouldn't be back home until late that evening. He had never lied to her before, and it made him feel extremely uncomfortable – a feeling that was to remain with him during the whole day. He knew that he hadn't given his best at the interview, but the recruitment agent must have picked up on it and asked him if he was feeling unwell. Steve thanked him, and said that he had been under the weather for a day or so – another lie, and this one was easier than the first. He hoped that this was not the start of a trend.

He arrived home to find the place empty. There was a note from Tracey saying that she had gone to her parents and would be back the following day. It was late, and after a shower and a bite to eat he went to bed, but sleep did not come easy and he spent the whole night tossing and turning. He wondered how he would explain it to her if he were to be offered the position. Steve slept in the next morning, and didn't hear the front door open and close as Tracey returned from her visit. When he got up she was in the kitchen sitting at the table with a cup of coffee, and it was clear that she had been crying. She had tried to contact him at work the previous day, and had asked to be forwarded to his mobile messaging service. They told her that this would not be possible as he had booked the day as one of his annual holidays, and that as the mobile was company issue it was still on his desk.

Tracey asked him if he was seeing someone else, and his evasiveness only made the matter worse. When he did eventually tell her what he had been doing the previous day, it must have sounded like some kind of excuse, and she called him a liar, went to their room, packed her things and left. He was devastated and wished now that he had told her all about the appointment - at least that would have got the matter out into the open, and he could have dealt with her anger on the spot. As it stood, there was now the added complication that she neither believed nor trusted him any more. There had to be a way around this.

Over the next few days he tried to reach Tracey at her mum and dad's, but she had left instructions with two obviously distraught parents that he was not to contact her and that she would not be returning to him. At the end of the week the agency rang to offer him a position in the States with their client company, and indicated that an answer was required within the next seven days. The starting date for the new job was in three months' time, and all travel arrangements would be made for him along with temporary accommodation whilst he found something more permanent. It really did seem to be the kind of opportunity which comes along just once in a lifetime, and he made one last attempt to see Tracey and discuss it with her.

He called at her parents' house a few days later and although they were pleased to see him, there was an uncomfortable edge to the meeting. They explained that they could not persuade their daughter to change her mind, and that she wouldn't tell them what had gone wrong. Steve showed them a letter from the agency which had arrived only that morning confirming the offer of the position in Seattle. He said that she would not believe his explanation of the events surrounding the interview, and that she suspected that he had been cheating on her. She was due back later that evening and they said that he should leave and let them talk to her when she arrived.

Steve went home and waited. Time was running out and he now had only two days left before his deadline for accepting the offer. There was no reply from Tracey, and he wrote to the agency confirming all the arrangements for the new position. He saw his boss the same day and gave three months' notice – plenty of time to hand over all his project work to other members of the software development team. From that day on there was no contact, and Steve concentrated on tying up all loose ends at home, saying his farewells to friends, reassuring his mum and dad that he would keep in touch and making preparations for the journey to America. When the day of departure came he still expected some late call which would have stopped him from going, but it didn't come and a vast emptiness filled him through the ten hour flight to the north west of the USA.

To say that Steve made a success of his career in Seattle would be an understatement. He rose quickly through the corporate system, heading up several teams involved in critical software programming and progressed to the position of Regional Head of Software Development. After a few years in this post, the company asked him to head up a new division in Washington looking at security systems for the US Government. He grabbed the opportunity with both hands and was very soon living in one of the best neighbourhoods on the kind of salary which he had never even dreamed of. It was here that he met Sadie.

He had never forgotten Tracey, but letters from home indicated that she had settled down with someone else, was married and had two children. Her career in veterinary practice had taken her to the position of partner in one of the top local practices and all seemed to be fine. It was a thinly veiled message to leave well alone, and Steve had no reason now to go raking over the past. After an uneventful courtship he and Sadie were married, but over the years it became clear that they were not destined to have any children of their own. They adopted Jason, a three year old whose parents had died in a plane crash and loved him as if he had been theirs all along. They watched him grow and develop and when he passed out of West Point with an officer's rank, they were very proud. His death in the first Gulf War came as a devastating blow and Sadie never seemed to recover from it.

Their lives carried on, and Steve's career peaked with the position of company Vice President over the entire eastern software development division. His professional life was now complete, but when Sadie developed a brain tumour in late 2002 their world started to dissolve again. She died in February 2003 leaving him once more alone, and Steve took this opportunity to retire and come back to Britain. His pension settlement was extraordinarily generous, and the company awarded him a final bonus payment in gratitude for the years of work he had devoted to the corporate cause. At the age of 52 he wound up his affairs and prepared for his return 'home'.

His parents were now in their early eighties and still living at the same house where he had said his 'goodbyes' years before. He had installed a computer and showed them how to use it to keep in touch before he left, but it wasn't the same as being there and their meeting up again was full of emotion. He stayed with them until a suitable house could be found, and conversation inevitably got around to Tracey. The room went very quiet and he sensed that there was something which they had been instructed not to reveal to him. Despite his insistent probing, it was nearly a week before he got the merest hint from his mother that she was no longer around, and when they both caved in and told him about the car crash three months earlier he sobbed uncontrollably.

Tracey, her husband and their son had been returning from a day out at a theme park, when an articulated lorry crossed the central reservation of the dual carriageway and collided with their vehicle. They were all killed instantly along with several other motorists behind them. Their daughter Samantha had not been with them that day, choosing instead to go shopping with friends. Steve sensed something else from his parents' uncomfortable manner and pressed home the issue of the girl. It was his mother who broke the news that Samantha was actually his daughter, and had been born five months after his departure for Seattle. Steve was speechless and asked why no-one had told him over the years. The explanation was that Tracey had met Bill, her husband, shortly after Steve had left for the States and had made it clear to everyone that he was not to be told about it.

Bill had been delighted to bring Samantha up as his own, and they arranged formal adoption proceedings to prevent the possibility of Steve returning and taking her back to America with him. Samantha had been kept in the dark about her natural father and his whereabouts. Steve's parents cautioned him against contacting her, advising that it would be best left alone as Samantha had her own life and was still trying to come to terms with the death of the family. Steve agreed to their wishes and set about finding somewhere to live and something to do in order to occupy his time.

Old friends from his days at the UK software company got in touch, and one of them offered him part-time work in a medium sized software company in Birmingham. Steve was pleased to be involved at grass roots level again and relished the challenge of setting something up from scratch. His search for a house had produced nothing concrete, so telling his parents of the new situation he accepted the position, packed up his stuff and made the travel arrangements for the following week. There was one last thing he felt that he needed to do. Buying some flowers from a local shop, he made his way to the cemetery which his mother had told him was the location of the grave of Tracey and her family.

He stood before the headstone placed there by her parents, reliving the early part of their lives together, going over once again the events leading up to his departure for the States, and wondering what would have happened if he had not made that fateful journey to the recruitment agency in Birmingham. He found all the old feelings returning to the surface and knew there and then that he still loved her, and that he should never have gone to America despite all the success it had brought him. Placing his flowers carefully on the ground he stepped back, wiped the tears from his eyes, said a silent 'goodbye' and walked slowly away. He made his way to the cemetery gates and turned for one last look. The scene was silent – there wasn't a breath of wind and he couldn't even hear a bird singing. He shook his head, took a deep breath and a moment later was gone.

A woman in her mid to late twenties entered the cemetery from the opposite gateway and noticed him walking towards the far exit, but gave the matter no thought as she approached the headstone with her own bunch of flowers. Her disinterest turned to curiosity when she read the message on the card with the flowers – 'So sorry for all the things we never did. Steve'. She looked from the flowers to her own bunch. They were both pink carnations, her mother's favourites. Who was this man, and how could he possibly know of Tracey's preference? She ran to the end of the cemetery where Steve had disappeared only to find him getting into a taxi some two hundred yards down the street. Her calls went unanswered and the vehicle pulled away, turned the corner, and Steve was gone.

THE BEST SUMMER

*T*hrough the throng of excited holidaymakers at Glasgow Central Station, I noticed that my dad wasn't wearing a tie – and I knew, there and then, that he wouldn't be wearing one for two whole wonderful weeks. He was always gone when we got up each morning and worked long hours, not returning home until well after the rest of us had gone to bed, leaving mum alone downstairs to prepare his supper. Our holidays were a rare and special time, when the entire family was together and all the cares he must have had at work seemed to drift away. Weekends were OK, but he always seemed too tired to play with us, and mum was always careful to make sure that we didn't disturb him when he dropped off for forty winks.

But the two week summer break was different. He seemed to come alive as if he had been saving up all his energy for us and the trip to Mrs Brown's B&B in Scarborough. We had been there before and it was within easy reach of other seaside resorts on the North Yorkshire coast. Oh, excuse my manners, but I was so excited that I forgot to introduce you to the rest of my family. There's dad, of course (Billy to his grown up friends), my mum whose name is Brenda, Sharon my older sister (she's 15 but thinks she's much older), our William who's only a baby at two, and then me – I'm Tommy, twelve years old and dad says I'll play for Partick Thistle one day if I practice a lot (they're his favourite team).

We all like the Yorkshire resorts, but Scarborough is my favourite and we hadn't been there for two years – see, we all got to choose each year and this was my turn. I wondered if it would have changed much since our last visit, and I must have been daydreaming because I let go of mum's hand to look at some comics on the newspaper stand. When I turned back round she wasn't there, and with so many other people at the station I suddenly felt very small and afraid. Dad had always told me that if I ever got lost I was to find a policeman and tell him, and there was one near the tea stand. I went up to him and was about to deliver the well-rehearsed lines which we had all been taught, when I felt a touch on my shoulder. I turned around to see dad's smiling face and buried my hand into his gigantic fist. I always felt so safe when he did that. Got some real stick from Sharon when we got back to mum, though.

Our train arrived soon after, and we managed to get a compartment all to ourselves. I liked that because we could spread out without having to bother about anyone else, and dad could drop off for the whole journey while we read books or comics, or played a very quiet game of I-spy. It was a long trip, but we all enjoyed it as part of the holiday, and it built up the excitement of arriving at Scarborough and finding Mrs Brown's. She was a very nice lady who liked children and always made a fuss of us. I didn't mind all that, but she did insist on giving us all a big hug, and seemed to reserve a very special kiss for me – 'my little man' she would call me, and there would have been serious trouble back in the playground if my mates ever found out.

Dad would always spend the first day sitting on the beach in a deckchair, mainly asleep, while he recovered from work, but from the second morning on it would be different as he took part in all our games, dug enormous holes in the sand and helped us build sand castles. I told him that he would be in trouble with the council if the sea came through the hole and flooded the town, but he just gave me one of those great big grins and dug even deeper. He would suddenly stop digging, get out of the hole, dust himself down and announce ice creams for all. He said you couldn't work in the midday sun without food, and the best seaside food was ice cream. It was a race to the van and dad always won (actually we always let him because he had the money, but I think he knew that).

Now, years later, the memories are as clear as if the events happened only yesterday. We never left Scarborough without at least one visit to the castle up on the headland, and dad had always carried me up the steep hill on his shoulders for as long as I could remember, but when you get to twelve it's time to make the effort for yourself and this time he didn't argue. We always went the back road through the town on the first trip because mum liked to look in the shops on the way, but dad insisted on going the other way next time – it was steeper and he said that all real explorers should go the hard way. It's an impressive place, and even now years later when I take my own children the feeling of awe is always present.

We would run around the battlements and in and out of the keep, playing fighting games with pretend weapons like halberds, swords and spears. Dad would always get in the way of a sword thrust and die a horrible and prolonged death. Mum always said he overdid the agony bit, and that he was not to give up his daytime job. He would get up and run after her with a pretend spear – she would squeal and disappear into the ladies toilets until it was safe to come out. It made us all laugh and then he would come after us. After that we would sit down in the castle grounds and eat the picnic which Mrs Brown had prepared for us. She was a very generous lady and always seemed to pack far too much but dad said we would walk it off in the afternoon. There were lots of penny arcades on the seafront, and we must have spent hours in them but mum and dad never complained, especially since I always seemed to come out with more pennies than I went in. Mum said that I could pay for a trip on a boat with my winnings and I was never sure whether or not she was serious.

It was like this for day after day and the sun always seemed to shine, it was always hot, and the ice cream sellers never seemed to run out. We had fish and chips most days, and although dad said it wasn't good for us to eat so much fried stuff, I didn't see him refuse in all the times we went on holiday. By the time we got back to Mrs Browns each day we were tired out, and after a quick bath we only seemed to have enough strength to get into bed. Mrs Brown's beds were the old fashioned metal framed ones with thick mattresses and soft fluffy pillows. It was like slipping into a cotton wool cocoon, and you were asleep before you knew it.

All too soon it was time to pack up and return home, and the last day was always the saddest. We would say our goodbyes to Mrs Brown and promise to see her next time, give her a present which we had spent all week choosing and was just what she had always wanted, and then make our way to the station for the trip home. This was always the quietest day of the fortnight when there was nothing to look forward to except another year of dad being tired before our next holiday. I didn't know it then, but there was not to be another holiday with dad. He had been tired for a while, and this had been because he was sick and getting sicker all the time. He died in the November, and although we had enough savings to tide us over while mum found a job, there was never enough for any more holidays. Scarborough was the last one and all my memories of him were of that last, wonderful, special fortnight.

HIT AND RUN

*T*oo fast, he was definitely travelling too fast, and a number of other motorists had flashed him and blared their horns as he flew past them in the outside lane. This was madness and he couldn't even remember who he was or where he was going – there certainly didn't seem to be any vehicle chasing him. Recovering composure and slowing down, he pulled right over into the nearside lane of what the last blue information sign had told him was the M1 southbound, and counted himself fortunate that he had not been stopped by a motorway patrol. The next sign indicated Watford Gap services in nine miles and the eight minutes he took to reach it seemed to take forever.

He pulled into the car park and stopped in the corner, well away from any other vehicles or members of the general public. He was now aware that he was shaking and perspiring profusely. A search of the vehicle revealed no clues as to his identity, the only clothes being those he stood up in and a jacket in the rear seating area, and that contained nothing more than some loose change and a comb. He sat on one of the picnic benches for a while, trying to figure out what he should do. The speed of his journey convinced him that he was trying to get home at the earliest possible time, so perhaps there was someone waiting for him and getting more worried by the minute.

He needed help, and the police squad car across the parking area now came to his attention. He walked over to it but found no-one inside – typical, never one there when you wanted a copper. His head had started to spin, when he heard footsteps approaching from behind and a voice asked

"Anything wrong, sir?"

He blinked several times. Trying to get his eyes to focus.

"Sir?" came the voice again, a little more insistent this time, and he saw two of them about ten feet away. Close enough to subdue him if things got out of hand, but far enough away to evade attack. He noticed that one of the officers had withdrawn a cosh from his belt and was looking around, possibly for a confederate. It was a warm day, and as he wiped the sweat away from his brow, he noticed the crimson stain on his hand – it was tacky and clearly fairly fresh.

"I....er..." he heard himself say, and then things really began to spin, and he blacked out. The next thing he saw when he came round was the green clad figure of a paramedic who had him on a stretcher and had placed an oxygen mask over his face. He tried to pull it away, but stronger arms than his restrained him, and he felt himself being lifted into an ambulance. He couldn't make out what anyone was saying, and minutes later he was being whisked away with sirens and lights clearing the route. He passed out again.

He awoke in the accident and emergency department of some hospital, and heard a doctor talking to one of the police officers. Apparently X-rays had revealed no fractures, and apart from the concussion and a cut at the back of the head there didn't appear to be anything wrong. Nevertheless they would be keeping him in overnight for observation. The officer said that he would return the following day and take a statement from the patient. He drifted back off to sleep and must have needed it – he didn't wake until the next afternoon. They asked him all the questions he was unable to answer like who he was, where he lived, where he'd been and where he was going. Why were they so stupid?

Nothing in his car had been found which identified him, and after being discharged, he was taken to the local police station to be interviewed. He still had no idea what he had been doing, and was unable to help the police in their efforts to get to the bottom of his condition. The officers whom he had met at the service area had submitted his car details to DVLA in order to trace the name of the registered owner. Apparently he was George Wilkinson, and an address in Northampton had been given to them. They said they would take him there and his vehicle would follow on behind. As they approached the suburbs of the town, he started to become aware that he had been there before, and on a number of occasions. An icy chill crept down his spine and he began to feel nauseous.

They pulled up outside a large house with a double garage in a leafy area. The gardens were immaculate and there was a Porsche sports car in the driveway. He now remembered quite clearly, he wasn't George Wilkinson at all - his name was David Bryant and he was George's driver. They had been in Leeds collecting 'subscriptions' from customers of Wilkinson's protection and prostitution rackets. Everything now moved on apace. He had coshed George and tried to snatch the briefcase containing the takings from him, but he wouldn't let go. In the scuffle, George must have hit him on the head with the briefcase, but went down under a rain of further blows. Bryant remembered running for it without the bag when he saw people approaching – obviously drawn by the noise of the attack.

Now he was between the devil and the deep blue sea, with four coppers behind him and goodness knows what beyond the front door which they were rapidly approaching. One of the officers rang the bell, and it seemed to be ringing out his death knell. George would have had plenty of time to get home, and was probably now sitting inside at his study desk waiting to take out his revenge. The door was opened by a blonde in a two piece with matching accessories, and a wide-eyed look of surprise and relief.

"George baby, you're safe. Oh come here and let me look at you. What have you been doing and where have you been? Thank you officers for bringing him home, I've been worried to death."

The police smiled amongst themselves, saluted and left, with Celia (for this was George's wife) waving them tearfully away. She pushed him inside after checking that they had disappeared, and locked the door. He stood there in the middle of the hall waiting for the inevitable rush of Wilkinson's heavies, and his transportation to one of the well-known 'reception rooms' where he would surely be worked over into a pulp before being disposed of at the bottom of some lake or in the foundations of a high rise block well away from Northampton. Nothing of the sort happened. Celia turned to him after what seemed an eternity.

"You killed him then? Of course you did, we saw it on the news – 'Unidentified male found beaten to death in Leeds city centre car park. Police are still searching for clues.' They won't find any, the clear up team were in as soon as you had gone, and nothing was left on his body to trace him down here. We even got the briefcase that you left behind."

"It was a set-up?" He asked, now knowing full well what the answer would be, but still unsure of his immediate fate.

"Of course, we talked about it two weeks ago after I found out about that bimbo he'd been sleeping with. You'll be safe as long as you do as you're told. We keep our noses clean down here, so the local plods will never make the connection."

He now became aware of the presence of others in the room with them, and he turned around to see two gorillas standing by the door – he hadn't even heard them come in. It was clear that they were there to ensure that the rest of the arrangements went according to plan. Celia beckoned him to another room and the two heavies followed at a less than discrete distance.

"There's a change of clothing here, it looks as though you could do with one and all the papers you'll need are in the envelope in the overnight bag. Check that everything is there because this is a one-way trip. The money has already been transferred into the account we set up in Jersey, and you should be able to access it immediately. The passport is in your new name. These two 'gentlemen' will assist you in your journey to the airport and will make sure that you board your flight without any problems."

She smiled as she turned to leave the room, safe in the knowledge that with George gone, she would now be able to run the organisation properly. Maybe she should take out the bimbo as well just for good measure. Nice idea – she'd keep that one on ice for the future – you never know if she started asking awkward questions.

"In a few weeks time, I'm going to file a missing persons report which will detail the removal of a significant amount of cash from our joint account. I will be so upset that I shouldn't be surprised if they nominated me for an Oscar for the performance. Now get out and don't let me see you again unless you want to be saying 'Hi' to Georgie."

FALLING

*F*alling wasn't a problem. It was easy, all you had to do was to step out and let gravity take its course. The rest of it was firmly in the hands of the laws of physics. Falling wouldn't hurt, there would be the sensation of air rushing past with perhaps the vague feeling of breathlessness, but even that wouldn't matter in the end. Falling didn't kill you, it was the impact at the end of the drop that was the fatal stroke. Julie had thought about it for a long time now, and this was the only answer. There didn't seem to be any way out of the situation that she had allowed to germinate and develop, and it was now out of control. This was the way of reasserting that control, even if it was at the cost of her own life, and if anyone was unsure of the circumstances the note in her pocket would set them all straight.

She had met Joe at an office party and after a whirlwind romance they were married. She knew that he had been involved with a number of other women before, but he promised her that those days were all behind him, and that she was the only one he would ever love. Friends told her that he had a chequered past and that leopards never changed their spots, but she ignored them out of hand and lost a number of them as a result. She knew him and they didn't, after all he had asked her to marry him, hadn't he?

Her parents were a little concerned at the speed with which the relationship had developed, and cautioned her against any precipitate decisions on her future. Whilst they didn't dislike Joe, and he had always been very polite in their company, her mum in particular had said that there was something about him that she couldn't quite put her finger on, and which made her very uneasy. Julie made her feelings on the matter clear and although she respected her parents' opinion, told them firmly that she was going ahead with wedding plans and that she hoped they would be there for her.

Preparations all went according to plan, and when the day came everything went along smoothly. Her mum and dad had to admit that there was nothing obvious to support any feelings of unease, and in no time at all the newlyweds were away on their honeymoon - a fortnight in Greece. The time flew by, and on their return it was the considered opinion amongst all of Julie's friends that she positively glowed. A few sly nudges and winks from those closest suggested that it might not be too long before additions to their household were apparent, but she blushed and ignored them.

The house they had bought in Margate was perfect. Not small and yet not expensive. Joe seemed to have all his ducks in a row, and there were no signs of extravagance. It wasn't until they had been married for six months that he began making noises about her giving up work – after all, he was on a salary level that could support them both plus any additions to their family. Julie resisted, telling him that she liked the feeling of contributing to the monthly budget, and that her wages would provide for any luxuries that came along. It was obvious that this didn't please him and he became more and more insistent; one evening after he had been drinking steadily since dinner the matter descended into a full blown row, and he struck her. It was a punch to the eye and she was lucky to have fallen across the settee. He didn't even apologise until late the following day, but the first step had been taken and things got worse from that point.

If she had only told someone immediately and before the bruising had disappeared she could probably have stopped him going any further, but she took to wearing sunglasses outside the house, and it was weeks before she discussed it with her parents. Her dad was all for confronting Joe, but Julie told him that it would only make things worse and anyway there was no proof but her own testimony that it had actually happened. They reluctantly agreed on condition that if anything like it happened again she would come to them straight away.

It didn't of course, and for a while things returned to normal. They had been trying for a family for a while but after having been married for eighteen months it was becoming apparent that something was wrong, and medical tests revealed that Julie was sterile. This was a devastating blow to her personally and for their marriage in general, and Joe started taking it out on her. He wasn't careless enough to use his fists any more, but the constant psychological barrage every day was starting to take its toll. He would blame her for ruining his life, calling her 'barren', 'sterile' and 'frigid' when she refused sex. He then started accusing her of being a lesbian and asked her how many 'dyke' lovers she had.

It was inevitable that depression would set in, but she held back from seeking medical advice, thinking that she could handle the situation herself.

Then came the anonymous telephone call telling her of Joe's involvement with a woman at his office. The person (Julie couldn't make out whether the voice was male or female) even gave details of the places, dates and times of their meetings and said that she would be better off without him. She started to drink, just the odd glass at first, but as the weeks drifted past in her increasingly lonely existence they became larger and more frequent, until one day she made the decision to follow him.

His meetings with the woman were regular at a specific hotel, and Julie made sure that she was sitting in the reception area half an hour before their next 'scheduled appointment.' She had decided that she would not show any emotion when they appeared, but could not suppress the sharp intake of breath when they walked through the door. He spotted her immediately and just stood there at the desk smiling that seductive smile of his, but she knew that the feeling behind it was far from friendly. Having checked in they went on to their room. The woman hadn't even noticed that she had been there.

Julie left immediately and drove out of the area to a secluded spot. She broke down and sobbed hysterically as the full realisation that their marriage was over dawned upon her. What was she going to do? She couldn't tell her parents, it would be too shameful and her dad would almost certainly go out looking for Joe. No, there had to be another answer and the one she came up with was that if she were no longer around the whole problem would go away. She went home and sitting down in the lounge, poured herself a large glass of whisky. She had always believed that suicide was a coward's way out of a problem, but that was before she fully realised what kind of situation could drive a person to contemplate it.

When Julie finally decided on jumping, it seemed that the only remaining fact to consider was location. There were plenty of places in town which could be used, a car park for instance, but that would almost certainly cause distress for any witnesses. No, somewhere on the coast, and there were plenty of high cliffs along the footpath. The sooner the better she thought, and picking up her car keys she set out for the Kent cliffs. It wasn't far, and parking in one of the long stay car parks, she walked the short distance to the place of her destiny.

It was a cloudless, sunny day with a light breeze, and Julie thought it odd that she should have noticed the weather in the circumstances. Inching closer to the cliff edge she went through the events of the last year and a half – was there any doubt in her mind? No, it was now or never. The only thing to look forward to was a life of unending misery with a husband who no longer loved her and who would, in all likelihood, return to violence as their marriage disintegrated.

She stepped forward, one foot into the void, one step from oblivion. The fall would be a silent release from all her troubles, she whispered 'sorry' to her mum and dad and then at the end there would be blackness. The arm pulling her back nearly carried them both over the edge, but Julie found herself spinning around into the welcoming arms of her father.

"We followed you from home, love. Come on, we'll take you with us, he's not worth even this. It never happened."

She collapsed into his arms and he carried her to the car.

Out of the Frying Pan

Mark knew that he was for the high jump as soon as he got the summons to head office from Burt Travers, the head of corporate HR. He had failed on a number of potentially lucrative contracts, and the work required to seal each deal had been neither complicated nor time consuming. Someone of his ability should have had them nailed down and signed weeks ago, but instead he had let them slip away to the company's main rival by a combination of laziness and lack of attention to detail. He had been warned by his regional manager, Steve, that unless he pulled himself together there would be serious consequences, and to be fair to the man he had gone out on a limb in his efforts to turn Mark around.

Now it was time to face the music, and as he sat in the company's reception area of the 38th floor of the World Trade Center in New York, he started to worry about how he was going to explain things to his wife Selma. They had been married for twenty-two years and although they had no children, his was the only source of income and they had a hefty mortgage to pay on their Philadelphia home. It was a riverfront property off St Columbus Boulevard, and he had gambled on his commission to pay off the interest on the loan. He was snapped out of his reverie by a call over the reception intercom.

"Doreen, send Mr Carston in please."

"Sure Mr Travers." and she waved Mark down the corridor to room 3810.

Travers was standing facing the window, looking out across the New York skyline when Mark entered. He told him to take a seat in that blunt, dead, no-nonsense voice of his which Mark had heard on a number of occasions when Travers had visited the Midwest offices in Philadelphia. It always sent a shudder down the spine even when you weren't the one being addressed, and the man had the reputation of being the corporate butcher. He turned around and stubbed out his cigar in a large ornate marble ashtray, went to the door and asked Doreen to bring in a cup of coffee, and leaving it open took a deep breath, shook his head and sat down.

"Carston, normally in circumstances like this I would have the cops standing in the corner ready to take you away after what we've found out about your activities, but it's your lucky day. With the merger coming up we don't want any jitters affecting the stock price now that we've almost got pen put to paper."

He went on to explain that although Mark's insider trading activities had been cleverly concealed, a routine computer diagnostic run had been made using the new prototype software which had only been installed at head office a month ago. No other sites were using it, and a number of transactions had fallen into the random sample selected by the program. There was incontrovertible proof that he had been siphoning off funds for a number of years into his personal bank account, and all the evidence was there on Travers' desk in front of him. The only thing left to decide was how to terminate Mark's employment without causing too many ripples in the merger proceedings.

Travers' suggestion to the board was going to be relocation for Mark to Oregon, to the regional offices in Portland as deputy to the manager of the smallest operation in the firm. From there he would be quietly retired without pension after an appropriate time. Any failure to agree to this option would result in prosecution for abuse of company privileges. Travers would, of course, ensure that some incriminating evidence of a minor financial irregularity would surface in order to justify immediate termination.

Mark sat frozen in time for what seemed like an eternity. It doesn't matter how well you are prepared for the consequences of any actions, the final statement always comes as a shock. Travers had to jolt him out of his 'trance' with a sharp tap on the desk in front of him, and asked if he understood what had been said. Before Mark had a chance to answer, there was what sounded like a loud explosion from above, and a cascade of debris falling past outside the office. Travers went over to the window, closely followed by Mark, to see what had happened and leaned out to look upwards. He was caught by a large piece of falling masonry and plummeted thirty-eight floors downwards to certain death. Mark had tried to reach out to grab him as he went over the window ledge but he had been too slow.

Not believing what he had just seen, Carston stood staring at the window and was only shaken out of his trance by more falling debris. His immediate reaction was to get the hell out of there, but with unbelievable calmness he picked up the documents left on Travers' desk, put them into his briefcase and walked slowly out of the office, closing the door behind him and almost colliding with a static Doreen in the process. There were a number of people hurrying to the reception area and making for the elevators, and Mark's instinct told him to ignore them and head for the emergency stairways. They were clear at present, but he could hear screams coming from above, telling him that large numbers were descending to his level with great rapidity.

Taking the steps two at a time he was soon down to the 30th floor where an empty elevator was standing open. Against his better judgement he got in and punched the ground floor button. The doors closed just as a crowd of terrified people came around the lobby corner. Self preservation is a primal feeling, and Mark descended alone to the 10th floor where the elevator stopped and a flood of people rushed in. He pressed himself into the front corner and when they hit ground level, held his nerve and waited to avoid being crushed. It was abundantly clear that something catastrophic had happened, but his only concern now was getting clear of the building and in the fastest time possible.

It was like a sea of humanity, with terrified people all heading in the same direction and there were now the first clouds of dust-like material coming from above. There was no chance of running, so he went along with the pace of the crowd which quickened as the main entrance doors appeared. Everything now appeared to be happening in slow motion and a series of ominous rumbling sounds came from above, increasing in volume and intensity with each passing moment. Suddenly he was out in the street amid clouds of flying debris, and he headed for the nearest cover to avoid falling masonry of the type which accounted for Travers. He made it to a coffee bar and looked around for means of further escape. The sidewalk to his left appeared to be clear and led down the street and away from the World Trade Center – he ran as fast as his legs could carry him.

He had to find a telephone to call Selma. Looking around him, this was a major disaster and the news media would be all over it like a rash. He had to tell her that he was OK, but there was no answer from home so he rang her mother's house. She had been there when the news broke, and knowing that he had an appointment in New York that afternoon, was glued to the TV set in the lounge. Selma was nearly hysterical with relief, but he calmed her down and said he would be home that evening. In the confusion, no-one seemed to be bothered with survivors escaping the worst of the damage, and he made it back to the lot where his Buick was parked without anyone giving him so much as a second glance.

On the way home Mark mulled over what had happened. Travers clearly stated that the software which had picked up his transactions was a prototype version, and not on general release throughout the corporation. Mark knew that he was in possession of the only hard copy evidence, and Travers had been swept out of the window to certain death thirty-eight floors below. Who, therefore, was left to corroborate the findings Travers had made? He had told Mark that he was going to make a recommendation to the board, so it was reasonable to assume that the investigation had not yet reached that level. He could still be in possession of his job, the private account was still known only to him, and if he acted as if nothing had happened it was conceivable that he could get away with it.

Selma raced down the driveway and threw herself into his arms as soon as he pulled up outside their home. She was gabbling incomprehensibly, and it took Mark half an hour to calm her down. He didn't tell her about Travers or the details of the meeting, but just said it was a follow-up to performance related issues, and they had suggested he apply for a position at head office. He, of course, had declined and said that he was happy where he was. From what he saw on the newscasts, everything inside the Trade Center had been destroyed. All he had to do now was steel his nerves, return to work the following day and face down the barrage of questions.

Three months later and the carnage of 9/11 had been all over the world's press every day, but for Mark everything had returned to something approaching normality. Normal, that is, until a knock at the door one evening saw him faced with two federal agents. They had an arrest warrant bearing his name for the murder of Burt Travers on the morning of September 11th 2001. A sworn statement from a witness had him pushing the head of HR through the office window on the 38th floor.

A Shot in the Dark

*O*ne clear and uninterrupted sight line would be all that he required. One shot would complete the job and then he could pack up all his kit and leave. Exit would be a lot easier than getting in. There would be no need for radio messages – radios were too bulky anyway, would only get in the way and might even lead pursuers straight to him. No, one brief coded line in the form of an encrypted e-mail bounced off a satellite from his Blackberry to a secure IP address, and arrangements would be activated for a collection at designated co-ordinates known only to himself and the client.

The job had taken a fair amount of setting up due to the ultra tight security which surrounded the target at all times, and entry into the country had been by means of a covert action within a set of scheduled army movements in a neighbouring territory. Arrangements had been made for him to go AWOL whilst on manoeuvres, and his 'name' and serial number never appeared on any roll call sheet. He simply slipped away during the darkness hours, making his way across country and keeping off all roads. The thick vegetation afforded ample cover from prying eyes, and after he changed out of his army fatigues into the special uniform which he had carried in his back pack, all unnecessary equipment was buried deep enough so as not to attract any unwanted attention.

Now it was a case of keeping out of sight and away from all settlements between him and the border. He reckoned it would be a three day hike, and he would have to live off the land on the way – not a problem, as this was what all the Special Forces training had taught him to do in the seven years he served with the unit. The real difficulty would be the approach to and the crossing of the frontier, as regular border patrols, with orders to shoot first and ask questions later, ensured that very little human activity went on undetected around there.

He reached his first destination point half a day early and settled down under cover to monitor patrol activity for the next week. The border guards were heavily armed, regular and very efficient in their routines. All local buildings were checked, rechecked the following day and, he was sure, booby trapped to catch any unsuspecting travellers seeking concealment. They rotated their shift patterns, but he was able to work out very quickly when the next visit was likely, and they were always on time. On day eight he decided to make his move and used a dried up river bed for the initial part of his journey. The guards were clad in standard olive drab uniforms which made them highly visible against the scrublands, and maybe that was the point – visibility in itself being a potent form of deterrence.

His own clothing was a reversible olive drab and khaki, and the latter shade was currently keeping him out of the immediate sight of any government army units. Nevertheless this was a time for caution, and the slightest slip would find him inside one of their infamous interrogation compounds; he had never heard of anyone coming out of there alive. Time was on his side, as the target was not scheduled to be in the area for another week or so. The man was fastidious in his insistence upon reviewing army units himself, and this caused obvious security problems for his personal guard. Army camps were always located in open ground, thus denying cover to any would-be assassin and last minute forays into neighbouring undergrowth had always been used to flush out potential snipers. This tactic had been successfully used on a number of occasions in the past, and the remains of several corpses were hung from trees around the country as messages to the locals.

He was not a local. He had no name. He carried no identification, and all labels and serial numbers had been carefully removed from every item of equipment. He simply didn't exist and no government on earth would acknowledge him. This was what made him special, and he had operated in all of the world's war zones since the early 1990s, coming out of each assignment completely unscathed and undetected. This one was no different – the target was merely an embarrassment that certain powers wished to have removed, and their reasons were none of his business. As long as they paid for the service he was more than happy to be their agent.

He had acquired the target's itinerary, and had insisted upon choosing the location of the hit himself to avoid any possibility of detection. He selected a camp two days travel from his current hideaway and had allowed himself plenty of time to disappear into the undergrowth. Range would be a distance of some six hundred metres from the site of the inspection. His specially built, high-powered night vision sniper rifle came fitted with its own laser sight and silencer. Guards surrounding the target would have no idea where the shot came from, and he was certain that a single bullet would take care of this assignment.

He spent a couple of days setting up his line of fire from a number of possible sites in the undergrowth, and the pile of bones buried in a shallow grave was the only evidence of his presence and its impact upon the indigenous mammal population. Finally he was ready and settled down to await the arrival of his victim, a wait which was to last two more days. This was the main problem in his line of 'work', and there was always the danger of boredom setting in and disrupting all his preparations. It was another area where his years in the Special Forces had trained him - the art of patience, an asset which had come in handy on many occasions.

At last, in the gathering gloom, there was a sudden burst of activity in the camp compound, and an advance army unit quickly spread out into the immediate area of bush. His camouflage rendered him invisible to the naked eye, and complete stillness made him impossible to detect. The soldiers returned to their troop carrier, and a message was obviously sent out that the area was clear and safe to enter. The dictator's convoy now entered the camp, and after several bodyguards had made a protective shield, he stepped down from the vehicle to be greeted by the local commander.

The sniper had the target in his sights immediately and tracked every movement to ensure that he had a clear shot. With his breathing under control and his finger squeezing the trigger very slowly, he waited for the first stationary moment. The recoil from the rifle was minimal and the sound of the gunshot barely discernible. Keeping the target in sight he watched as the uniformed figure of the president crumpled and fell with a single, but fatal, wound right between the eyes. Panic was instantaneous, and automatic gunfire peppered the area in all directions, fanning outwards from the camp. He took no notice – there was no chance of his position being located; he packed up his gear, removed all trace of his position and carefully backed out of the tree line until he was clear.

The assassin had three days until the pick up he had arranged from his palm top computer, but he had chosen a very different route out of the country from the one which brought him in. A forty mile march across open scrub after dark in a northerly direction took him far away from the hive of activity along the border to the west, and the chopper arrived at exactly the time arranged. No words were exchanged between him and the pilot – they both had jobs to do and saw no profit in idle conversation. His arrangement had been for a drop just inside the border of the northern neighbour, giving him ample time to cross over and lose himself in a friendly country.

He watched the helicopter depart and held his position for an hour, listening with heightened senses for any signs of pursuit. Satisfied that he was clear, he gathered up his belongings and headed for the crossing. He never got there. An army troop transport appeared to his left, and he knew that it would be useless to try to outrun it. He put down his kit, laid his rifle clearly on the ground and raised his hands. If he anticipated execution on the spot he was to be mildly surprised. The soldiers collected his things, dropped the tailgate of the transport and assisted him inside. The journey lasted about two hours, and apart from being offered a drink, nothing was said to him.

They pulled up outside another army camp; he was escorted inside, taken to the main building and shown into a room where a single figure stood looking out into the grounds. The man turned around.

"Mr Sharpe, that was certainly a very impressive display of covert operations, and a highly efficient method of disposal. I assume that I have your permission to examine the rifle?"

Sharpe, for that was his name, stood unblinking before the dictator whom he had assumed to have been the victim of his assignment. Joseph Maninga smiled a broad toothy smile and poured two glasses of Jim Beam, offering one to his captive.

"Do not be disappointed Mr Sharpe, I have a number of doubles around my country. Men who are willing, for a price to put their lives on the line. You were not to know that your target was one of them."

Sharpe stiffened, took the drink in one go, and prepared himself for the inevitable torture and execution which had been the fate of so many before. Instead, Maninga waved him to a leather armchair and sat down opposite in an identical one.

"A man in my position, Mr Sharpe, makes many enemies in the course of his lifetime and I have the need of someone with, shall we say, a certain level of skill. You are that man, and now that I have found you, there is really no option but that you will work for me. No government in the world will open its doors to you, and I have a little job that requires some attention, and your agreement to carry it out, before you will be allowed to leave my country..."

AT YOUR COMMAND

Sinai
31st July

Dear God

Further to our little chat on the mountain the other day and the instructions you gave to me for forwarding to the masses, there are a few things that have been puzzling me. I think it's best, if it's alright with you, that we sort this out before I release them for publication. I know you are our God Almighty, Omniscient, Omnipresent and all that, I appreciate that a lot of planning must have gone into them and I am sure you haven't just dashed them off in a moment of blind thought. However, as I am going to be the one facing all the questions I feel that I ought to have the answers ready – they can be a funny lot sometimes, these children of Israel.

Anyway, here goes. The first and second commandments are a bit long-winded, and it sounds as if you are laying down the law a bit too strong, bearing in mind what comes a little later. I think they will all understand how the land lies with you, and that you have been around since way before Adam's day. We are all grateful, I am sure, for our deliverance from the Egyptians – they really were a load of slave drivers, and the food was a bit too spicy for some of us (you didn't want to be around on a Saturday night). We don't need any other gods, one will be quite sufficient thank you, but it might be helpful if you could supply some signed photographs so that your folks down here will know what you look like. This could kill the 'idol' thing stone dead, and it would not conflict with item six on your list – you know, the 'murder' thingy.

Also, and excuse me for being a little forward, visiting the sins of the fathers upon the heads of future generations is unlikely to get you many votes in the public relations area, so if you could rethink that one it might be helpful in convincing your followers to love you for the thousand generations you mention. I don't mean to be picky, but maybe you could use a little help in the subtlety department – I believe I have some time free next Wednesday afternoon.

Moving on, taking your name in vain is not a very nice thing to do, and I appreciate why you would like this to be clearly understood. Could you let us have a list of acceptable expletives which can be used without fear of retribution of any kind? Please understand that hitting one's pinky with a hammer is apt to invoke some form of verbal release, and we would all appreciate some guidance on this matter.

Next – The Sabbath. Good plan, we all need a day reserved especially for talking to you, and if you could devise some form of rota it would be appreciated. This would avoid the situation where we all try to talk to you at the same time, and I know from experience with all the kids around here that you can't possibly make a decision with everyone twittering on together.

Also, I like the idea of one day each week when we can all chill out and rest – this is a big vote winner. If this is the day you would like to schedule for talking to you, all the better. However, could you leave off the bit about you creating everything in just six days please? We know you work hard, and it just comes off as bragging and I could do without the aggravation of facing a barrage of insults when I try to make your case. All mums and dads have a special place in our society as you must be aware, and even though the kids sometimes take us for granted we are always around when they are in need of a few shekels for the odd drink or night out now and then. I suppose you must know how that feels – or perhaps not as your only son hasn't been born yet (must swot up on those Prophets pamphlets again). It would be helpful if we could clearly understand if this is restricted to mums and dads, or is also extended to grandparents – there are one or two clever dicks down here who might take it as a free licence to take the mickey out of some of the older members of our little group.

The instruction not to murder is a bit of a 'gimme', but does it apply to your enemies or are you going to take care of that as you did with those plague thingies in Egypt and the Red Sea demo (I know that it wasn't really me doing it)? I mean, if you are going to be watching over us and protecting the group from enemy attack that's all well and good, but what happens if you're not looking one day or are busy with something else? Do we defend ourselves, or ask any belligerents to wait for a moment while we get a message to you? Perhaps you could have a think about that one and get back to us.

The adultery thing is a bit of a tricky one. I'm not too worried personally, and I think the rest of us 'wrinklies' will be OK with it. It's the youngsters I'm a bit concerned about. They've been born and brought up in Egypt, and some of their customs were a bit dubious to say the least. Maybe a seminar on the dangers of unprotected sex would dampen their ardour a bit, together with a list of forfeits and/or penalties for breaking the rules. Nothing too draconian you understand – no cutting bits off or anything, and no putting things in their food and drink after that last time with the laxatives please.

Stealing – again, does this apply to the world in general or is it limited to just amongst ourselves? We've not exactly had the best time of it of late, and I keep coming back to the Egyptians as an example of how we have suffered at the hands of a pretty unscrupulous oppressor. Taking from the likes of them surely cannot count as anything seriously wrong; after all, a lot of us died while we were constructing their fancy buildings for them – fair's fair, you know.

'Bear false witness' – if you mean telling lies it would be best if you just come out with it instead of beating about the bush. (Talking of bushes, I've still got the burn marks from that last one you appeared in, so I'd appreciate it if you could tone the visions down a bit in the future). There are a few down here who won't understand if you use flowery language; although I could probably interpret what you mean, there's still the chance that I might get it wrong and then your laws could be up the spout for who knows how long. Also, could you please be a little more precise as to who exactly you mean by 'your neighbour'? Is this the family in the next tent on either side or is there some wider meaning to the statement? I'm sorry to labour the point, but you surely aren't including the Egyptians in this, are you?

I'm glad we've got to the last one, because this is the item I found most confusing. If you go around using words like 'covet' it is always a good idea to define your terms first. I mean, I have looked it up in my thesaurus and that lists a number of alternatives such as 'desire', 'want', 'long for', 'yearn for', 'crave' and 'hanker after' and whilst all of these could be easily applied to humans, I would be a little careful about their usage where animals are concerned. There are some oddballs amongst our number, and if you give them as much as an inch they'll take a mile. Any recognition of their 'special needs' is going to cause mutterings of discontent amongst the rest if you are seen to be giving special consideration – see where I'm coming from?

So, I hope that you won't think I've been too forward, but I reckon if I am going to be your spokesperson to the masses, it really is important that I understand clearly what it is that you want from us. I mean it's not as bad as it must be for the Greeks and Romans, with a god for this and a god for that. At least you're the only one we've got, so we know more or less where we are. Anyway, I'm going to put these tablets away (out of the reach of children – get it?) until you've had time to think about what I've said. If you need me at any time, just bellow my name and I'll make myself available – don't take any notice of the wife and any of her excuses. I sometimes wish I'd never brought her along.

Yours grovellingly,
Moses

PS

Joshua says to tell you that the parting of the Red Sea was the coolest thing he has ever seen, and could you make it an annual event for the kids? If that's possible, we could run day trips from the Promised Land each year.

AND DID THESE FEET

*M*y feet are killing me – I've been on them all day at that market stall and it's been hot enough to fry an egg on a Roman's breastplate. Mind you, frying a Roman would be preferable right now considering all the restrictions they put on us these days. That Herod's no good, he's just a patsy, kowtowing to the governor instead of standing up for his own people – still, I suppose someone's got to be 'numero uno' as the Latins say.

I'm just so fed up with the constant bickering over prices though. Don't these people realise that I've got a living to make? Three kids all at school and a wife with fashion tastes certainly takes it out on the pocket. Dear Miriam, I shouldn't complain really, she does her best and the Romans pay well enough if you know what I mean. Not too sure about our Brian though. He's the youngest and I haven't quite worked out when his birthday actually is. I'm sure I was doing my stint at national service at around that time, but there's no-one to complain to anyway. The Romans just laugh at you if you do.

What I need now is a basin of cold water for my poorly tootsies and a read of the daily blurb. I suppose we could go down the inn after dinner, but it'll only be packed out with the ninth legion – I think it's their quiz night tonight and I'm rubbish at Latin so there'd be no point in joining in. Sitting at the bar would be no good either – you can't gossip with Augustus's spies everywhere – God my feet ache and I'm famished!

Maybe I should have stayed on at school instead of going into the family business. Family business! Don't make me laugh. One fruit and vegetable stall on the central market where every other trader is trying to cut your throat – what kind of business is that? If I didn't supplement my income with the odd bit of wacky baccy, where does Miriam think she'd get her new designer headscarves from? I tell you money's so short at the moment that even the dwarves can reach it.

Oooooooooh, that's better. Doesn't take long for this water to take effect. Is that a bunion? I wouldn't be surprised if it was with all the time I spend at that stall. I wouldn't mind if it were one of the newer ones, but dad wouldn't pay the rent. Oh no, not him – tight fisted git. 'There's years of life left in this one.' Never any consideration for anyone else – he'd turn in his grave now if he weren't already dead!

"Oh, hello Miriam dear – just thinking about you. Have you had a nice day? Me? Oh not bad you know, takings a bit down. But we won't starve."

That's the wife, Miriam, just back from her mother's. Spend all day flipping through the latest catalogues from Rome they do. Have you seen those prices? It's Ok for the troops, over paid, oversexed and over here. They've got money to throw away. Trouble is, precious little of it gets thrown at me – all they do is walk up and down pinching produce off the stalls, and you daren't say anything or they'll have you off to jail PDQ (Pilate's Palace we call it).

Still, I shouldn't complain too much. It could be worse – could be stabbed, as they say. Talking of pinching, they nicked this guy the other day for writing all over the amphitheatre walls. Rumour is he belongs to one of these pressure groups who keep looking for a fight with our glorious Roman benefactors. Don't know what it was that he wrote – I can't read the language, but its still there despite all their efforts to clean it up. He hasn't been seen for a while – in fact since Cyril sold him that false beard when the local plods were chasing him. Silly sod paid full price, but then again I suppose I would too if the filth were after me.

Oh, here comes trouble – school's out and the kids are home. Wait for it, they'll make a beeline straight for my wallet without so much as a 'by your leave' or 'Hi dad, had a good day?' Mind you, could be wrong, could be wrong. They've gone straight upstairs, wonder what they're up to now. You never know with the youngsters of today. One minute they're all over you like a rash, the next you're a complete stranger. Count your blessings Simon mate, you could still end up in pocket today.

Really need to get my eldest, Jacob, interested in the stall but he's only got thoughts for that Rachel at present. She's Paul's daughter and they live next door. He fishes the lake, and he's been seen knocking around with some chap from Nazareth just recently. They've been spending a lot of time with the poor and sick, and one or two folks have been saying that a number of illnesses have mysteriously cleared up when they've been around. It's not going down too well with the local quack, I can tell you. There'll be tears before bedtime, just you mark my words. I need to make sure that our Jacob steers clear of any of that – the Pharisees are a funny lot, and I can see them complaining to the governor if a stop isn't put to it, and you never know where that will end up.

Right, a nice towelling down and a fresh pair of sandals. That's better – now for some grub. I'm sure I heard Miriam preparing dinner just now, so if I sit down and keep quiet she won't ask me to help. I'm a firm believer in keeping out of things I know nothing about, and I've spent a lifetime learning nothing at all about cooking. Anyhow, I'd just get in the way and then she'd shout at me and tell me to go and sit down, so I'm already doing as I'm told without the aggravation – simple isn't it? I used to be expected to help with the washing up at one time, but Aunty Ivy taught me that if you 'accidentally' broke a few things, you would be shooed out of the way and it works like a charm. Haven't washed up for years – must have a word with the two lads about that sometime.

Mind you, a funny thing happened today and I've only just remembered it. The stall's on the corner of the Via Dolorosa and Market Street and trading had been slowish, but there's been a lot of folk about for the time of the week. Anyway, this chap comes up and starts poking and prodding at the produce and when I asked him what he was playing at, out comes this parchment with some fancy official stamp on it. He says he's from the council (don't ask me which one) and is 'inspecting the foodstuffs to ascertain fitness for human consumption'. I tell him to pay up or leave it alone, but then he gets all high and mighty and tells me he can close the stall down if I don't cooperate. I call him a Roman scivvy, but luckily I don't think he heard.

So then there's a sudden crush, the stall very nearly goes over and if I hadn't got round the front sharpish the local urchins would have been away with my best stuff. I'm just restacking some oranges when this centurion barges into me and doesn't even have the manners to apologise. When I told him what he'd done, all I get is a shove, a mouthful of abuse and the back of his hand – fortunately I'd already ducked. They can be a bit slow sometimes these NCOs and I nipped round the other side out of his way.

I'm just trying to ease myself around the back of the stall, when this great chunk of wood catches me behind the ear. Well I'd had enough by then; I spun round, set myself, stuck both fists up and let him have it.

"Jesus, bloody hell mate, watch where you're going with that or I'll sodding well crucify you."

Well there's this bloke on his knees in the dirt see, and he looks in a bit of a bad way. I go to help him up and the same centurion muscles me to one side. You could have knocked me down with a feather when the chap replied:

"I think you'll find, my friend, that the Romans have beaten you to it."

THE CRACKER

George Edward Marshall was a safe cracker, and a very proficient one at that. He prided himself on keeping abreast of the latest developments in security and was more than familiar with all the latest standards of locking mechanisms. He could take apart and reassemble any of the current models and no-one was safe from his activities. He liked to think of himself as a sub-contractor, hired for his particular skills rather than an outright thief. Thief – the very word left an unpleasant taste in his mouth and he tried, at least mentally, to distance himself from that kind of criminal group. He was a craftsman, and comparing him to some kind of bandit would be tantamount to saying that all joiners were really no more than DIY enthusiasts.

He had even gone so far as to have made all his own tools, in order to avoid detection through some vendor who couldn't keep his mouth shut. It needed a couple of small lathes of course, but he had been able to pick those up for cash at a liquidation sale years ago. Installing them into a workshop at the back of his garage had been tricky though and had been carried out during darkness hours. Fortunately he had no nosey neighbours to contend with, and the whole process appeared to have gone unnoticed. The only piece of equipment he couldn't make was the stethoscope, and distasteful as it was, he lifted one from the local hospital when visiting a friend.

His was a profession which went undetected largely because the activity itself, if carried out properly, would leave very little trace that he had been around until it was too late and the commodity 'removed' had long gone. The real skill lay in leaving things exactly as the victim would have expected to find them. He could neither understand nor abide the 'amateurs' who would leave a trail of devastation in their wake. That level of burglary would be likely to create too much noise and this was the enemy of the safecracker. He also made it a policy to take nothing but cash. Anything else would have to involve a third party to fence it for him, with the inevitable risk of traceability and also another individual who could give him away.

No, you needed to get in as quietly as possible, know exactly where in the property you were going and get there within the shortest possible time, touching nothing outside of your ultimate object. Get used to working in the dark unless you wanted the police feeling your collar before you'd even got started, keep your tools in one place and neatly laid out, and for goodness sake remember to take them all away with you. Finally, make sure that you wipe clean any surfaces you touched, whether you had gloves on or not. Lock up after yourself and always remember to go out the same way you came in.

He had decided long ago not to work as a part of any 'gang' wherever possible, whether he was simply required to open up or take a larger role in the activities. Involvement with other members of the criminal fraternity would leave him exposed to any or all of their inefficiencies. The last thing he needed was an informant after all the years he had worked without a single conviction to his name. The trick was not to be greedy, and never extend yourself beyond your known abilities. Keeping a low profile was what had kept him under the police radar for so long, and he wasn't about to throw that away.

He always preferred to work alone, unaided and on targets which he had carefully selected for himself. He was an ordinary looking man getting towards late middle age and tended to blend into the background. He was never one for starting up a conversation, so you would neither notice him nor recognise him in a crowd and he liked it that way. Still, things were inevitably becoming more hazardous as age slipped its cold fingers around the cardiovascular system, and he wondered if it was time to quit while the going was good. He could do one last safe and make it large enough to provide for him and Nancy, his wife, in their retirement. He had limited himself previously to small/medium sized jobs, and his current thinking would involve much greater risk and require considerably more care at the planning stage.

He knew where the best properties lay, and they weren't always those with the highest profiles. You could keep your footballers and TV celebrities – their perimeter security systems were far too complex to justify the effort. No, you needed somewhere much less ostentatious and yet far enough from any built up area so as not to attract attention of any passing constabulary. He'd had one particular location in mind for a while, but had always considered it too risky – maybe now was the right time. Jim McKee had run the 'Organisation' for around fifteen years since the death of his father, but he wasn't a patch on the old man. George had been asked a few times to name his price for a number of 'tasks', but had always politely declined, and it was good PR to be polite to this guy.

It had been a while since contact had been made, but George knew that it would only be a question of time before his expert skills would be requested again, and on this occasion he would be ready. Sure enough McKee sent one of his messenger boys to the match one weekend where it was common knowledge that George spent every other Saturday. After a brief exchange, details were given verbally – nothing was ever written down. George turned up for a meeting at Mckee's home a week later and details of the job were discussed. All eyes were on him as the expert cracker who would gain entry to the selected premises, but one look at the plans was enough to convince him that there would be no difficulty in opening up the site and cracking the strong room. His one condition, as always, was that there was no mess and he took all his tools away with him. Payment would be up front of course. He said 'Yes'.

The job went like a dream and they were in and out in just under an hour; George pocketed the pair of gloves carelessly discarded by one of the gang. There was no evidence left to tie anyone in the group to the robbery, and the only damage inflicted was to the dignity of the security guard who was tied up, gagged and left in the office. All proceeds were taken back to McKee's premises for fencing at a later date. The group split up and everyone went home – apart from George that is.

He returned to the house two hours later, and concealing himself in the back garden, switched on the miniature intercom set which he had planted in the property during the planning meeting. He smiled to himself as he realised that the family were to be away for the next forty-eight hours at McKee's wife's mothers, and that all the robbery proceeds were stashed away in the safe. Of course, George had made himself quietly familiar with the location of the strong box and he knew that he would have no problem in opening it. His M.O. would be quite different this time though, and he packed up and made his way home for a good night's rest.

The following evening, two hours after dusk, he made his way to the McKee house, parking a mile away from the premises and walking across open fields to the rear of the property. McKee's security system was very good, but nothing that George couldn't handle, and having watched whilst the passcode was entered on a previous visit, he knew that he could disarm it before it went off. It paid to have an eagle eye and a good memory in this game. He could, of course, have cut the wires to the box but that was crude and against all his professional 'ethics'. McKee, like the rest of the residents, had also paid for a private security firm to keep an eye on the place, but George knew that they were lazy and had become careless with the timing of the patrols, so avoiding them would be easy and he had just missed the last one. He now had about three quarters of an hour to complete the job.

Putting on his gloves, he set to work. Getting past the external door locks was a piece of cake for a skilled cracksmith like him, and he was careful to lock them after himself. He needed no time for darkness acclimatisation, and went directly to the study where the safe was situated. Standing still for a moment he made sure that no-one was snooping around outside, and then went to work. In ten minutes he had the door open and all the contents in his holdall. He had to clean it out to make the job look like the work of another one of the gang – everything but cash would be dumped on his way home. Now for the part of the job which would throw everyone completely off the scent. He locked the safe up again and planted the gelignite with its remote detonator around the lock. In the course of the next twenty minutes, a trail of damage was very quietly laid through the house to the back door, where George carefully smashed a pane of glass in one of its panels to simulate the break in. He even trod it through the house to create a more convincing impression, before resetting the alarm system, leaving the premises and cutting the external wires— something he would not normally have done.

The final coup de grace was the explosion, set off remotely, just after the next patrol had departed, giving him plenty of time to get back to his vehicle and drive home, even allowing for the return of the guards alerted by the blast. Passing over the river he made one stop – to drop the rest of the safe contents, together with the remote device, into the water inside a weighted bag. He knew that he was in possession of over £250,000 in used notes, and as long as Nancy was ready with their cases packed and the passports and tickets ready when he got home, they would be away on the night flight to Barbados before anyone was any the wiser. Along with the half million he had accumulated over the years, they wouldn't be short of a bob or two during their retirement, and he'd even been paid for the raid itself.

No-one would be looking for them after they found the gloves he 'carelessly' dropped at the scene, together with the wallet he had lifted from one of the gang during the operation. He had 'trained' as a pickpocket but didn't fancy it as a career – too crude. Came in useful in the end though, and it was rather nice to know that he hadn't lost his touch.

A Sporting Chance

When you are cold, homeless and alone with no job to provide a source of income, you are inclined to desperate measures in order to make some kind of a living, and Colin Sharp fitted all these criteria. At 17 years of age he had come down south from Manchester to make his fortune. His parents were both dead and he had no other relatives, so shaking the northern dust from his feet wasn't a problem, but the fact that he had bragged to all and sundry that he would return some day a rich man meant that he couldn't go back now that things were drastically different from how he had anticipated.

He hadn't eaten for two days as a result of a lack of money, so desperation was now forcing him to take the kind of action which repulsed him. It was dark, and he had been watching the house from a concealed position for over an hour. There had been no lights showing during that period and he decided that it was time to make a move. Walking to the rear of the property, and keeping all senses on high alert, he forced an entry into one of the back rooms. Pausing briefly just inside, he listened for the telltale sounds of footsteps approaching and was relieved when all he heard was the ticking of a clock. All he needed was something he could sell quickly in order to buy food and some better clothing than the stuff he was wearing. Moving swiftly through the downstairs without much success, he found himself in a room filled with glass cabinets, but was unable to see their contents clearly until the light came on.

"Can I be of assistance?" A voice from behind shook him rigid, and after what seemed an eternity, he turned to see a man in his mid forties standing by the light switch. "Don't think of running, you wouldn't stand a chance", he continued.

Colin looked around the room, the trophy room to be more exact, at display cases full of boxing awards and memorabilia. His blood ran cold as he realised that he was inside the house of none other than Eddie McGiven, former British, European and Commonwealth welterweight champion – he was unlikely to get away from here unscathed. McGiven approached him slowly with a boxer's assuredness until they were standing just a few feet apart. Colin met his gaze, but couldn't hold it and resigned himself to a thrashing before being unceremoniously dumped out on the streets somewhere. McGiven looked him up and down and offered him a startling choice.

"I can either make a call to the local police, which will involve a prosecution and likely jail sentence, or offer you a job to get you off the streets and out of the reach of the low-lives who run them. Let's call it a sporting chance."

Colin looked at him in puzzlement until Eddie explained the similarity in their situations. Back in the 1970s he too had been out of work and destined for the scrap heap, until someone gave him the chance to make something of himself. The opportunity which he grabbed with both hands propelled him to fame as undefeated champion by the time he retired in 1981, at the age of thirty. Colin's immediate reply was a resounding 'yes', but Eddie cautioned him that it wouldn't be easy, there would be sacrifices to make in the form of his free time, the food he could eat, and the tough, and extensive training required to bring him up to the level of fitness needed to survive in the boxing ring. To Colin this was a gift horse and he was staring straight down its throat; there was no changing his mind. The first job McGiven gave him though, was to replace the broken window he had used to gain entry.

Over the following six months with Eddie as his trainer, Colin went through the usual routines of road work, weights and sparring in the ring. Building up his strength had been an initial priority, and the normal boxer's diet soon had him approaching the 147lb weight category for a welterweight – one of the glamour sections of the boxing world. Eddie pointed out the now familiar legends in this category – Sugar Ray Robinson, Jose Napoles and Sugar Ray Leonard, telling Colin to focus on them for inspiration, but for the moment it was all down to sheer gut-wrenching hard work - with the finer skills of the art of boxing to come at a later stage.

Eddie had quickly seen potential in the young man's ring work, but he was raw, clumsy and predictable. These were the kind of traits which had to be eliminated in order that Colin wasn't picked off at an early stage in his fledgling career. In an attempt to demonstrate the art of defence, the former champion had both his arms tied behind his back during a sparring session and invited Colin to land a blow. The lad couldn't touch him, and Eddie seemed to know instinctively where every blow was coming from, forcing Colin into to more and more desperate attempts. In the end McGiven called time out and showed how it was done. From that day Colin picked up every technique very quickly, and from defence they went on to the various forms of attacking strategy. By the time they had been training for nine months, Eddie decided that Colin was ready for his first test.

All the necessary paperwork had long been sorted out to enable Colin to box competitively, and one of the local gyms where Eddie used to train was holding an evening of amateur contests. The owner was a friend and agreed to put the lad in against another young prospect over three rounds. Colin was understandably nervous and was caught a couple of times in the opening round, but with Eddie in his corner he settled down and took the second with some delightful defence and counter punching. In the third he stepped up a gear, landed a few tasty blows, and finished the contest with a right cross which appeared to come from nowhere. He was elated and it took Eddie the rest of the evening to bring him back down to earth. On the way back home (Colin now regarded Eddie and his wife as family) they talked over the fight, and the youngster was made to understand that a more experienced opponent would have finished him off in round one.

Notwithstanding this first expedition into the world of boxing, Colin's education continued with increased effort, and the skills Eddie taught him were used to maximum effect in the next contest two weeks later. This time the opponent was a real bruiser, and the training was all about close contact and how to avoid it by using jabs in conjunction with the defensive weaving that Eddie had used in the training ring. From the first bell he was faced with an onslaught of attempted punches, shoulders and elbows. Nothing touched him, and the first round was all about staying out of the way whilst using a stinging left jab to keep the opponent off balance. The opposing corner had no answer to the tactics, and half way through the second round a short distance uppercut took the bruiser's head back, stopped him in his tracks, and set Colin up for a finish with the now familiar right cross.

Out of his initial ten fights only one went the distance, and he won that on points. Eddie decided that it was now time for more serious competition, and having attached Colin to the local boxing club, he was entered for the upcoming ABA Championships. Now all training was refocused, and Eddie pointed out that this was the big opportunity which could lead to a place in the next Olympic squad. Success at that level almost guaranteed a career in the professional game. They had twelve weeks to prepare and fights were limited to one per month only. At the end of this period Colin was as physically and mentally prepared as Eddie had seen him, and was unrecognisable from the waif who stood in the trophy room less than a year ago.

Colin Sharp was becoming one of the names in amateur boxing, and meteoric success at the ABA's which saw him win all contests, including the final, inside two rounds catapulted him into the Great Britain team for the next Olympic Games. The competition was tough, and training reflected that fact with Eddie making up ever more demanding work routines. Colin's overall fitness was giving him the stamina for performance way beyond the three round limit set by the amateur game, and his eventual victory in the welterweight category was a foregone conclusion. His name was in all the papers, and he was hailed as the golden boy of British boxing.

At an age approaching twenty, Eddie now gave him the option of remaining in the amateur game in order to defend his title at the next Olympics, or of turning professional with potentially ten or more years' earnings before him. Colin chose the professional route, and Eddie smiled and slapped him on the back – that was exactly what he had done. With his own corner team, and Eddie as his manager pulling strings to get the best fights, Colin progressed quickly through the early contests and no-one seemed able to lay a blow on him. Eddie had always cautioned against 'showboating', and the young man's concentration was one of his strengths. A year down the line he was ten fights older and unbeaten, with none of the contests going the distance.

Half way through Colin's second year the reigning British and Commonwealth champion retired, leaving the BBBC to set up an elimination contest to fill the vacancy. Sharp's name was first on the list along with seven other hopefuls. The fights took place over four weeks and he emerged with the title at the ripe old age of twenty-one. Now he was being touted for a contest against the European champion, with the inevitable barrage of publicity which had followed him since the ABA championships. This time it was not to be, and the champion himself seemed to go to some pains to influence the selection of a suitable opponent – it was to be a further six months before Colin got his own chance. During this time he kept busy and two more opponents went the way of the rest, while speed and skills were honed to something approaching perfection.

By the time of his biggest contest yet, for the European crown, Colin was 22 years old and at the peak of his physical fitness. The champion, a German by the name of Schnell, had reigned for four years with very little credible opposition. He made it his policy to demean Sharp's performances, predicting a very swift end to the match. Eddie had prepared Colin for all the pre-match hype, and the lad dealt with the press conferences and the customary eyeball-to-eyeball meeting at the weigh-in with the calm of a seasoned professional. The German's predictions came unceremoniously unstuck in the second round after Colin had taken a good look at him in the opener. All of McGiven's training on the reading of an opponent's eyes and body shape came to the fore in a second round of unremitting punishment for the champion, and he returned to his stool after a three minute battering with a cut above one eye and the other rapidly closing. The referee gave both a close inspection during the break, but allowed him to continue into the third round. Eddie had schooled Colin well in going in for the kill, and the lad was on to it in a flash at the bell. The fight was over inside thirty seconds as the German was completely unable to defend himself. Champion of Europe at 22 and the world at his feet, Colin was given a three month break and told to relax – if only that had been possible.

Colin had asked Eddie why he chose to retire at thirty when other fighters had carried on well past that age. McGiven had smiled at the youngster's probing into his private life, but answered honestly. A partially detached retina had forced him to either quit or risk losing his sight in one eye; the decision was a 'no brainer', and with earnings placed wisely in a portfolio of investments he and Carol, his wife, had more than enough to live on for the rest of their lives. When the accident happened, it tore the life out of young Sharp. Eddie and Carol had gone up to Scotland to see friends for a week, and were travelling south west on the A9 from Aviemore to Kingussie when a Transit van coming in the opposite direction swerved in front of them, sending their car off the road and into a tree. The vehicle exploded on impact and both of them were killed instantly.

Sharp was devastated at the loss of what had become his only family. Eddie had joked just recently that the time was coming soon when Colin wouldn't need his help and advice any longer. It seemed like that time had come earlier than anyone expected. Sharp stayed at the McGiven house – he had nowhere else to go, and a week after the funeral came the phone call from Martins McBride, the solicitors handling Eddie's estate. Colin had to sit down – as Eddie and Carol had no children, they had made an alteration to their wills three months ago naming him as sole beneficiary. The official reading was to take place in one week's time, and more details would be given at their offices.

Despite the loss of his mentor, Colin carried on his boxing career asking Brian Carroll, the chief corner man, to take over as his manager. Eddie and Brian had been together for many years and he had Sharp's complete trust as they scaled further heights in the boxing world. Six successful defences of his British title gained him two Lonsdale belts outright, and there was no-one to touch him on the European stage. When the chance came for a crack at the vacant WBA world title, Colin's name was at the top of the list and the contest at the Wembley Arena lasted all of three rounds. With his foot now firmly on the world ladder, it would be easy to get access to the other three associations in order to unite the crown under one champion. Over the course of the next two years he had added the WBC, the WBO and the IBF title belts to his growing trophy cabinet. He was 24.

Eddie's philosophy always seemed to be to quit while you were ahead before some lucky bruiser caught you with a sucker punch. He did it in 1981, and Colin started to consider how long to give himself in the game before calling it a day. His inheritance from the McGivens meant that he was now independently wealthy, leaving him to box for the fun of it and quit when the work became too hard. There was no shortage of challengers, but he had vacated the British, European and Commonwealth titles at the end of his successful campaign to unify the world championship. His defences of these belts were mandatory and came along at intervals of between three and four months. None of the bouts lasted above half way, and he made the decision to carry on until someone put him on the floor – this would be the sign that he was losing some of his edge. That time was to be another three years coming – April 2004 in Las Vegas. Colin won the fight on a technical KO, but not before he had been caught by a left hook which he never saw coming. After a standing count of eight, he ended the round and the fight with a ferocious barrage of punches which saw the referee step in to save his opponent from further punishment.

Back home, he sat with Brian over dinner and discussed retirement. At the age of 27 he had nothing more to prove and everything to lose, and although his former corner man tried to persuade him into one more year, Colin shook his head and told him that now was the time to go. There was the expected news frenzy and speculation of a career in Hollywood, but he laughed it all off and slowly but surely the media drifted off on to other more interesting stories. He had had very little time for female company over the last ten years, Carol being the only regular contact, but now that his boxing life was drawing to a close it was time to give that matter more attention. There had been the normal round of photo shoots which every successful boxer gets involved in, but these would only have proved to be distractions from a career which demanded focus. Out for dinner with friends one evening, he met Liz and they clicked almost immediately. In six months they had married and were living a life out of the public eye.

One evening about a year later, they were approaching Colin's BMW in a multi storey car park after a night out. A figure with a knife stepped out of the shadows and demanded Colin's wallet. Stepping in front of Liz, he set himself in the familiar boxer's stance and told the guy to come and get it.

One forward pace was all that he was allowed to take. A straight left jab full on the nose sent the youth careering backwards, whilst the knife went spinning out of reach. Sharp was on him in a flash and pinned him to a stone pillar with a right cocked to finish the job. He dropped his hands at what he saw before him. This was a mere lad, scruffily dressed with holes in his shoes. His hair was unkempt and he looked like he hadn't washed for a week. Something very familiar resurfaced from Colin's memory, and he brushed the lad down; over the next half hour Sharp learned his whole life story. At the end he made him a startling offer.

"You have a choice, I can either make a call to the police which will involve a prosecution and likely jail sentence, or offer you a job that will get you off the streets. Let's call it a sporting chance, shall we?"

STICKING THE KNIFE IN

Joe stood staring at what he had just done. The slit across the throat he had made with the twelve inch blade was deep and wide, and the knife was now hanging limply in his blood-soaked fingers - she definitely wasn't moving any more. His clothes were a mass of red and he was standing in the middle of an ever increasing pool of thick, crimson blood which was making its way steadily but surely towards the half open door. He closed it quickly, glad now that he'd had the presence of mind to lock the front door an hour earlier. Cleaning up was going to take quite a while, and he would have to put the body out of the way into the freezer until he made up his mind what to do with it.

That the situation had come to this didn't surprise him much at all really. Ever since school everyone in authority had seemed to have a down on him, and he never had the knack of being able to keep out of trouble. He was always the one who got caught, the fat lad who either didn't see the danger coming or who couldn't run fast enough when it arrived. Let's face it, the ones who got away only had to be able to move faster than the plodder at the back, and maybe that was why he was invited along in the first place. Academically he had been at the back of the door when the brains were given out, and progress through primary and secondary education had been painfully slow, so when the chance came to join the army and learn a trade, it seemed to be a lifeline.

He left school in 1970 with CSEs in woodwork and metalwork and joined the army, signing up for three years after basic training. That first stint extended in due course to ten years, and by the time he came out of the service in 1980 he was fit, trained in all the usual physical disciplines, and with a trade under his belt. The army had seemed to give him the kick up the backside he needed after his wasted years in school, and he had revelled in the camaraderie. He had been in Northern Ireland during arguably the bloodiest period in the province's recent history, and had seen the kind of things which young men of his age were not accustomed to.

Returning to civilian life afterwards had, like for many ex- squaddies, been an uncomfortable transition to 'normality'. There had been periods of employment with a variety of security firms, and he had even tried a couple of years in the police but had been unable to settle into the more flexible lifestyle outside of the forces. He had met and married Sonia in 1986, and for a while they muddled through on a fairly comfortable basis, but when money became tight and the arguments started, their relationship commenced on a downward spiral. He took to drinking more than he should, got in with some unsavoury characters, and during a bungled robbery attempt one night barely got away by the skin of his teeth. This time his army training had taught him to be on the lookout for problems, he had been the first to make a run for it and appeared to have come out of the encounter unscathed.

It was to be his first and last brush with the criminal world, and when his mother and father both died within a short time of each other, the legacy they left solved all of his financial problems and went a long way towards putting his marriage temporarily back on an even keel. Like all good things in his life however, it didn't seem to last very long and Sonia was at the heart of it with her constant demands on their newfound wealth. The money was firmly under his control, but her incessant whingeing and whining was beginning to take its toll on his fragile temper, and there had been a number of occasions when neighbours had summoned the police after hearing raised voices and threats coming from their property. Divorce was out of the question as she would claim half of their combined assets, and at times when the drink got the better of him he had considered severing their relationship on a permanent basis in a less than legal manner. Sobriety had always returned him to a more stable frame of mind and the subject had not been considered for a while, but how long he could hold out was anybody's guess.

He decided to use the inheritance to start up his own business using some of the skills he had acquired during his time in the army, and after taking advice from his new bank manager friend, submitted a five year plan with all the necessary forecasts and projections. He was amazed to get the go ahead almost immediately and set about canvassing for business, firstly through friends and ex-army buddies, and later using mail shots and fliers. Sonia came into her own here with her computer and accounting skills acquired at evening classes, and their increased level of activity even kept quiet her incessant demands on the financial front. The business began to take off, and pretty soon the increase in trade necessitated the recruitment of staff in addition to the two of them, to ensure that the whole enterprise didn't fail for lack of customer care.

As money flowed into their accounts expansion became a reality, and Joe had to devote more and more of his time to driving the business forward from the top, and fewer hours on the premises dealing with day-to-day matters. He was able to renegotiate the bank loans to pay them off earlier than expected at better interest rates, and his business dealings with suppliers increased to the extent that he was able to demand better prices for his orders. One evening after a particularly busy week, Sonia took the opportunity to raise again her demands for more money to satisfy what she regarded as her increased status in their community. Joe had thought that the whole matter had gone away in the midst of their business success, but here it was once again coming around to bite him.

He tried to explain to her that during the early years of their new company, all profits needed to be ploughed back into the business to ensure its future survival – 'Jam Tomorrow' he said, was the phrase that all small businesses used as their mantra. Sonia wasn't having any of it, and insisted that her allowance be increased so that she could keep up with the activities of her newly discovered social circle. The discussion descended into an argument, and culminated in a full blown row with a variety of household items being thrown around the room. It wasn't very long before a knock at the door revealed the local constabulary who had, once again, been summoned by neighbours. This time the previous warning which had been served upon them activated a visit to the local station where a formal caution was delivered as to future behaviour. They were released, but the matter got into the local press, and Sonia used this as a stick to beat Joe with, pointing out the embarrassment she would suffer as a result.

He was coming to the end of his tether, and called at his local on the way home from work to sit and consider his options. Over a period of three hours, and a quantity of more than a few beers, his steady descent into inebriation brought him to the conclusion that he would probably be better off without her. He left the pub at the end of the evening determined, in his now less than rational state of mind, to put the matter to bed once and for all. The only question left for him would be the manner in which he was to dispose of her. That, he determined, was a question to be resolved with a clear head and rational thought. He went home and slept soundly – more soundly than he had done for some time.

That was last night, and he had got up this morning with an amazingly clear head, sure in the knowledge that he was about to commit an act that would rid him forever of the bane of his life. This, however, was before he found the note. The note from Sonia telling him that she had left him and would not be returning, that she had met someone at one of her social meetings, that this person would provide for all her future needs, that he was encouraged not to look for her as the two of them would be leaving the country, and that he could keep his little business all to himself. He smiled and couldn't remember the last time he had felt so good. Even slaughtering the pig hadn't managed to take the shine off the morning. He had always prided himself on his butchery skills – it was a trade that he had picked up very easily in the army catering corps. He now had an increasing network of butcher's shops together with the wholesale trade which he had been building up for the past six months, and no Sonia to drive him up the wall.

Race Against Time

*W*hat a complete waste of time that was. A four hundred mile round trip to St James' Park and a whole day out to see them play like a bunch of nancies and lose five nil to Newcastle. It wouldn't have been too bad if the opposition were something special, and now this filthy weather all the way back home if, that is, he could get out of this infernal road works traffic jam. Barry Marshall was in a really bad mood. Not only had his team just been trashed, but his girlfriend had chosen the previous evening to tell him that they were finished. They had been seeing each other for about three years and he thought the relationship was OK, but clearly he was wrong. At thirty-six, and in a steady job with the possibility of promotion, he didn't exactly want for anything, but like many males approaching middle age, change was not something that he welcomed with open arms. Change hit him like a thunderbolt when one of his rear passenger doors opened, a body dived inside, shut and locked it after them. He had heard the stories about car-jackers, and was cursing himself for not taking the precaution of securing the car before leaving the north east. For a moment there was no sound, but then a female voice hissed:

"Help me, I must get away from here!"

"What? Who are you? "

"They are after me and I must escape. Is there anywhere in this car that I can hide?"

He told her to pull down one of the back seats, climb into the boot area and reset it behind her. The fabric cover would conceal her from any prying eyes, and they were not too long in arriving. Two men appeared out of the darkness and in the now driving rain, were peering into a selection of vehicles including his own. Fortunately at that moment the lights controlling the queue of traffic changed, and he was away from the place. All this had happened so quickly that Barry had no time to consider what to do other than vacate the scene as fast as possible, but now that the initial events had passed, he took the opportunity to pull in at the next lay-by to confront his new passenger.

The rain had eased as he got out of the car, and having walked slowly round to the rear, he raised the tailgate. There, in the corner of the luggage compartment, curled up in a ball and shivering in the cold, was a young woman in her twenties. The dim light bulb caused her to shade her eyes as he reached his hand in to help her out of her hiding place. Giving her the blanket which he had always kept in the car, he told her to wrap it around her and get in the front passenger seat. She was of medium height, slim and had brownish hair. Her clothes were soaking wet, and she would need to change out of them as soon as possible. He pulled off the road at the next junction, having seen a sign for a designer outlet site with late opening hours. Returning to the car some thirty minutes later, she was kitted out in new, dry clothing and shoes together with a cheap overcoat, all at his expense.

Now was the time to find out exactly what was going on. Her name, she said, was Danielle Moureau and she had been kidnapped during a day trip with friends to Calais. Her father, Phillipe Moureau, was a wealthy French industrialist and her captors had issued a ransom note threatening to kill her if their demands were not met. She showed him a photograph in the locket which was around her neck, of a man in his late forties or early fifties. She had no idea where she was, except for the fact that she was somewhere in Britain and asked Barry if he could return her safely home, saying that her father would be extremely grateful to him. They lived in a large house in the Bois de Boulogne area of Paris and she said she needed to contact him urgently, but when questioned further would not give the reason. Barry frowned and agreed to take her to the nearest telephone – he was starting to get a bad feeling about this, and was half tempted to drive away right now. She was in and out of the phone booth in five minutes, thus rendering his dilemma irrelevant. Her expression was calmer, but she said that she would need to get as far away as possible from the place where he picked her up.

The rest of the journey back home to the Midlands was uneventful and quiet apart from the usual polite conversation. There would be plenty of time to find out more about his guest when they got there, and he figured out what he was going to do. It was late evening by the time they reached his flat, and in the continuing bad weather, no-one seemed to notice that he had company, as they entered the apartment building and closed the door behind them. The following day being a Sunday, they had plenty of time to discuss her plans for returning home, but Barry insisted that she stay inside the flat at all times in case her pursuers had managed to trace them from

Newcastle. Her father, she said, had developed a revolutionary new process in the engineering field which would render obsolete a number of well-known products, and cause serious damage to a variety of high profile companies in the industry. The men chasing her had been hired by a group of competitors to obtain the specification from her father's company, and somehow prevent him from marketing it. She had no doubt that they would have killed her if demands were not met, and the call to Phillipe Moureau had been to tell him of her escape and forestall any action which he may have been planning.

She was sure that if they got as far as Calais the rest of the journey to Paris would not be a problem, and reiterated her father's assured gratitude for Barry's bravery in bringing her home. His initial fears started to dispel as her story became more plausible – if it was a fabrication she was certainly an accomplished liar, and looking at her over the breakfast table now he found that difficult to believe. Barry decided to go along with her explanation of the events of the previous day and her ideas for getting home. He would phone into work tomorrow morning to take some of the leave which his boss had been nagging him about for the past three months. This would give them time to plan the journey across the Channel via Dover towards the end of that week. The problem was that she had no papers, and so would need to be concealed amongst the luggage in his car. His own passport was up to date, and he was fairly sure that they would pass through the document checks at the port without any trouble.

They decided to make their move on the Friday afternoon when the rest of the occupants of the apartment building would be out, planning to get to Dover in time for the evening crossing to Calais. Once across the Channel she would be able to travel openly in the car instead of concealed in the boot area. During the time Danielle had been with him, Barry had found himself becoming more and more attracted to her, and she did nothing to dissuade him. He wondered if this was the result of his being on the rebound from his former girlfriend, and decided to play things slowly and carefully until he met her father. Consequently he had given up his bedroom to her, choosing to sleep in the lounge for the duration.

He did all the shopping during the week so as to avoid her being seen by any nosey neighbours or, more seriously, the men who were so intent on recapturing her in Newcastle. It was on the Thursday when he had gone out, telling her that he would be back in a couple of hours, that he was intercepted. It all happened so fast that he was taken by surprise. Coming out of the Crown and Anchor where he had stopped for lunch, he was approached by a couple of men posing as friends. They made all the usual noises of people who hadn't met for a while, and he felt a sharp pain as a needle entered his arm. A sense of dizziness enveloped him and he slumped into the arms of one of them. Passers by would just assume that he had been drinking too much, and that these friends would be taking him home. As Barry was ushered into the back of a waiting car he lost consciousness.

He opened his eyes sometime later and took in a small but clean and well-furnished room, containing a uniformed police officer who immediately radioed that Mr Marshall had woken. He was served with a cup of tea and shortly afterwards two plain clothed men entered the room, introducing themselves as a Mr Brown and a Mr Green of Special Branch. Brown spoke first.

"Mr Marshall, you've given us quite an interesting time since Newcastle, and at one point we thought that we'd completely lost you. There's no need for concern but I'm afraid that you have been led up the garden path by Miss Moureau which, incidentally, is not her real name."

Barry looked at them both with a furrowed expression, and Green picked up on it as he continued the conversation, placing a photograph of Phillipe Moureau before him.

"Her name is Maria Charkov and her 'father' is Dimitri Ostrovsky, I assume this is the man whose picture she showed to you. You have been the unwitting victim of a plan to return her to her handler in France. She is a spy in possession of certain information stolen from one of our nuclear research establishments in the north. It is vital that we not only recover what she has taken, but also that the cell from which she operates is eliminated before further damage can be caused. I can see that you need some convincing of the situation and we were prepared for this eventuality."

Stepping outside the office, he summoned a uniformed officer.

"Constable, would you ask Detective Inspector Marks to join us, please?"

The uniformed officer returned with a man whom Barry recognised immediately. DS Marks (as he then was) and Barry had been friends for some years, and he started to relax at the sight of a familiar face. Marks shook hands with the two Special Branch officers and confirmed the facts which they had related. He also pointed out that, like himself, Barry would be required to sign the Official Secrets Act before they could proceed any further. The appropriate documents were produced from a briefcase and, after the formalities were completed, the briefing (for that was what it was) continued. Marks remained whilst Brown took up the story.

"We believe that you have been requested to take the lady 'home', and can ensure that your passage through whatever port has been selected will go unhindered and yet remain convincing. Do not doubt the fact that when Miss Charkov reaches her destination there will be no further use for you. They will kill you and ensure that no trace of your body is ever found. However, we need you to carry through your plans in order that we can eliminate the threat at the other end. This will be dangerous, but we can assure you that both the French Sûreté and Interpol will have agents watching you every step of the way, along with our own Special Branch officers. In any case since you are now involved in the matter, it is likely that even if you pull out, certain foreign parties will ensure that your silence is rendered permanent. Do you understand?"

Barry took a few moments to absorb what had been said, and turned to look at Marks who nodded. It was clear that he had no real option other than to proceed as planned whilst remaining as casual as possible in Danielle/Maria's presence. They provided him with instructions relating to his point of departure from Dover, and what to expect in Calais. He was then to follow precisely the instructions given to him by the woman as to the route to Paris. They would be tracked continually by a series of vehicles so as not to raise suspicion, and he was asked to travel in the manner he would use whilst on a holiday. The real problems would be at the end of the journey, but Barry was to hold his nerve and act as surprised as if he knew nothing at all of the true facts.

Returning to the flat after being dropped off a few streets away, Barry composed himself as well as he could, and explained his slight lateness as being due to meeting an old school friend for a pint and a bite to eat. Danielle (he had to remember to call her that) accepted his story, and later over dinner they went through the details of their journey south the following day. She said that she had called her father again from the flat, hoping he didn't mind, and had told him that she would be home within the next day or two. Barry smiled and waved away her apologies as they went to pack a couple of bags to make the journey look realistic. He explained that she would have to ride concealed in the luggage compartment, but that he would make it as comfortable as possible. Once on the ferry she could travel as normal for the remainder of the trip, and the way would be relatively clear along the E15 through Lens to Paris.

They left the flat at 4.30pm the next day, arriving at Dover half an hour before the evening sailing. Customs checks were as cursory as Barry had been told, whilst remaining official enough not to raise suspicion, and he was aboard the ferry shortly afterwards. Once in the parking bays, Danielle emerged from her hiding place after all other passengers had moved to the upper decks. Barry was certain that Special Branch had operatives on board, but avoided any attempt to identify them with Danielle at his side. They made their way to the restaurant and settled down for the crossing. He had to admit that she was good, maintaining the appropriate level of nervousness required to keep him assured of the validity of her story, whilst periodically looking around for any signs that they were being followed.

Disembarking at Calais, they were waved through the port by the local Gendarmerie, and headed off down the E15 towards Lens on the two or three hour journey to Paris. They had been travelling for about an hour when the police car sirens alerted Barry to a potential problem. The distinctively marked vehicle moved alongside and an officer indicated that they should pull over immediately. Barry had no choice, and a glance at Danielle revealed what he believed to be a genuine look of concern on her face. The police officer got out of the car which had pulled up some twenty yards behind them, and was pulling a notebook from his pocket when a speeding black Citroen roared past them, swerving wildly from side to side across all lanes of the motorway. The gendarme immediately got back in the squad car and charged off in pursuit amidst a cloud of smoke and burning rubber, leaving them in the lay-by where they had stopped. Disappearing back into the general traffic, Barry wondered if the forces of law and order had just given them a lifeline to Paris, and that somewhere further down a slip road the local police were being 'clued in' to what was happening. They certainly weren't bothered again.

After making one further stop at a service area, they continued on the rest of the trip to Paris arriving at the outskirts of the city at around nine o'clock. Danielle took over the navigating at this point, and some fifteen minutes later they turned up the driveway of an imposing house set in its own grounds in the Bois de Boulogne. Barry wondered how the security forces were going to effect entry to the premises without being seen, but since he hadn't spotted them during the entire journey (with the possible exception of the Citroen) he didn't give the matter too much thought – he had to focus his attention on appearing to be what Danielle believed him to be, a knight in shining armour. They were met at the door by a butler whom Danielle called François, and he escorted them to an imposing drawing room. The walls were lined with a collection of oil paintings, and although Barry was no art expert, he recognised one or two notable items amongst them. Behind an ornate desk towards the window, a silver haired man in his fifties was rising from his seat to meet them. He and the woman exchanged the traditional greeting of a kiss and Danielle introduced him to Barry as her father, Philippe Moureau. They were ushered towards three leather chairs at the other end of the room, and the butler was called and instructed to serve tea. When he returned, it was in the company of another man whom

Moureau greeted and introduced as George Watkinson. Barry's feelings of unease now started to return as they had done at the telephone booth near Newcastle - a lifetime ago.

A sudden commotion outside the room banished all such thoughts from his mind, as he went back to the statement made by Brown and Green that 'the real problems' would unfold at the end of the journey, and that time was now. Whatever had happened outside the door was very loud and over very quickly, with Barry expecting to see the two Special Branch officers burst through the door backed by whatever law enforcement agencies had been following them on their journey. He was dismayed instead to see them both restrained and in some disarray, accompanied by four burly individuals wearing dark combat clothing. He turned back to Moureau to see him holding a small pistol and it was pointed in his direction.

"Yes, I suppose you are a little surprised Mr Marshall, but this is not the time for regrets."

He pulled the trigger and Barry winced in the expectation of pain and, ultimately, death. Instead, a small orange flame appeared at the end of the barrel, which was then extended to the man introduced as Watkinson.

"Let me light your cigar for you George, you never do carry matches do you?"

The whole scene began to turn into some surreal dream, as Barry looked around him for someone to make sense out of the last week of his life. The two prisoners were now brought forwards into the room and stood before the assembled group. A number of other uniformed men had appeared at the door, and were now making their way towards them. It was the man named Watkinson who spoke next.

"Now that our little game has played itself out, it is time to explain to you, Mr Marshall, what exactly has been happening. I am George Watkinson, the head of an 'appropriate' department within the British government, the name of which you do not need to know. The two men before you whom you know as Green and Brown are, in fact, agents of a foreign power bent on the elimination of key members of NATO staff. They had managed to infiltrate the British security services, but became noticed by us at an early stage. We have been aware of their activities for a while, but were not completely sure of their ultimate objective until last week when they did, in fact, kidnap Danielle. Their intention was to lure her father away from this place and kill them both after extracting whatever information they could. Thanks to you, and a little deception on our part, they were allowed to believe that they were approaching their final objective."

Moureau now joined in the conversation.

"You see Mr Marshall, with your help we have been able to identify and eliminate a dangerous spy cell. Unchecked, its activities would have had serious consequences throughout Europe and the Middle East. Danielle really is my daughter, and also an agent working within an area of NATO which must, by its very nature, remain covert. The man known to you as DI Marks was on our team from the outset and makes himself available to us as and when he is needed. This was something of an elaborate trap, and the incident with the Citroen on the E15 nearly derailed the whole thing – we do not know the identity of the occupants of the car and they have yet to be traced. Now that the matter is finished, I would be pleased to extend the hospitality of my house to you for the rest of the time you are in France. Who knows, as you have actually signed your country's secrecy legislation, we may be calling on you again some time."

"Papa, I'm ashamed of you, stop teasing him. He saved my life and you should be grateful for that – don't push your luck. Come on Barry, you look like you could do with a drink."

Danielle delivered the ticking off as only a daughter could do to a father. Taking Barry by the arm she steered him past the now helpless Brown and Green and headed for the lounge. Outside in the grounds of the house it seemed like the entire French security forces had taken up residence, and there were several other individuals wearing handcuffs and bearing the signs of a struggle. Going back to work in England was going to be extremely dull by comparison.

TOMMY

Dave could not recall exactly when he first noticed Paul's odd behaviour. It might have been last week, a month ago or even longer, but the fact of the matter was that it was becoming frequent enough for neighbours to have commented upon it. Paul was the son of Dave's wife Rachel whom he had married three years ago. The lad was just over seven years old and therefore not a blood relative to him. Nevertheless they had built up a bond as any father and son would, and Paul was too young to have remembered his natural father, who had been killed by a drunk driver whilst waiting for a bus some six years earlier. Dave had fallen in love with Rachel as soon as they met, and although it took her a little longer to realise that his intentions were strictly honourable, their relationship blossomed quickly and she had no qualms about introducing him to her son.

Paul was a happy, bright boy and a quick learner. His nursery school teachers had all remarked upon his ability to read and write way in advance of his peers, and this they put down to the amount of time that had been spent with him in his pre-school years. The three of them formed the archetypal 'perfect' family and Dave could not remember a single instance of unruly or petulant behaviour from his now adopted son. He was a popular child at school and had a variety of friends, many of whom had spent time at the house with him, and this in itself made the current situation all the more difficult to understand. Paul had somehow acquired an 'invisible' companion. Rachel and Dave had both heard and read of similar situations, and one of their friends had a daughter (now in her teens) who had passed through what psychologists label as a 'phase'. Their GP had reassured them on the same score, and merely advised that they go along with it until Paul outgrew it.

As Dave watched Paul playing in the back yard from the kitchen window, it was clear that a series of prolonged and detailed conversations were taking place up and down the garden, both on the move and stationery whilst a face-to-face explanation of some matter or other was happening. Dave hadn't taken the opportunity as yet to question Paul about this person whom no-one else could see, but now felt a growing need to discover more about the new addition to their family unit. He discussed it with Rachel, and although she had her reservations about his planned action, she shared his increasing concern for her son's well-being. Dave went out into the garden on the pretext of doing some weekend tidying up. In truth he had been neglecting it of late, so this was unlikely to unsettle Paul as he carried out his conversation with the newcomer. He made a show of noisily searching the shed for the correct tools for the job he intended to do, and coming back out into the sunlight made a comment to no-one in particular about the state of the lawn. Paul had been at the other end of the garden, and was returning to the swing near the back door when he saw Dave appear suddenly out of the shed. He jumped in surprise and dropped the cricket set which he was carrying. After picking up the stumps and bails, he looked around in puzzlement and shrugged his shoulders.

"Oh he's gone, I wonder where. Perhaps you scared him off dad, he said you might."

Dave stood in silence as his son strode past in a very matter-of-fact way, put the toys in the shed and went into the kitchen where he poured himself a drink and sat down at the table with a comic. This was the chance that he and Rachel had been waiting for – they had been told that allowing Paul to be the first to broach the subject of the new friend was the best way of finding out more about the situation. Dave followed him into the house, sat down in a chair opposite at the table, smiled and was rewarded with the most perfect expression of trust and innocence which could ever be imagined.

"Paul, is this new friend of yours going to be stopping for tea? I mean we'll need to do some more shopping if he is, and we'll need to know what he likes to eat, won't we?"

Paul looked up from his comic book, cocked his head on one side, put one hand under his chin in a perfect imitation of Dave's own mannerisms and replied thoughtfully.

"No, don't think so. He says he can't eat since the water got into his lungs, and to be honest dad, he doesn't look very well to me. I've told him that I'm a bit worried about him, but he says there's nothing anyone can do about it, and that you'd know what he meant."

"What's his name, I mean..............where does he come from?"

"Well, he won't let me tell you his name just yet, but he says that he used to live around here a long time ago, but I don't understand that and he won't explain it to me either."

The conversation ended, Paul smiled again and went back to his reading. Dave went to find Rachel and told her of the conversation he had just had. She asked him how their son could have made up such an elaborate story, he was bright but this went beyond simple cleverness, and there was something strangely worrying about it. Paul obviously had no more to tell them at the moment and they agreed that a further attempt would be made in a couple of days. Paul had clearly stated that Dave would know what the new friend meant with reference to the water, and Dave was puzzled by the fact that this 'person' was a local, albeit from sometime in the past. He shook himself and laughed – was this the beginnings of paranoia? He let it go for the time being and dismissed it from his mind, but the matter was not long in rearing its head again.

They were sitting one evening during the following week watching television, when Paul turned to Dave and asked if he could go fishing with Tommy. Up until then, their son hadn't displayed the faintest interest in the sport and wouldn't have known one end of a rod from the other, let alone how to deal with a writhing fish on the end of a line.

"Tommy? Who's Tommy, one of your school friends?"

"No, don't be silly dad, Tommy's my home friend. He said that if I told you his name it would be alright with you for me to go fishing with him."

"Tommy...............sorry Paul, I don't know anyone named Tommy, and unless your mum and me know who he is we can't let you go anywhere with him, after all you're only seven."

"He said you might say something like that, but you do know him. Tommy Watkinson, he used to live on Wellington Road with his mum and dad, and three sisters."

Dave froze, and Rachel noticed the change in him. A cold sweat broke out on his forehead and his hands started to shake. He excused himself and went up to the bathroom where he filled the washbasin with cold water and splashed it up into his face. Drying off, he looked in the mirror not knowing what to expect staring back at him. Tommy Watkinson, a name coming back to haunt him from the mists of time in his childhood. Rachel was knocking at the door and asking if he was alright – Dave told her he'd be out shortly. She was waiting in their bedroom for him with a very worried look on her face. He started to explain but the words wouldn't come out in the right order, and she had to shake him and made him start again.

He took a deep breath and began a story which went back twenty years to his childhood. He and Tommy Watkinson were best friends, went everywhere together and outside of school were inseparable. He disappeared one Saturday afternoon after they had been fishing down by the canal. There had been a widespread hunt for him which had covered larger and larger areas as the time went by. It was six months before the police scaled down their efforts, but the file had remained open and a young sergeant, going back over it some time later, came across two references to a man named Ronald Williams who was well-known to the youngsters in the area. Williams ran a local youth club, and was the trainer of a youth football team of which Dave and Tommy were members. They had been to his house on a number of occasions and he had always seemed to be harmless. Nevertheless, the sergeant built up a circumstantial case against the man and when it came to court he was convicted of the abduction and murder of the youngster. Tommy's body was never found and Williams died in prison after receiving a great deal of attention from other inmates. Dave paused, obviously in great distress but Rachel wanted to know more, and specifically what it had got to do with their son.

"I lied to the police, Rachel. They asked me where we had been the day Tommy went missing and I told them about the canal, but that he had gone straight home afterwards and that I didn't see him again. It wasn't true. We went fishing alright but we took our swimming gear with us as well."

"So what? There's nothing wrong with that, is there?"

"We didn't swim in the canal, it wasn't deep enough to use for diving so we went to the old quarry. Dad always said that we should keep away from there because people used it as a dumping ground, and that it wasn't safe to swim in. He'd have taken his belt to me if he found out that we had done. Tommy must have got caught on something in the water because he didn't come back up after one dive. I didn't know what to do, I waited and waited but he never surfaced, so I put my clothes on and went home. I got rid of his fishing rod to hide what I'd done. I should have gone in after him and tried to help, but I didn't and when the police asked me if I'd seen him later that day, I lied."

"So Ronald Williams had nothing to do with it?"

"No, he was completely innocent, but by the time he came to court I was so scared that I didn't say anything. They're both dead and it's all my fault. Now Tommy's back, talking to Paul and I don't know what he wants."

"Perhaps we should ask him, then."

It was three days before Dave built up the courage to ask his son about Tommy again, but this time the response was considerably less evasive. Paul told him that Tommy had said he wanted to talk to Dave alone, and that he couldn't explain what he needed to anyone else. He looked a little upset that his new friend wouldn't share this with him, but told Dave that if he was in the garden after tea, Tommy would come and find him.

"I don't understand what he wants dad, and he's starting to frighten me. What's the matter?"

Dave told him not to worry, and that everything would be alright once he and Tommy had met. He went down to the bottom of the garden after they had washed the tea pots and his stomach was churning with the anticipation of meeting a ghost from his past. He sat on the bench under the apple tree and waited. The temperature of the warm, sunny late August afternoon dropped suddenly and there at the side of him was the vision of Tommy Watkinson exactly as he had been on that afternoon twenty years ago. Rachel watched from the kitchen window at the strange sight of a grown man deep in conversation for over half an hour with no-one. When Dave returned to the house he was pale and clearly shaken. They took Paul over to his grandparents and drove to the local police station. The young sergeant of twenty years ago was now running the station as Chief Inspector and remembered the case clearly. What he was not prepared for was Dave's revelation of facts not disclosed during the original investigation. He organised a team of divers to search the quarry and there, six feet down in the muddy water at a spot indicated by Dave, they found the skeleton of a young boy of approximately ten years old – Tommy Watkinson.

Dave wasn't charged with any offence by the police even though he lied during the original investigation. His dad was a known bully and beat his mother regularly, so his reticence over Tommy's whereabouts was understandable, they said. Mr and Mrs Watkinson had been dead for over ten years so identification of the body was made by one of his sisters from the contents of Tommy's pockets. Ronald Williams' name was cleared posthumously and although no-one apportioned any blame on to Dave, the high profile coverage in the national press kept him in the spotlight for quite some time.

Tommy made just one more appearance, and it was to Paul. Dave saw the conversation from the kitchen window one afternoon and at the end of it his son came running into the house in tears.

"Tommy's going away now dad, and he says I won't see him anymore. He says to tell you that you're not to blame yourself and that he'll look after Ronald. What does he mean?"

A Shot Too Far

Sharpe sat in silence for what seemed an age as the president strolled over to the large bow window which looked out across an acre of green and well-watered lawn. The empty glass in his hand had been refilled by his captor prior to the issuing of the thinly veiled threat.

So that was it. He had been suckered in to the dictator's web of power and intrigue merely as a pawn in some larger game known only to the man himself. For the moment then he was safe, which was more than could be said for a considerable number of other souls whose paths had crossed with the figure now approaching him from the far end of the room.

"You see Mr Sharpe, my country is going through a transition, a series of changes which do not meet with the approval of certain governments in the west. The imperial powers of the past hundred years have not taken kindly to their grip on this continent being loosened, and we have become something of a target for their wrath. It is time for a gesture, and I have decided that I am the man to make that statement."

He dropped a file in front of the assassin and removed a Havana from the box on his desk. Lighting it, he blew out a cloud of blue smoke and sat down once more opposite the sniper. Sharpe opened the folder, one eye focussed on the man's face for any reaction.

"But this is………."

"Yes, I know who it is Mr Sharpe. The man has been at the forefront of European condemnation of my regime, and feelings have begun to polarise around him. The time has come for a gesture. He must be silenced, and the message to all those of a similar opinion stifled."

"You know he's a cabinet minister."

"The workings of your government are no mystery to me, and its ministers should not consider themselves above reproach. You will kill him and send a warning out to the rest of his kind."

The statement was cold, clear and unambiguous. Take the assignment and disappear freely. Refuse and disappear here, never to be seen again. He nodded and his captor smiled that toothy smile once more. He raised his glass.

"To success, and your freedom of course."

Sharp reciprocated and downed the Jim Beam in one swallow. The president picked up on the frown which played across the assassin's face.

"One final word of warning, Mr Sharp. Do not for one moment even consider an attempt to vanish once you are out of my country. I have contacts in many lands, and should you attempt to double cross me, you will be found and executed. Clear?"

This foray had clearly been in the planning for some time. He led Sharp out of the room and down to a basement area which was kitted out like something out of an Ian Fleming novel. All that was missing was the figure of "Q" to demonstrate the equipment now on display.

"You will be provided with all of the necessary documentation to get you back into Britain, and passage through your country's security systems will be very easy."

He handed Sharp a package, and the sniper had to admit the papers were of the highest quality. He focussed on a table where a rifle was being assembled by one of the dictator's staff. It was a weapon straight out of Forsyth's "Day of the Jackal" and could have been made for him.

"You will be shown how to assemble it, and we have a testing range for final adjustments to be made. After that you are on your own, so to speak."

One week of briefings and 'final adjustments' later, Sharpe was leaving the Arrivals lounge at Heathrow. With hair now dyed a different colour and a suitable growth of beard, he would pass unnoticed through the airport security checks. The plaster cast around his right leg also lent an air of 'ordinariness' which had baggage handlers and airport staff alike fussing around him like a group of mother hens. Little did any of them realise the lethal nature of the contents of the crutches which now supported him on his journey to the assignment that the president had given.

The Minister's itinerary and appointments schedule had been included amongst the documents given to Sharpe before leaving Africa, and a visit to Nottingham, together with timings and travel details, had been highlighted. This was obviously the location of choice, and he had no option in the matter. Making for the hotel where he had reserved a room, he was now anxious to rid himself of the cumbersome cast which had hindered his progress.

Removing the rifle parts from their concealed position within the steel crutches, Sharpe marvelled at the ingenuity of the planning which had gone into this assignment. He would have to carry the rifle with him, and the camera case brought through airport security was now adapted to suit the needs of its more dangerous cargo. He cut the protective foam to fit the new purpose and disposed of the Nikon. Later that day he was aboard an Intercity 125 from London St Pancras and heading for the Midlands. Nottingham would soon have a place in history quite different from anything that had gone before.

The day was warm without being uncomfortable, and a light breeze blew from east to west across Old Market Square, where the minister was due to speak that afternoon to a Trades Union rally. There would be a considerable number of participants and onlookers, and Sharpe saw no difficulty in merging with the confused masses after the kill had been made. It was now one week after his return to the UK, and he had taken three to four days in selecting the position from which to make the shot, and it would only be one shot.

The roof of the office block gave him a clear and uninterrupted view of the podium where his target would stand, some hundred yards away in front of the Council House. He had posed as a maintenance engineer and made his way to the top of the building via the emergency stairways. Securing the door behind him, he had started to lay out the rifle parts when noises from the stairwell had him quickly packing them away. The security guard bursting through the door on to the roof missed Sharpe by seconds as he hurriedly concealed himself behind one of the air conditioning vents. Reaching into his pocket, he withdrew the garrotte and looked at his watch – time was starting to run away. The man pulled out a pack of cigarettes and lit one.

Sharpe's relief at the impromptu break was tempered by the incursion into his timing. The choice was clear – either pass up the opportunity and suffer Maninga's wrath, or take the intruder down and risk an early discovery. In the event he was rescued by an irate voice from the stairwell.

"Briggs! Put that bloody fag out and get back to work. One more bit of skiving and you're fired!"

The man jumped as if he'd been shot, crushed the Marlboro beneath his size ten and hurried back down the stairs. Sharpe breathed a sigh of relief. Pausing only briefly to assure himself that there would be no more interruptions, he resumed preparations – now more urgently than before, as crowds started to gather in the city centre square.

The kill would be easy. Broad daylight and with no need for night vision equipment, he had only the minimum of kit with which to burden himself, and the downhill shot would be a piece of cake. As the minister stepped up to the raised platform, Sharpe's steady breathing took over and he squinted down the telescopic sight. Sweeping across the assembled group, he homed in on the figure whose picture had been given to him in Maninga's stronghold – there was no doubt as to the identity of the target. He settled down into his firing position and took one long breath. Releasing it very slowly he brought the cross hairs perfectly in line with the man's head.

A sudden commotion in the surrounding crowd to the left almost took Sharpe by surprise, but with consummate professional skill he squeezed the trigger and felt the gentle kick from the rifle as the armoured round sped unerringly towards its destination. He watched, very briefly as the suited figure fell, and then began his clear-up routine. Time was now of the essence, and with commotion and panic already rife in the city centre, he was down at ground level in a matter of minutes. Now outside the office block and immersed in the confusion, Sharpe failed to notice the black, smartly dressed 'executive' who had been watching him since his arrival at the site. The man began his approach and removed a syringe from his inside jacket pocket.

Sharpe collided with one of the fleeing pedestrians, and asked what had happened.

"Guy on the platform got shot. Looks dead to me, and I'm getting out of here while I can!"

What no-one had mentioned was the Arab student now in police custody. He had moved forwards in the crowd at the last moment with a pistol in his hand. A round had been fired in the direction of the minister and it was this that had set off the panic, not Sharpe's precision shot which actually killed the man. The assassin smiled to himself at this stroke of good fortune and, carried by the crowd, was spun away into the middle of the street. He never saw the oncoming tram as it ran down the hill from the Royal Centre, once beneath its wheels there was no hope and Sharpe's screams went unheard amidst the general panic. His weapon case went spinning on to the pavement area right in front of his tracker. The 'executive' picked it up, replaced the cap on his syringe, smiled and disappeared into the crowd. Nothing left at the scene would connect the killer to his principal.

"You did very well." The president smiled his toothy smile at the figure before him. "That was quick thinking to remove the gun from the scene. I will ensure that you are suitably rewarded."

The man bowed in deference, smiled in return and left the room. Charles Adebe stood up from the president's desk and looked at himself in the full-length mirror which Maninga used to feed his vanity each day. Never in his wildest dreams had he imagined that he would, one day, be running his country. Sharpe had been quite correct; Maninga had not survived the assassination. The dictator had chosen that occasion to go off on one of his unpredictable forays into the countryside, leaving one of his carefully chosen doubles to 'hold the fort'.

Secrecy had been the man's byword, and none of his staff were aware of this last minute change of plan. Now that he was dead, who was to question the word of the man who was, to all intents and purposes, The President? His word was law. Maninga's body would disappear in some unmarked grave and Adebe's family would be told of the disappearance. A suitable monetary amount would be sufficient to keep them quiet. The only remaining problem was Serena, Maninga's wife. She would be the only one able to identify him as an impostor. An unfortunate motor accident would take care of that.

For a man living at the edge of poverty not twelve months ago, life now seemed to hold out so much promise. He smiled that toothy grin which Maninga had made his trademark, poured a glass of Jim Beam, lit a Havana and relaxed into the arms of the Chesterfield – these British certainly knew how to make good furniture.

BITTER SWEET

As she stepped down from the National Express coach, Liz's feelings of apprehension reached a new peak. One more journey by local bus and she would be at her destination after a trip of three hundred miles from her home in the north east. It was a fair distance to travel on nothing more than a whim, but the feeling had been growing stronger since her mum died almost a year ago. She had always assumed that her father was dead, and her mother Joan had done and said nothing to persuade her otherwise. However, in the final weeks of her futile struggle against the cancer which was consuming her, Liz's mum had let slip one or two things which had stirred her daughter's interest in their family history. Going through a box of old photographs one day, Liz came across one of her mother in her mid to late thirties at the seaside and in the arms of a man of around forty years of age. She turned it over and read out the writing 'Margate – July 1975'.

"What's this, mum?" she asked.

"Give it here, love." Joan replied, and smiled as she took in the faded image. It was one of those calm, wistful expressions which always comes with pleasant memories half forgotten.

"Mum?"

"Oh, sorry love, I was somewhere else for a moment just then."

"Well, who is it?"

Joan coloured up, and for a terminally ill cancer sufferer the change in her complexion made her look almost well. She looked down again at the photograph and began humming a tune to herself. Liz recognised it as 'Leaving on a Jet Plane' – a favourite of her mother's down the years, the source of which she had always refused to divulge, but now that her time was coming she released the memory.

"It's your dad. We met on holiday in Margate. He was there with his brother and family and I'd gone with my mum and dad and your aunty Pat. We had a wonderful time for a fortnight, and I'm afraid he swept me off my feet. The song was popular at the time and we adopted it as ours."

She went on after some encouragement to elaborate the story. They exchanged the usual addresses at the end of the two weeks, and Joan half expected that to be an end to it. She got a pleasant surprise shortly after returning home to North Shields when a letter arrived bearing a Bristol postmark – it was from Tom, the man in Margate, and he wanted to see her again. To cut a long story short, they met and picked up where they had left off in Kent. A whirlwind romance ended abruptly when he found out that she had cheated on him whilst he had gone back to the south west for a few days. It had been a stupid thing to do, but there had been no way of repairing the damage. He left on the morning after she told him about it and she never saw him again. Nine months later Liz was born. Joan was sure that she was Tom's daughter even though, in those days, there was no way to prove it conclusively. She was christened Elizabeth Jane after her grandmother, but no attempt was made to inform Tom of the event. Joan ended up marrying Paul Williams, the man with whom she had the brief relationship, but they were never in love and their association only lasted eighteen months.

Joan died a few weeks later, leaving Liz as her only surviving family member and sole beneficiary in her will. Apart from the house, she had few possessions of any great value and her savings, though sufficient for her own needs, amounted to little more than modest sums. Liz lived in the two bedroom semi for a while, but the memories of her mother became too strong and after a quick sale she moved into a new city centre apartment purchased with the proceeds. This kept her in touch with friends and work colleagues, but she was becoming aware of a growing sense of curiosity about her father and she felt that an attempt should be made to trace him and get in touch.

Joan had told her that his name was Tom Parsons, he was forty when they met, and this would now make him sixty-four. She also knew from her mother that he had been employed as a draughtsman with a Bristol firm, so Liz decided to take some leave from work and make the trip down to the West Country to see what she could discover – in any case one of her college friends lived in the city and it would give her an excuse to get in touch again. That was a month ago, and as her bus pulled into Bristol city centre she felt like a small child arriving at the seaside for the very first time. She knew the name of the firm where Parsons worked and clung to the slim hope that he was still there, albeit nearing retirement. The lateness of the hour gave her time only to find accommodation for the night, together with somewhere to eat. This being a Monday, tomorrow would see her at the doors of Barton and Wallis at the start of business for the day.

Enquiries at reception revealed that a Tom Parsons did, in fact, work for the firm as Project Director, but Liz's excitement was tempered by the fact that he was tied up in meetings all morning and would not be free until 2.30pm. She was advised to leave her name and an address, and call back in the afternoon. Her morning trip around the city delayed the return to the offices, and by the time she arrived at three o'clock he had left for an appointment with a client, and would not be back until the following day. Disappointed, Liz returned to her hotel where she showered and changed in preparation for dinner in the Brasserie restaurant. When she later returned to reception for her room key, it was to discover that a visitor had made enquiries after her. A change of shift had meant that no-one knew she was still in the hotel, and the man had departed half an hour earlier. He was described as being in his sixties and said his name was Parsons – she had been within yards of him, and now he was gone who knows where.

Frustrating as it was, there was nothing left but to return as planned to the architects' offices in the morning, and hope that he would have time to see her then. She spent a restless night tossing and turning as sleep evaded her, and rose early the following day with her mind still buzzing in anticipation. Breakfast was a non-starter, and after a quickly consumed coffee she set off again for Barton and Wallis. Arriving at 8am, she was admitted into the building by a security guard who sat and chatted with her until the receptionist arrived half an hour later, but she couldn't for the life of her remember anything of their conversation. The receptionist recognised her from the previous day, and said that Tom Parsons was due in at nine o'clock. She checked his diary, and confirmed that apart from normal work commitments the morning appeared to be clear. Liz breathed a sigh of relief and resumed her seat, picking up a magazine which she knew she would be unable to read.

At around nine, people began arriving and Liz looked anxiously amongst them for someone matching the description given to her by hotel staff the night before. She had begun to think she may have missed him once more, when a silver haired man in a dark blue suit entered, signed in at reception, chatted pleasantly with the girl behind the desk and headed for the staircase. He was called back by the receptionist.

"Oh, Mr Parsons, I'm sorry I nearly forgot, there's a lady to see you over in the corner."

He turned to face Liz, smiled politely and offered his hand in greeting. She took it nervously and introduced herself. They made their way up to his office on the first floor where he asked for tea and coffee to be served, and waved his arm in the direction of two armchairs over by the window.

"Now then, Miss Williams, what it is that I can do for you? It seems that we were destined not to meet yesterday."

"I hardly know where to begin; it's a rather personal matter really. My mother died some months ago and amongst her possessions were a number of photographs – this is one of them."

She passed over to him the snap taken in Margate in July 1975 and watched as he studied it. The smile on his face vanished instantaneously as he turned it over to read the writing on the reverse side. He pulled out his wallet and removed an old photograph of his own.

"We had two printed you see, and kept one each. The handwriting is mine, and the woman in the picture is Joan Taylor. You say she was your mother, so your name is Williams because………………"

"Because the man mum married walked out, leaving her to bring me up alone. I wasn't two at the time and never knew him. I had no idea until just before she died that you even existed. Mum told me that you are my father."

Tom Parsons sat back in his chair and sipped at his coffee absently whilst he thought. Joan had written to him after he left but he had never replied to any of her letters. Looking back, it was probably not the kindest thing to do, but how was he to know that she was pregnant when there had been no mention of it? Had he been aware of the facts, things might have turned out differently. Too late now, except for the fact that before him sat an attractive young woman who claimed to be his daughter. He and Joan certainly had a passionate relationship, and no-one thought too seriously about contraception in those days – you were just unlucky if you got caught. There had been a number of women in his life down the years, but he had never married and the thought of having children had never crossed his mind. He looked across at Liz and could see the resemblance to Joan in the 1975 photograph – his heart started to melt. Pulling himself together he spoke again.

"Well Miss Williams, I really don't know what to say. This has all come as a surprise to me as you will appreciate, and whilst I am sure that you believe the story your mother told you, I think proof of our relationship is required before we go any further. I can schedule blood tests with my doctor at short notice if you wish. DNA profiles are the best way of resolving such matters."

Liz had no option but to agree. If nothing else it would ease the increasingly fond feelings which she was experiencing for this man. The appointment was made for early in the evening at a private surgery across the city, and the day seemed to drag interminably until they met up again at five thirty that afternoon. The procedure was quick and relatively painless, and a quiet word in the right place ensured that some urgency was attached to the results. They would know by the end of the week whether or not they were, in fact, father and daughter. There seemed to be no point in taking up any more of Tom Parsons' time than she already had for the moment, so Liz made her excuses and headed off back to her hotel. She decided to call Sheila, the friend from her college days at Warwick, and catch up on old times. They met up for a meal at the hotel and spent the rest of the evening reliving past glories and disasters. As the time wore on and the wine flowed, Liz related the story of Tom Parsons to her old friend, and Sheila was intrigued by the whole matter. Liz was glad of some supporting opinion in her 'quest', and by the time Sheila left her spirits had brightened considerably. They made arrangements to meet during the rest of the week until the deadline for the DNA results arrived.

That day was surprisingly quick in coming, and when she got a telephone call from Tom Parsons it caught her slightly off-guard. She was to meet him at his offices, and they would travel to the private surgery together. Arriving just after four o'clock they were shown into a private consulting room immediately where Tom was greeted by John Grant, his GP. After explaining the unusual situation of Liz being there, Grant agreed to discuss the case with both of them present. The results proved conclusively that they were, in fact, father and daughter and Liz could hardly conceal her delight at no longer being alone. She threw herself into Tom's arms and called him 'daddy' – a word she had never had the opportunity of using before. He responded to her embrace awkwardly at first, but as she looked up at him with tears of joy in her eyes, he opened up and clasped her firmly to him. As they thanked John Grant and turned to leave, he called Tom back for a moment to discuss another matter. Liz left the room to wait outside.

"Tom, we've now got the full results from your earlier tests and there's no easy way of telling you, but the outlook is not promising."

Parsons was stunned. In one instance his world had been built up and then instantly demolished. Grant explained that the condition was fairly well advanced and would inevitably lead to a rapid deterioration of his health – he was dying. How was he now going to explain all this to Liz?

One year later, a young woman is pushing a wheelchair occupied by an ancient man in his mid sixties along the seafront of a small Devon resort. Liz and Tom had sold up and moved there to spend whatever remained of his now severely curtailed life. They had crammed an enormous amount into the brief time since their first meeting, and the bond between them was now complete. He was resigned to his fate, and she was his rock as he slid slowly but inexorably downhill towards his destiny. She had made him very happy in the months since the meeting with John Grant, with stories about her mother and their twenty years together, and he had developed a kind of serenity as he accepted his situation. Liz parked the chair at the side of a bench close to the railings near the sea wall and sat down. She looked at her father and smiled, noticing that he had dropped off to sleep. Leaning across, she stroked his thinning hair and planted a kiss on his cheek. As she looked out across the sea to the horizon, a tear made its way slowly down her cheek.

"He's coming home to you mum, he's coming home."

FOOT IN THE DOOR

*D*avid Marsh had always wanted to be a salesman, and despite all the advice from the teachers at school he was adamant that his career path would take him down that road. Leaving at sixteen he took the first job he could find in a sales office, and his enthusiasm and willingness to learn landed him a place sponsored by his employer at a commercial college. He excelled in the subject, passing all the exams with flying colours and moving up the albeit small corporate ladder with a rapidity which surprised all of his colleagues. Inevitably, with further progress hampered by more senior staff, it became time to move onwards and upwards. His next job, for a much larger company, was in the area of home improvements and specifically the double glazing field.

Again he applied himself diligently and very soon knew all that there was to know about the industry. Single and in his late twenties, he had what he thought to be the perfect job. Perfect that is, until one morning in late May in the North Yorkshire coastal resort of Scarborough, where he made the acquaintance of Jennifer Riley. He was well up with his sales targets for the month so he wasn't trying particularly hard to gather in extra business, and this calmness in his demeanour was one of the secrets of his success, making him appear less pushy than competitors in the industry. Nevertheless he was always on the lookout for anything that appeared to be an easy sell, and number fourteen Walsingham Gardens fitted the bill exactly. The house was large and in a quiet cul-de sac, but the wooden windows and doors had seen better days and were starting to let the rest of the property down.

Straightening his tie in an almost ritual way before facing a customer, he walked up the gravel drive, put on his best smile and rang the door bell. The woman who opened the front door took his breath away and for the first time ever, he was momentarily lost for words as she returned his smile. She was a brunette, with hazel eyes and a figure which harked back to the days of Marilyn Monroe. At about five feet eight, she was slightly shorter than him and had the kind of hands which had never seen a day's manual work in their lives.

"Yes, can I help you?" She had the kind of voice which could charm the birds down from the trees.

"Good morning Mrs…………?"

"Riley, Jennifer Riley."

"Good morning Mrs Riley, my name is David Marsh from Surebright Home Improvements. Would you be interested in replacing your existing frames?"

She looked him critically up and down, stepped out of the porch and gazed at the windows and door with a frown on her face.

"They do look rather tired, don't they? Why don't you come inside and let me take a look at your brochures – perhaps we can come to some arrangement."

Over tea and cakes they spent the next hour exploring every aspect of Surebright's portfolio, and David was left with a quotation to prepare for a complete refit throughout the house. The job was larger than any of those he would normally have dealt with and would earn him a tidy commission. As he rose to leave, he noticed a change in her manner and she appeared to be crying. Unsure of how to deal with the situation, he extended a hand and placed it upon her shoulder. She was in his arms immediately and dissolved into floods of tears as she began to explain the position in which she found herself. She had been married for fifteen years, and over the past five had known of her husband's affair with a woman in Thirsk. She had attempted to discuss the matter with him, but all of her efforts had been brushed aside and she was now left alone most of the time, as he always seemed to be away on business. There was no love left in their marriage and if she could find a way out of it there would be no regrets.

He remained there for the rest of the afternoon comforting her in the only way he could think of, assuring her that he would return in a few days with the figures which she had requested. There was no shame in his mind relating to a brief affair with an unhappy, attractive woman even though she was his senior by at least ten years, and he was looking forward to their next meeting. George Riley was at home when he made his return call and you could have cut the atmosphere between Jennifer and him with a knife. He glanced at the quotation in a cursory manner, and with a wave of his hand told his wife to please herself. Picking up his golf clubs from the hall, it was clear where he intended to spend the rest of that day and probably the majority of the evening. Left alone together, the formalities of the paperwork were completed quickly and he returned the signed contract to his briefcase.

"Do you see what I mean?" she asked. "He's like that all the time and it's come to the point where I would be better off without him. If I could find some way of freeing myself I'd do it in a flash. I wish he were dead."

David was at a loss for something to say in a situation which he had never encountered before, but was sure that there was more to Jennifer Riley than met the eye. He was not to be disappointed.

"What should I do? If I divorce him he'll fight me all the way and move in with his fancy woman. He's extremely wealthy and employs lawyers who could keep me tied up in court for years. Even the insurance policy only covers accidental death."

"What if he did have a fatal accident?"

"In that case, everything goes to me. There are no other beneficiaries in his will, and he has no family. What are you suggesting?"

For a moment, David thought that he might have overstepped the mark and turned to stare out of the back window into the large well-kept garden. She continued.

"If I could find someone who could arrange for him to somehow suffer accidentally fatal injuries, there would be a considerable amount of recompense for those kinds of services. Do you have anyone in mind?" She smiled and cocked her head on one side.

He was now getting in too deep to pull out without facing embarrassing consequences. Knowing that George's mistress lived in Thirsk and that he called on her regularly, his route would probably have to take him along the A170 from Helmsley and down the treacherous incline of Sutton Bank. A brakes failure along this stretch of road could have serious consequences for any unwary driver, and it would not prove too difficult to engineer some wear to the fluid cables underneath the car. Dave's dad had been a mechanic, and so all of his teenage years had been spent in and around the series of vehicles which occupied their drive and garage. It was time to take the bull by the horns. He stared at her intently.

"If a person knew the likely timing of the next visit, arrangements could be made to change the reliability of the brakes on George's car. A fractured brake pipe could be lethal in a place like Sutton Bank, and if a payment for that service were to be made in an untraceable manner, no-one would be any the wiser."

Jennifer looked at him long and hard, turning the matter over and over in her mind. She had only known this man for a matter of days and had poured out her life to him in that time. Were they to go ahead with this, there could be serious consequences for both of them, and yet the alternative for her would be a lifetime of misery and loneliness. She asked him straight to his face if he would do it. For David it could be no more than a business transaction and whatever had happened between them so far would have to stop. She said she understood that, and that all contact would cease, just as it would following the completion of the double glazing installation.

The driveway to the house front was long and isolated from the roadway, giving David cover from prying eyes as he quickly worked on the brake cables three nights later whilst the Rileys were out. He knew how to make fractures look like accidental damage done by a loose brick, and had even taken the precaution of providing one as evidence. Laced with brake fluid and left lying in the road outside the house with a trail leading up the drive, it would ensure that any accident investigator came to the correct conclusion. Regular as clockwork, George departed the next day and headed out of Scarborough with David following him at a respectful distance as far as Helmsley. Now he and Jennifer simply had to bide their time and carry on as normal.

She called his mobile two days later, confirming that George had been taken to hospital after leaving the road unaccountably half way down Sutton Bank. He was pronounced dead on arrival, and after a consoling visit from the local uniformed police, she was left as sole beneficiary inheriting everything. The payout from his insurance policy should net £1.5 million, of which £100,000 would be transferred to an offshore bank account in payment for the service. At more than double his annual salary, this amount placed David in a situation of some comfort and he returned to his normal lifestyle convinced that he would hear no more from Jennifer Riley – how wrong he was.

By August, he had left Surebright along with Roger Harding to set up their own business, and initial deals indicated that the company was moving quickly in the correct direction. They had set up in the Home Counties, away from any contractual restrictions imposed by their former employer, and David was relaxing at home after a meeting with the bank when his mobile phone rang. Usually it was from Roger to remind him of commitments for the following day, but the number displayed did not look familiar. The voice at the other end made him sit up with a start.

"David, its Jennifer. Look, don't worry, there's no cause for alarm but I have a friend who could be in need of the same sort of service to the one which you provided for me earlier this year. The 'installation' would be similar to mine and she is flexible with regard to contractual terms. Are you interested?"

He was dumbstruck. He was a salesman not a fixer, and the job for Jennifer had been more out of sympathy than with any thought as to financial reward. Now here, out of the blue, was an opportunity to expand what could become a pension fund for his old age. Jennifer had told him over the phone that no names had been mentioned at this point, but that the woman was in a similar position to that which she had occupied a few short months ago. He bought himself a new mobile on a 'Pay As You Go' package and told Jennifer never to call him again on his normal number. She gave him details of her friend and he agreed to call her to set up preliminary discussions. Telling Roger that he would be away up north for a few days on a sales trip, he set out up the M1 for Chesterfield and a service area meeting with Rosemary Davidson.

The facts were almost identical to Jennifer's situation, and the fee for completion and the method of payment were identical. It was almost too easy to believe – the man (David declined the offer of his name, preferring to remain distant) worked in Manchester and after parking his car made the final leg of the journey from Trafford Park into the city centre by tram. From an earlier trip to the North West, David knew that trams had become very popular and were always packed. It would be quite easy to engineer a terrible accident for someone caught up in the crush of passengers for an approaching vehicle.

The job was over and done with minimal planning involved. David simply positioned himself two rows back from his target and 'stumbled' into the man in front of him under the weight of a 'heavy' suitcase, apologising profusely for his clumsiness. Instinct had forced this passenger into breaking his forward movement by placing hands upon the back of the person in front who in turn pushed Rosemary's husband into the path of the approaching tram. By the time of the impact, David was away from the scene with all other eyes on the horror unfolding before them. Back in his car outside Manchester United's Old Trafford ground, he rang Rosemary with the result of his action. Three months later, with the insurance claim finalised, he was £100,000 richer and back on the road in his normal business. He called Jennifer to ensure that no more recommendations were likely and chose to believe that he would hear no more. He didn't, at least not from her.

The business set up with Roger Harding was progressing very nicely, but David's accountant partner was becoming aware of the lack of paperwork relating to his business trip to Lancashire. At one of their weekly meetings he broached the subject, and finding himself in a corner David lamely explained that he had paid his expenses on his personal credit card, and that recompense could take place at the time of their annual bonuses. Roger frowned and let it pass, deciding instead to file it for future reference but to keep an eye on his associate's movements from now on. A phone call to his new mobile a few weeks later had David hurrying out early one afternoon with a vague 'see you in the morning' parting line. Accountants are curious creatures by nature, and Roger was soon in David's private office looking amongst the papers on his desk. There was nothing of unusual interest there but his partner had, surprisingly, left his laptop switched on and logged in with just the cover pulled down. He had obviously forgotten about it in his haste to leave. Raising the cover, Harding was faced with a set of files which he had never seen before, one of which contained a list of passwords – he printed a copy of this. The eyes nearly popped out of his head when he came across David's offshore bank account and the amounts of cash it contained.

Like all partners, they knew the details of each other's remuneration package, and these figures couldn't possibly be any part of that. Within his hands he held much of David's private wealth and the means to acquire it without leaving a trace. He used the passwords to access all the files, and satisfying himself that he had full and complete control over all funds, closed the computer down for the day, tidied up and went home to consider his next move. At the same time, David was on his 'private' mobile to Rosemary, the mystery caller that afternoon. Like Jennifer before her, she had a 'friend' who required the help of someone discreet and willing to benefit by a six-figure sum for certain services. He tried to explain that this was not something which he had ever intended to carry out on a regular basis and that he would, regrettably, be unable to office any assistance. After a muffled conversation at the other end, during which time David deduced that the 'friend' was present, Rosemary relayed the message that the fee would be double his usual charge.

Leaning on his elbow and with his head in his hand, he tried one last time to dissuade both women from the course of action which they were contemplating, but when the final offer of £250,000 came back as a reply he couldn't refuse. This, he stated, was to be the final job and no further recommendations were to be made to any more deserving individuals. Both women agreed, and arrangements were made to meet with customer number three to discuss details. On his way to another 'business trip' which Roger accepted rather easily, David wondered where all these women were coming from, and was sure that somewhere a smart detective would make a connection of some kind to link him to all three events – or was he just becoming paranoid?

When an overweight man falls from a ladder forty feet up the side of his house and dies as a result of a massive skull fracture with no-one else anywhere near, there is not usually much cause for suspicion of foul play. For David, this was an unexpected bonus since this was not the method which he had planned to use in disposing of the unwanted husband, but since he had not informed the wife of his chosen technique it really made no difference, and in the course of time he collected his fee for a job well done. He became a little uneasy some time later when a call came from Cecily (the beneficiary of his latest assignment) informing him of a visit to the house by the local CID. A neighbour had reported seeing an unknown man at the house during the days immediately prior to the fatal accident, and further enquiries had revealed the name of his company on an advertising sticker in the rear window of his car.

Back home, he had no option but to sit tight and wait for the enquiries to hit a dead end, but when a connection was made back to Rosemary and then Jennifer, things took a turn for the worse. He received a visit from Inspector Dennis Marks, head of homicide and his sergeant, Peter Spencer. Questions as to his relationship to Jennifer Riley and Rosemary Davidson were detailed and lengthy, but any evidence of a connection beyond that of a business deal for double glazing was circumstantial at best, and the detectives left with nothing more than when they had arrived. Still, Marks had started to get one of his feelings that there was more to this than some randy salesman and a few desperate housewives. Like all criminals Marsh would slip up, they all did in the end, and it would just be a case of putting the pieces together.

David decided to take the rest of the week off, and left a message for Roger at work to say that he would be back in on the following Monday. When that day came he returned to the office to discover that Harding had, himself, decided to take a leave of absence but had left no indication as to his proposed date of return. Initially this was no cause for concern, but when he switched on his laptop and accessed his private files Marsh got the shock of his life. His on-line offshore account had been emptied of its entire contents including the newly received funds from Cecily – a total of £450,000; a call to Roger's flat was redirected to the House Manager's office where he was informed that Mr Harding had vacated the premises the previous week without leaving a forwarding address.

He put the telephone back down in its cradle as his attention had now been drawn to flashing blue lights outside the office window. Two police patrol cars had pulled up behind an unmarked vehicle from which DI Marks was exiting with a smile on his face. They entered the salesman's office to find him sitting at his desk with his head in his hands.

"They all screw up in the end, Mr Marsh. Overconfidence breeds sloppiness – what made you think that a hole drilled through a ladder rung wouldn't be spotted? I'm sure that the power drill we found in your victim's garage will match it. I said to my sergeant that it would only be a matter of time. We already have statements from the three ladies concerned implicating you in all of the deaths. You'd better be coming along with us. Cuff him please, constable."

As he sat in the squad car on its way back to the station, David pondered upon the irony of being caught as a result of the only death of the three for which he was not responsible. He wouldn't even have the comfort of knowing that he had £450,000 waiting for him when he eventually did come out of jail.

FACING THE DEMON

*T*he light streaming into the room through a chink in the heavy curtains sent a rapier-like pain through what masqueraded as his brain at this time in the morning, or was it afternoon? Since he had no reason to get up each day at a regular time any more, setting the alarm clock had long ceased to be one his daily rituals. He turned over to look at the dial, but came so close to the contents of his stomach in the bucket at the bedside, that the automatic heaving and retching which had become a normal part of his life kicked in once more. After the excruciating pain in his abdomen had eased, he rolled back over on to the bed, picked up the cigarette packet from his bedside table and lit up for the first one of the day. He couldn't face any kind of food, and the nicotine would suppress any appetite planning to creep up on him unawares.

Brian Powell knew that he was a disgusting mess, that former friends now avoided him like the plague and that unchecked, he was heading for the inevitability of disease and death. The plain fact of the matter was that at the moment he didn't really care. Out of work and unemployable in his current state, all his benefits went into feeding the addiction which was surely killing him – the only question remained was the timing of the end. He struggled out of bed and dressed – no point in washing or showering any more, there was no reason to waste valuable drinking time in unnecessary activities. Most of the public houses in the neighbourhood had banned him from their premises, as his mere appearance caused an exodus of customers. He was therefore reduced to park benches and curious mixtures in plastic bottles.

He didn't speak to passers by, not that they would have been able to understand him anyway, and the local police just kept moving him along – the last thing they wanted was to keep him locked up for the night in a cell which would need cleaning and disinfecting the following morning. It hadn't always been like this, and he couldn't say for certain when his party drinking descended into alcoholism – that was the way with booze, it played funny games with your memory, like making sure that you didn't have one. There had been countless times when he had woken on some street, or in a back alley with no recollection of the events of the preceding evening; it was as if that part of his brain had been wiped clean like a blackboard when the lesson was over. The depression was probably the worst aspect of the whole matter. He would go for days wandering around in a morass of self pity, becoming extremely belligerent with innocent bystanders for no apparent reason, and he always felt guilty afterwards.

Stepping out of the front door of his filthy flat into a bright April morning, he squinted in the glare of the spring sunshine. A sunshine which meant so many different things to so many people, but to Brian it represented only pain. He staggered, part blinded, into the street, off the pavement and straight into the path of an approaching vehicle. There was a screech of brakes and an angry horn blaring in his ears before the collision which sent him reeling backwards, head over heels and into the unforgiving concrete structure of a lamp post – he blacked out. He never saw the ambulance, and was totally unaware of the paramedics loading him on to a stretcher for transportation to one of the few hospitals still prepared to take in the drunks and time wasters of the district.

The usual procedure would have been to patch him up and get him through A&E as quickly as possible and out of the way of normal people, but this time it was different. He had sustained a broken arm and was suffering from concussion, so they were obliged to keep him in at least overnight for observation. The regular medical staff were not on duty at the time, and he was seen by a young, fresh faced university graduate who took a more serious view of cases than the time-wearied veterans. He looked at Brian's chart with a frown on his face, leafed through a file which resembled case records and sat down at the side of the bed.

"Mr Powell, you have a multiple fracture of the right arm which we have put in plaster, and there's a deep cut at the back of your skull which we have managed to stitch. I see from your records that this isn't the first time that you've sustained significant injuries, and that you have been advised to seek help for your alcohol dependency. If you don't make some changes pretty soon your life expectancy will be very short."

Much as this sounded like a sermon, Brian knew in his heart that the doctor was right. He hadn't eaten a thing in days, relying on cigarettes to suppress any need for food – it would only end up in the street anyway. The doctor continued.

"I'd like to refer you to Alcoholics Anonymous; there's a branch in the town and I'm sure that you would benefit. Their details are on this card."

Brian had tried it before but had more pride in those days. He didn't see why he should share what he couldn't regard as a problem with a bunch of mamby-pamby do-gooders, and told them so to their faces. It dissolved into a full scale shouting match and he stormed out. Now his soul was stripped bare of any care for what others may think of him, and when you are at the bottom of the pit staring up into the blue sky it just can't get any worse. He agreed, and took some details of the time and place of the next meeting before being discharged that day. He hadn't had a drink for over twenty four hours and it seemed as if the thirst was sending an ache into his very soul. The meeting was not until the following evening and, try and resist as he may, he had to have something now. Using the last of his change he bought two cans of strong lager and took them back home to his wretched bolt hole. They were gone in an instant and he drifted off to sleep for the rest of the day.

Halfway through the night he awoke for the ritual emptying of his gut into the foetid smelling bucket which had become a fixture in the bedroom. Every time it exhausted him and he knew that there had to be some way of breaking the cycle, but the constant craving for booze outweighed any sense of reason. In and out of sleep for the rest of the early morning, he awoke at around ten and resisted the habitual reaching for the cigarette packet. Showering for the first time in weeks, Brian dressed in what were his only clean clothes and left for the address given to him at the hospital. He was late and they had started when he arrived. No-one criticised, and with a smile the leader invited him to take a seat and join the group. They were taking it in turns to 'share' with each other their progress in the intervening period since the last gathering, and all too soon it was his time to stand up.

He knew the drill – state your name and confess to all present your failure to control the substance which had become the driving force in your life.

"Hi, my name is Brian Powell. I am thirty-nine years old, and I am an alcoholic."

Thirty-nine! Thirty-nine and he looked a haggard old man of fifty. He had looked in the mirror too many times to be surprised by what he saw staring back at him, but to speak his age out loud and in front of a room full of strangers was more than he could bear. Slumping back into the chair, he shook with sobs which racked his fragile body. Hands and arms were suddenly around him, coaxing and soothing voices purred in the air and he looked up with a tear-stained face to see smiling, understanding faces all around. In one instance he had more genuine friends than he had ever known before. He stood up again and they all returned to their places to sit hanging on his every word.

"It's OK, I can do this. I am Brian Powell, thirty-nine, and I am an alcoholic. I've been drinking for ten years and I would like to quit."

His ears rang with applause as the entire group stood in approval at the admission. Brian smiled, wondered when was the last time that had happened, and couldn't remember. After the meeting, the leader spent half an hour with him alone and outlined a well-tried plan for freeing him of his dependency. Robert Briggs his name was, and he too was a recovering alcoholic. It seemed that you were never cured once the booze got a hold of you, there was only perpetual recovery and no halfway house - you could never touch another drop for the rest of your life. The first week or so would be the worst and there was no alternative to the 'cold turkey' of complete abstinence from day one. He knew that the cigarettes were also bad for him, but that would be a fight for another day – he would need something to get him through the initial withdrawal period.

The fags on their own would not be enough of a distraction in the early weeks, and if he were serious about the booze other aspects of his life would have to change as well. He knew he couldn't carry on living in the pig sty of his current lodgings and decided on a complete clean-up of his physical surrounding as well as his health. It would be a job big enough to occupy his mind and suppress the craving (he hoped), but nothing would be achieved without money – he needed a job and took the first one that came along. From the position of Engineering Services Manager with a company car, to General Labourer was a fall of monumental proportions and served only to bring home to Brian the desperate nature of his situation.

Robert's contact with local employers had landed him the position and there were no secrets as to the nature of his 'affliction'. Brian threw himself into this lifeline of a job with an enthusiasm which surprised his line manager, and a careful watch was kept on his activities during the initial two weeks of his employment.

It was during the periods when he was alone that the alcoholic cravings began in earnest, and if it had not been for Charlotte he may well have sunk back into the pit of his now gradually fading addiction. She was a rock, herself a member of AA and a leader of some of the meetings when Robert could not be there. She helped him with renovating and cleaning his flat, so that his previous lifestyle and any reminders of the filth in which he had lived were consigned to the past. A relationship beyond mere friendship began to develop, and he found it becoming easier and easier to disentangle himself from the nightmare of his last decade of heavy drinking. He had been 'on the wagon' for four months when the annual company Christmas dinner came around, and Charlotte suggested that this might be the ideal test for his newfound strength of character, and 'Yes', she would be delighted to come along with him.

None of his workmates were aware of Brian's condition, and although he had politely declined all offers of anything other than fruit juice, one or two of the younger members of staff had become increasingly insistent during the evening. On Charlotte's advice they had both refilled their glasses only when buying for themselves, but during one of the dances his drink was spiked. There had been half of his last orange juice left in the glass when the boss came around with the offer of a refill. As he knew about the AA membership, Brian had no qualms about accepting and downed the rest of his glass in one go. He knew instantly that there was something wrong, and Charlotte saw the look on his face with horror. She grabbed him as he slumped backwards and half carried him out of the room as he desperately tried to suppress the feeling of bile rising in his throat. They never made it to the door before a stream of vomit hit the floor, covering several items of clothing on the way. Brian was on his knees by the time the boss returned and surrounded by a group of laughing drunks.

He couldn't remember how he got home that night, and the following morning when the memory of the evening returned, was sure that his time at the factory was now over. Dragging himself to work he headed straight for the manager's office to face the music and the inevitable P45. He was not alone when he arrived, and the queue outside it was six deep with faces staring straight down at their shoes. One of them, Tony, looked up as he arrived.

"Look mate, we're sorry about last night. We didn't know about your………..you know, drinking. We didn't mean any harm."

Brian nodded, said he understood, and took the remaining seat in the row. It wasn't long before he was asked into the office and Ron Holmes, his manager, smiled and asked him to sit down. Much had taken place after their departure the previous evening, and no blame had been apportioned to Brian himself – in fact Ron admitted that perhaps he should have acquainted the staff with the facts prior to the party in order to prevent just such an occurrence. One of the six had been given his marching orders – this had been the last in a sequence of undisciplined behaviour, and the lad had been on a final warning for a number of weeks. It left the company with a vacancy for an engineering fitter, and Ron knew from conversations with Robert Briggs of Brian's qualifications in that field. The 'interview' as it turned out, lasted for thirty minutes ending with an offer of the position.

It was the start of Brian's climb back up the social ladder to the kind of position which he had allowed his addiction to destroy. That destruction had been speedy and spectacular, ruining both his career and personal life, and he did not intend to let it happen again. The AA meetings had continued, and he assumed that they would form a part of his life for the foreseeable future. Charlotte was delighted at the news when he arrived home to the flat which they were now sharing, and the increase in his wages from the promotion would allow them to look for more spacious accommodation in what was becoming an increasingly likely life together. They decided to go out for the evening and celebrate. In a quiet, secluded and romantically lit Italian restaurant Brian ended the evening on one knee as he asked Charlotte, to the sound of a mandolin player, to be his wife. It had all the trappings of 'Lady and the Tramp' and, with tears of happiness in her eyes, she said 'Yes'.

The next few weeks passed in a frenzy of activity, as friends from the AA and also from Brian's place of work threw their weight behind the wedding preparations. It seemed to be only a matter of a day or so until they were at the altar of St Johns with the vicar performing the time-honoured ceremony. It happens at every wedding - the congregation hold their breath as the minister solemnly issued forth the challenge:

"If there is anyone here present who can give any reason why this man and this woman may not be joined in matrimony, let them speak now or forever hold their peace."

He looked over the heads of the bride and groom and into the body of the church for what seemed like an eternity, and in the surrounding silence you could have heard a pin drop. It was punctured like the shattering of a glass as a woman stepped out from a row of pews towards the back of the building.

"I can, the man is my husband and has been for fifteen years."

There was a thunder of whispered voices around the church as Brian turned around to come face to face with the woman who had walked out on him ten years before. It was Caroline his, as he believed, ex-wife about whom he had never thought to tell Charlotte. She strode up the aisle and spoke directly to the now confused minister, who had not faced this scenario before.

"You can't marry them reverend, and here is our licence and my wedding ring as proof."

She turned to Brian and explained that, in their haste to part, the Decree Absolute had never been properly served, and that as a consequence they were still man and wife. This was all too much for Charlotte, and she left the church with her family as the rest of the congregation slowly made their way home. He sat down on the front pew with his head in his hands, and the vicar returned to the vestry leaving them alone together. Caroline was not a vindictive woman and had stepped in to save the couple from a disastrous ceremony. Nevertheless, seeing an opportunity she presented Brian with a proposition which would rid them both of the problem permanently. The divorce proceedings could be resurrected and finalised in a very short time at his cost of course, and after she had been suitably recompensed for her trouble he would hear no more. She gave him a phone number where she could be contacted.

Brian could not take in what had happened, and his thoughts were only of Charlotte. He ran out of the church but the wedding party had dispersed and she was gone. Over the next few days he attempted to contact her, but none of his messages received any reply and she didn't turn up at the next AA group appointment. He spoke to Robert who agreed to try to arrange a meeting between them, and a call from him two nights later gave Brian the chance to explain everything to her. The atmosphere was tense and Charlotte was clearly still upset, but she listened in silence to all that he had to say. At the end he sat there facing her, holding his breath with Robert to one side like some referee. She sat with her hands in her lap, constantly clasping and unclasping her fingers, staring deep into his slate blue eyes for some sign of lies and betrayal. She shook her head and looked down at the floor and Brian thought that his last chance of happiness was gone. Raising her tear-stained face up to him she smiled.

"Give her the money she wants and tell her to sod off, you're mine now and she can't have you back!"

She wrapped her arms around him and they stood there in silence for what seemed like an eternity. Robert reminded them jokingly that they only had the hall for the one hour, and would they like a drink in celebration?

Caroline served the divorce papers as promised and this time it all went to plan, but strangely enough she disappeared shortly afterwards following the arrival in the area of a plain clothes detective asking questions as to her whereabouts. He had Brian's name on his list of interviewees as her husband, but was satisfied that neither he nor Charlotte was involved in any of Caroline's activities which he had under investigation. They were never to see her again, and their second attempt at the wedding went without a hitch. As they celebrated their silver wedding anniversary years later at a small gathering of friends, Brian wondered at the pain and suffering he had put himself through in his youth, and smiled to himself at the irony of his addiction. Without it he would never have met Charlotte.

THE VISITORS

Sometimes you wonder if your whole life has been planned out for you far in advance, and that there is very little that can be done to influence events which are pre-determined. Ray Taylor came from an ordinary background and had never considered that he had any special skills or abilities, and yet for as long as he could remember he seemed to have a flair for maths. His mother and father, whilst not stupid by any stretch of the imagination, were not academically minded and had always joked that he was way beyond their abilities in all of his school studies. This wasn't a problem, because whilst most of his classmates relied upon parental help with their homework, he always seemed to have the ability to work things out for himself. They say that ability has its roots in the individual's genetic make-up and that this can sometimes skip a generation, but his enquiries into family history had revealed no-one with the same capacity for learning as himself.

He was the only child of Derek and Susan Taylor, and up until June 1995 they had been a family of modest means and suitably prudent spending. When Derek won just over £500,000 on the newly launched National Lottery at the start of that summer, everything changed. Ray now found himself able to compete for places at the best universities which his academic prowess deserved, and having sailed through school he was offered a place at Oxford. In the course of what seemed very little time, he achieved a double first in mathematics and physics, and a very bright future seemed to be opening out before him.

He wasn't a swot and had always made time for the social side of university life, mixing with several different academic groups. One of these contained a stunningly attractive undergraduate by the name of Gwendoline Cholmondley-Smythe. She 'homed in' on Ray in a subtle sort of way, and it became clear to him very quickly that she had definite ideas about where they both belonged, and that was together. He was flattered and went along with the relationship, always assuming that it would peter out at the end of university life when everyone went their separate ways. Gwendoline was not one to let a minor fact like that stand in the way of her plans, and persuaded him that they had a future. Her speciality had been in Chemistry and Biology and, like Ray, she had achieved a double first.

Having been head-hunted at a very early stage following graduation, both went to work for government research establishments, he in propulsion and she in biochemistry. They married one year later and set up home in rural Sussex. It was then, for the first time, that he was introduced to Gwendoline's parents. He hadn't really given much thought until then to the fact that he had not crossed their paths before, but one day spent in their infectiously happy company dispelled all doubts that he may have had. It was as if some great cosmic plan had clicked into gear and was moving smoothly and effortlessly onwards. Gerald and Hermione Cholmondley-Smythe were of indefinable age, but confessed to being in their early sixties, retired and of no fixed abode. They oozed money, but any discussion of such a vulgar subject was actively discouraged in a very polite, old-fashioned manner.

It was inevitable that their chosen careers would take them to the places where the big money lay, and fairly soon they had pulled up their metaphorical tent and crossed 'The Pond' to America. Jobs at NASA are for the best talent only – for two relative youngsters this seemed like the beginning of some comic-book adventure. Once more, to Ray, it seemed that he was following some pre-determined path leading to who knows where, with a wife who always appeared to know more than she was letting on. Gwendoline simply smiled her beautiful smile and told him to take the good life whilst it was there, and within months of their arrival it was plain that the first of their children would soon be on the way. Harriet was born without complications seven months later, and perfectly formed, to the surprise of all at the local maternity unit. They came home less than a week later, and were joined almost immediately by Gwendoline's mother and father, who became 'live-in' grandparents.

Ordinarily, this would have bothered Ray, as his own parents could not possibly take any part in their new granddaughter's early life, but Derek and Susan assured him that there would be enough time in the future to catch up. Harriet developed quickly and surprised all their friends with her early walking and talking, although the Cholmondley-Smythes seemed to take it all in their stride with disconcerting ease. Just as well as it turned out, when Harriet was joined less than one year later by her brother Jonathan, who displayed all of the same traits. They grew up into two wonderful children, and under the care and tutelage of two brilliant academics and a pair of doting grandparents, progressed in leaps and bounds through school.

It was now 2005 and the children were both in primary school and far in advance of any of their peers. Their academic progress was so fast that Ray and Gwendoline enlisted the services of a private tutor to supplement their educational needs. It was at this point that Ray started to become concerned not only at the progress of their two prodigious children, but also at the close attention being paid to them by Gwendoline's parents. It was a week later that he sat one evening and voiced his concerns to her, but she had this way of smoothing out all worries and he found himself being gently and almost hypnotically drawn away from the subject. He shook himself, returned to the matter and, for the first time ever, detected a faint look of impatience cross her face. There was definitely more to Gerald and Hermione than met the eye, and it was time to find out exactly what it was. Gwendoline heaved a huge sigh and went upstairs to her parents' sitting room.

The three of them returned downstairs and the familiar happy, smiling faces had been replaced by those of people with a mission and concerns for its future. Ray felt instantly uncomfortable, but Hermione took great pains to attempt to put him at ease with a forced smile. The story they were going to relate was about to challenge all that he believed to be true, and would set he and Gwendoline off on a lifetime's crusade of preparation. He had been chosen, they said, for his exceptional abilities in the area of propulsion systems which, together with their daughter's skills in the fields of chemistry and biology, would shape and secure the future of the human race. Gerald took up the subject.

"We are all from your future, the year 2905 to be precise, and unless what we have started proceeds as planned, the human race will cease to exist by the end of the third millennium. We have a method of propulsion far in advance of anything imaginable in your day, and this allows us to travel backwards and forwards in time. What we have seen in our future forces us to change the past in the hope that humanity will survive."

Both of them elaborated to explain the emergence of a race, not unlike Homo sapiens, which had overtaken humanity in its exploration of the Galaxy. All attempts at peaceful contact had failed, and now that these Borelians had become aware of Earth's own technological advantages, the future of the human race was becoming more and more uncertain. Matters had come to a critical point when they perfected the Fortian Drive – a means of propulsion far in advance of anything which humans had at the time. Information relating to Fortian technology had been 'acquired' but it would be decades before any significant advances could be made to stem the relentless advance of this alien race.

It had been projected that, at best, humanity had less than one hundred years left. Gerald, Hermione and Gwendoline had therefore been selected to use prototype drive modules, capable of transporting individuals, to travel back in time and implant the technology into a suitable recipient. Ray Taylor had been selected due to his unique genetic structure, and enhancements to his DNA had been secretly made in his childhood to ensure that he progressed down a chosen path. His marriage to their own daughter had been arranged to ensure that their bloodline would, by the year 2550 produce an engineered individual, or individuals capable of discovering the properties of the hitherto undiscovered element, Fortium. It was a desperate gamble, but the only one left to ensure that the human race could survive. Hermione then took up the story.

"We calculated that it would take ten generations to evolve the skills and techniques capable of discovering and developing the technology, and a further century to research and mass produce the necessary equipment. The drive and fuel would then be available to enable humans to intercept and diminish the threat before the Borelians had the opportunity to pose a significant danger. Our only concern was the disruption of any pre-existing time line, but taking into consideration our current knowledge of the situation in 2950 we believed this to be an acceptable risk."

The couple looked in silence at Ray Powell for some positive sign. Their entire future rested upon whether he was prepared to go along with what must, it had to be said, have sounded as implausible as a story out of a 1950s science fiction magazine.

"How can I be sure that what you are telling me is the truth? I mean, you could simply be a pair of dotty old escapees from an asylum somewhere."

The old couple looked at each other and moved away out of earshot. There was a waving of hands and shaking of heads, and when they returned to Ray and Gwendoline it was Gerald who spoke.

"If it's proof you require, I suggest we take a short trip together. Will about nine hundred years be enough for you? It will be quite safe as long as you do exactly as I say and we'll be back in no time, if you'll excuse the pun."

What Ray saw in 2950 removed any doubts which he had, and the events in his childhood surrounding his family's good fortune now seemed to click into place. His father's luck with the lottery win and his own uncanny academic abilities were, in truth, small parts of some larger 'cosmic' plan to protect the future of humanity. He didn't see that he had much choice in the matter but to go along with what had been started. After all, what had these 'visitors' done over the past twenty years except provide him with nothing but the best? Gerald and Hermione were asking for his help, and yet it would have been just as simple for them to take whatever they had wanted in the first place, including both of the children, if they had wished. It would have been impossible for him to explain their disappearance, together with that of his wife, to a twenty-first century police force.

Thus the wheels were set in motion for a train of events planned to culminate in the discovery of the means which would enable humanity to explore and colonise the Galaxy. In a mere five hundred years time, the human race would begin to shake off the shackles of Earth's solar system and fulfil some kind of destiny geared to ensuring its survival. The 'visitors' would monitor events over that period, but had been forbidden to make any further interventions into the evolution of their species. When the day came, on August 14th 2550, that their ancestor Patrick Forthrop made the breakthrough which would make all previous space propulsion systems obsolete, the plan seemed well and truly set. They were even in New York at the awards ceremony which saw him receive the Nobel Prize for both Physics and Chemistry in July of the following year. No-one questioned their comings and goings, and it seemed to escape everyone's attention that they never appeared to age. They were always 'just visiting'.

SPRING ETERNAL

*T*he car shuddered to a halt and, despite all efforts to persuade it otherwise, refused point blank to restart. Rob knew that he should have had it serviced three weeks ago, but decided to wait until the following month when he would once more be out of the red at the bank. Funny how these things always seemed to come back to bite you. Knowing that it would be a waste of time, he raised the bonnet anyway and gazed imploringly at the contents of the engine compartment, hoping to spot a loose wire or similar problem that could easily fixed. Fat chance! Slamming the bonnet back down in frustration he took out his mobile. He was on a weeks' holiday, never told anyone at work where he was going, and always kept his phone switched off to prevent some over-enthusiastic colleague from calling with a 'Could you just…….'

Typical! No network coverage and no means of summoning help to get the car moving again. There was no alternative but to walk to the nearest telephone or find a house from where he could make a call. He couldn't remember passing anything suitable, and he had left the main road at least ten miles back, so the only way was forwards. At least the weather was OK, so picking up his jacket and locking the vehicle he set off. There was nothing to see but open countryside, and it was miles before he came to a fork in the road. An old weathered road sign told him that a place called Barton-by-Willows was six miles straight ahead, but that a place called Mannerley House lay only one mile along the left hand branch. Perhaps his luck was changing and he may even be able to get something to eat and drink whilst waiting for a mechanic.

The road was dusty and unmade, but eventually led to a pair of impressive gates and a lodge of some kind. They were open, and a driveway led away into the distance to what looked like a manor house set in a dip in the natural folds of the landscape. He waited for the lodge keeper to appear, but then noticed that the building appeared to be empty. Looking closer through the windows he doubted whether anyone had lived there for some considerable time. Nothing for it but to walk what looked like half a mile to the house itself. The day was warm and fine, but as he passed through the grounds of what must have once been an impressive estate, he didn't notice a single living thing. There were no birds, no deer or sheep which usually populated such areas, and no workers going about their daily tasks. Undeterred, he approached the large double fronted entrance and rang the bell.

After a few minutes he heard the approach of feet echoing through what must have been an imposing inner hallway, and when the door was opened by a youngish woman, his expectations of the interior were confirmed. The room took his breath away. Its floor was made of white marble and the walls were lined with tapestries and portraits. Here and there were dotted full sets of what looked like medieval armour each on a plinth, and highly polished. The ceiling was vaulted and decorated in the finest baroque style. A gentle cough brought his attention back to the person standing before him.

"Oh, I beg your pardon, my name is Rob Foreman. My car has broken down a few miles along the road and I wondered if I could call a garage from here."

"Please come in Mr Foreman, I'm Natalie Henshaw. I'm sure that Peter can get you moving again without the cost of calling out a mechanic. He looks after all our vehicles and there isn't much about the workings inside a car that he's not familiar with. I'll ask him to tow your car into the workshop if you tell me exactly where it is."

She was charming, and he accepted her offer of refreshments while he waited for his car to be recovered. They moved on to a room which was laid out for afternoon tea, and were joined shortly afterwards by two older people whom Natalie introduced as her mother and father. He was a distinguished-looking man in his early sixties and she the typical upper/middle class wife running the house in her businessman husband's absences. They chatted generally, and Rob found himself opening up to their gentle but persistent questions. In no time at all they knew more about him than he would ordinarily have divulged to strangers. Other people, whom he assumed to be family members, arrived in ones and twos as the hour for tea approached, and without obvious command a team of three servants brought in an assortment of sandwiches and cakes along with tea and coffee.

The time, several sandwiches and not a few cups of tea, seemed to pass very quickly and Rob didn't notice at first, but a figure appeared at the doorway and Natalie went over to meet him. After a brief conversation she nodded and he disappeared. Returning to Rob with a frown on her face she sat down.

"It seems that your car is in a worse condition than you may have believed. Peter says that the ignition system is faulty and that he will need to get a spare part before it can be fixed. That will not be until tomorrow, so why don't you accept our hospitality for the night? We have rooms to spare and you can stay for dinner – it isn't often that we have guests nowadays."

Rob was disappointed, but agreed to her kind offer and asked for his bags to be brought in from the car. He was shown to a double room on the second floor, and had to admit that there were worse places where he could be stranded for the night. Dinner was informal and the numbers at afternoon tea were swollen by one or two who had presumably returned to the house in the meantime. It did not occur to him at the time but there were no children present, in fact he appeared to be the youngest person there. The meal was a pleasant occasion, and more tea and coffee was served in the drawing room afterwards. Rob found himself becoming rather drowsy and put it down to the long journey he had made from Wiltshire to the Yorkshire Dales. Not wishing to appear impolite, he fought off the feeling of tiredness for a while but gave in when Natalie remarked upon his fatigued appearance. He took the opportunity to say goodnight and retired to his room.

He passed a night full of strange dreams and was 'aware' of a number of people in the room and standing around his bed. When he awoke in the morning he had difficulty getting up and felt as if the life had been drained out of him. When he didn't appear at breakfast, a worried looking Natalie called on him and offered to send for a doctor. He told her that he had probably just picked up a cold and that there was nothing to worry about. Nevertheless, he spent all of that day in and around his room, eating and drinking from a tray brought to him by a member of the serving staff. That night, the same odd and disturbing dream recurred, and he again awoke to feelings of exhaustion. This time he conceded to the offer of medical attention and a doctor arrived during the afternoon.

An examination lasting the better part of half an hour produced nothing more than a diagnosis of acute exhaustion, and a recommendation of complete bed rest. Medical opinion was that Rob should be up and about in a few more days, which was fortunate as he would be due back at work the following week. After another night of strange images, he awoke feeling considerably better and raised the subject of his dream again with Natalie. She smiled and said that the house was reputed to be haunted, but that none of the family had reported seeing anything remotely ghostly – was he perhaps psychically sensitive? Rob doubted it but still worried about the coming night's sleep. His fears were unfounded as the mysterious figures failed to reappear, and he was back to his old self. He told Natalie that he would be leaving the following day and wished to thank everyone for their hospitality and care whilst he had been unwell. Her entire demeanour changed, and she told him that would not be possible.

He laughed, but stopped when he saw that she was serious. Several other family members had appeared, and a cold feeling of unease swept through him. Natalie's father Paul stepped forward and ushered him towards a couple of chairs by the fireplace.

"My daughter was not exactly accurate when she told you that it is not possible for you to leave. Of course you may depart at any time you chose, this is not a prison – your car has been repaired and is available at a moment's notice. Before you take any action however, you must understand that once outside the boundaries of this estate you will be fortunate to survive beyond twenty-four hours."

Rob had risen from his seat at the start of Mr Henshaw's statement, but now slumped back into the chair as the man continued.

"You see when my people first came to your world over six hundred years ago, it was purely and simply a scouting mission and we managed to blend in with the indigenous population without much trouble. We really should not have stayed long, but by the time we chose to leave, several of our party fell ill once outside the immediate area. We isolated the cause as being due to the peculiar properties of the water supply to what ultimately became the estate, and we became trapped here. We were safe as long as each of us took in daily supplies of the liquid from the spring which feeds the house, but as for leaving the grounds I'm afraid that became inadvisable."

"So why am I here?" asked Rob. "What possible reason can there be for holding on to me? Do you intend to use me as some sort of stud animal to combine my DNA with your own in the hope that it may effect some kind of cure?"

"If only it were that simple." Henshaw continued. "There is a part of the human immune system which we need in order to be able to shake off the confines of the estate, but to achieve that purpose we have been forced into a program of harvesting individual humans and draining off their blood, replacing it with equal quantities of our own. In this way we are able to replicate an antidote to the component in the water supply, and will be free to return to our home."

Rob could not immediately take in what he had been told, and sat in silence for some minutes. When the full horror of the situation dawned upon him, he realised that his dreams were nothing of the kind. He had obviously been drugged and the 'people' he saw were a medical team performing some sort of bizarre blood transfusion.

"Let me get this straight. You can't leave here, so you use the locals or whoever else happens to pass by, to manufacture a cure for your condition. These innocent people are now either dead, or worse, still living somewhere on the estate with no hope of recovery or return to their families."

Paul Henshaw looked away from Rob's piercing gaze and stared at his shoes like some naughty schoolboy caught stealing from the kitchen.

"You must understand Mr Foreman, that our people have been stranded on this world for over eight of your generations, and that their families are now long gone. Whilst we are here our ageing process has suspended, and what we are going through is more or less a living death. Your race has been searching for the Elixir of Life for many years, and dreams of longevity as some kind of biblical Holy Grail – I tell you now, this is nothing more than a curse, and it is a situation from which we are desperate to escape."

Rob stormed out of the room and left the house in search of his car. This could not possibly be happening, and the sooner he was away from the estate the better. Natalie had followed him and caught up outside the front doors.

"What my father said is true, you will die if you leave. If proof of what has been done is needed, here, stick a pin in one of your fingers and see what colour you bleed."

He took up the challenge and the blood in his veins, he could not call it his, oozed out a pale yellow. He looked at Natalie and sat down on the steps.

"That is our blood, and is perfectly compatible with your body as long as you remain here and allow the water to keep you alive. Our early experiments with the local population resulted in the deaths of all of them and the illness of a number of us. The human race was not at the evolutionary stage where its blood could be used. We have had to wait a long time but now, at the end of your second millennium the conditions are perfect. The blood we took from you will allow the final members of our group to join the rest of us and return to our world. I am sorry but that is how it is."

"So what now, am I stuck here for the rest of my life? How long will that life be? Where are the others that you have used? What in God's name gives you the right to do this?"

"There's no point in becoming agitated, what's done is done and I am sure that you would have taken the same course of action in our place. The length of your life will be indeterminate as long as you remain here, and there are nine other people on the estate in a similar position to yourself. We assume that the same conditions which made us sterile will apply to you, so there will be no descendants. You may of course wish to contact the outside world with a tale of alien abduction, but without the facility of a telephone in the house that could take some time. I am sure that certain sections of your media will be interested, but without proof of our existence your story will not last for long. The locals will, of course, have nothing to do with you as they regard the inhabitants of the estate as latter-day vampires, which we are not of course."

Reluctantly Rob accompanied her back into the house and returned to his room as final preparations were in hand for 'curing' the remaining members of their party, and he gathered that the entire group was planning to leave within the next few days. He stood by the window and gazed out at the late afternoon sun bathing the estate grounds in a beautiful golden glow. He would have many, many hours to learn how to appreciate the sights and sounds of nature as it progressed through its annual cycle, and wondered at the mental stamina of the current inhabitants of what was to become his living tomb.

BOXED IN

*T*hey would be along soon, it would all be over and he would be able to start his new life as they had planned all those months ago. He mustn't panic. That would be bad; panic always made you do things that cold, hard reason told you would just result in your getting caught. After all the time spent planning and scheming, one mad moment of panic could bring the whole thing crashing down around him. Breathe slowly and regularly, that was the key. Keep the body temperature as normal as possible and try to conserve energy for later. How long had passed? He didn't know, and in the darkness it was always very difficult to keep a reliable check on the passage of time. Still, they would be coming soon, she promised and she had never broken a promise to him before. She wouldn't abandon him now, surely – would she? No, of course not, you're becoming paranoid he told himself. Look, you're starting to panic and we all know what happens when you panic, don't we?

This had seemed to be the only way out of the financial mess, and no-one would connect the four and a half year old insurance policy to the 'natural causes' of his death. Gary Porter's business had been failing for some time, but after fifteen long hard years of trying to keep it going, he was damned if a Meeting of Creditors was going to be allowed to take everything away from him, and a heart attack wouldn't be that surprising after all the stress he'd been under. He'd won the regional Businessman of the Year award five years ago, and his picture had been in one or two of the national tabloids with predictions of expansion, flotation and wealth. How quickly things change, and how fickle the business community becomes when your ship suddenly springs a leak. He'd tried furiously to plug the financial gaps in the business with bank loans carrying punitively high rates of interest and horrific penalties for default. All that would sink with the liquidation.

He'd believed all the hype and publicity which had projected his small electronics company into the big time, and had risked everything on a dash for growth on the advice of a venture capitalist 'friend'. Odd that when push came to shove, that 'friend' was nowhere to be seen. It had been quite simple really – an injection to stimulate the kinds of symptoms associated with a heart attack, a doctor's signature on the appropriate paperwork, with a funeral and interment within the week. All he had to 'do' was sit (or lie) it out in a comatose, death-like state six feet down waiting for his resurrection at the hands of his wife and a few friends with shovels. They would come, he was sure. They would have to fairly soon before he ran out of air in his normal revived state. Mustn't panic – that would stimulate his respiratory system and use up the available air too quickly. His pulse was racing; he could hear it inside his head. Must slow that down – breathe slowly, calm down, they'll be here soon.

Mandy, his wife, was the beneficiary named on the insurance policy and the payout was in excess of a million pounds. They had planned out to the last detail what they were going to do once he was free again from his current confined situation. Off would come his beard and moustache, and a radical haircut, together with contact lenses, would fool all but his closest friends and business acquaintances. He would then slip quietly away from the area and await Mandy's arrival with the proceeds of their scam, together with the funds from the sale of their house, which had always been in her name. The company would fold, unsecured creditors being left to fend for themselves in the feeding frenzy, and the two of them would slip out of the country with the false documents he had been provided with by the friend of a friend of a friend. That was the plan.

He felt around his wrist and swore at the lack of a watch there. He always wore a watch, and gently cursed Mandy's lack of foresight in not putting one on him for the funeral. 'It was his favourite watch – he would have liked to take it with him,' she could have said. No-one could have questioned it with the floods of tears that she would have been able to turn on – heaven knows there had been enough of those down the years. Now he was lying here with no idea of how long it had been since the funeral. He couldn't hear a thing; in fact it was as quiet as the grave. He laughed out loud at his sudden humour, and then wondered if anyone would be able to hear him at the surface. Imagining the sudden scare for grieving relatives placing flowers against a nearby headstone he laughed again. No, mustn't do that, there's not enough air for unnecessary respiration. Need to stay calm, they'd be along in a minute.

He couldn't remember how long after the burial they'd agreed that it would be safe to dig him up again. Was it a day? Two days? More? What was he going to eat and drink in the meantime – bloody hell, what if he needed the toilet? Bugger, now he had an itch on the end of his nose and couldn't reach with his arms pinned down by the coffin lid – why does that always happen? Stop it, you're rambling now, stay calm, must stay calm, and breathe slowly for God's sake. Try to go over the plans made with Mandy. She promised him that they'd come and dig him up as soon as they could, but what did that mean? What if something happened to prevent her from rescuing him? What if she got run over by a bus? Oh come on, pack it in, this is sheer panic, and we've been over this already haven't we? Just stay calm and she'll be here soon, very soon, very very soon. She promised, didn't she?

He'd always fancied Barbados, and a million pounds could buy a lot of coconuts there. He could see it all now, lying there on a sun-soaked white sand beach, with crystal clear waters and a bar within easy reach. They would live in a seafront property and make themselves busy doing nothing all day long. There would be servants to prepare meals and a variety of night-life and clubs to entertain them amongst all the other ex-pats who had escaped the rat race. Very nice, and just what he needed to calm himself down. It didn't last long though. With all his senses on high alert, Gary thought he heard something. It was a very faint scraping noise, and with six feet of soundproofing above him he couldn't be sure if it was the long-awaited rescue party. He held his breath and listened. Yes, he could now hear a distinct 'thud', like a shovel being plunged into earth – there was another. There must be at least two of them, and he could envision his dear wife Mandy, standing to one side urging the labourers on. It was getting louder and louder with each passing minute, or was that just his imagination? Wait, why has it stopped?

"Come on, get me out of here!" he hissed through gritted teeth, and he could feel his pulse starting to race again.

There was still no sound - perhaps he had imagined it all. Panic was now setting in big time and his breathing was becoming fast and irregular. Try as he may, Gary could not control his rapidly hyperventilating cardiovascular system, and the temperature in the coffin was rising quickly to an uncomfortable level. He could feel the pulse throbbing through his brain, and without the slightest warning his chest was seized by a burning pain, and suddenly he was struggling for breath. He lost consciousness.

Up on the surface, the two diggers returned from their drinks break suitably fortified by the four cans of lager that they had brought along with them. Medical students had to take subjects for autopsy study where they could, and this one was going to be a treat. Still fairly fresh after burial, it would be an ideal case for analysis back at the lab, and the dons at college turned a blind eye to the practice. They had used winos and derelicts in the past, but these presented no challenge – you always knew what the likely cause of death was. This one however, had been logged as 'natural causes' and no Post Mortem had been performed; it would be a fresh case for both of them, and a valuable experience in their progress towards a career in Pathology.

It was hard work though, and they were only half way down. They would have to work quickly now to recover the body and refill the grave before morning. A 'clunk' told them that the coffin had been reached, and it didn't take long to clear the lid and open the box. Neither of them had seen a fresh corpse before, and in the dark, one body must have looked a lot like any other that they had viewed on the slabs at the local mortuary. It wasn't until they started to lift Gary Porter out of the coffin that they realised how fresh he actually was. Surely he shouldn't still be warm after days in the ground, and now that he was back on the surface the colour and texture of his skin was not the classic pale, waxy and lifeless pallor that they had been taught. With a sudden gasp of breath, Gary's eyes opened and an involuntary scream pierced the night as he realised that he was free from his prison. The two hapless students dropped their shovels and fled in terror, leaving the re-born Gary Porter standing alone and spectre-like at the edge of his erstwhile tomb.

In the approaching dawn he replaced the coffin lid and refilled the grave with amazing speed for a man so close to death's door but a few moments earlier. His clothes were remarkably clean thanks to the plastic sheet conveniently provided by his rescuers, and brushing the few remaining grains of soil from his trousers, Gary calmly left the cemetery in search of his errant wife. Fortunately for him, he had a secret stash of funds which he had always been careful to keep away from prying eyes, little thinking that the need for them would arise in such bizarre circumstances. If he found out that she had abandoned him, there would be a reckoning for her to face.

Mandy Porter was, at this time, relaxing in a seafront apartment on the Cote d'Azure without a care in the world. She had put up with Gary's workaholic lifestyle for far too long, and the failing business, coupled with his life insurance, had provided the perfect solution to all of her problems. Along with the difficulties surrounding the electronics firm had come her husband's bad temper and lack of attention; when Markus came along with his charm, wit and fabulous body the contest was over. By now, her late husband would be conveniently disposed off six feet down in a Midlands cemetery and out of her hair forever.

Putting down her Piña Colada, she turned the pages of the English tabloid which she had delivered each morning as if she had never left the UK. She nearly choked on her drink when she read the strange story of the university students arrested after admitting to exhuming the body of a newly buried businessman. The story continued that the police, after a cursory look at the site of the grave, dismissed their claims when they both tested positive for narcotics and the equipment which they claimed to have taken with them could not be found. Gary was clearly now on the loose and after her blood and there was no way, short of admitting to the crime they had committed, that she could enlist the help of any of the law enforcement agencies.

REGGIE'S REVENGE

*R*eginald Davies was thirty-nine, a bachelor and lived alone in a two bedroomed semi in Ripon. He had been there all his life and when his parents died some years back, as the only child of their otherwise uneventful marriage, he inherited the property along with the rest of their estate. He was sad to lose them, but as they had shown very little in the way of emotional feelings for him, his grief passed quickly and he carried on with what was left of the rest of his life. The inheritance and his regular job at the engineering factory provided him with a comfortable life free from the encumbrances of any romantic attachments. Whilst he did not shun the company of the fairer sex, it was clear from his demeanour that he had no real interest in them either. He was not gay, and took whatever pleasures he needed commercially, and with the proper precautions which could be expected of a man with his quiet and unassuming background.

Childhood had presented its fair share of problems for a boy of his nature. He was the recipient of more than a little bullying at school, but his lack of response together with dedication to class work had earned him the protection of his teachers, and eventually the bullies tired of trying to catch him unprepared, contenting themselves instead with the odd bout of name calling. He could cope with that, and was happy enough to be ignored by boys and girls alike – he was accustomed to such silent treatment at home. He'd had the normal range of hobbies throughout his youth but the one subject which aroused a real interest in him was ornithology. Reggie had a burning passion for the study and observation of birdlife of all kinds, and had started out quite simply with a cheap pair of binoculars and The Observers Book of Birds. Every winged visitor to the back garden was watched, its behaviour noted, and the cycle of its life as the seasons progressed described in minute detail.

He was a true ornithological anorak in every sense of the word, and was intensely proud of the fact. He became a regular visitor to the North

Yorkshire Moors, and passed many a summer holiday camped out in the wilds around Fangdale Beck or Old Byland. He was in his element, and in the peace of these surroundings was able to watch as the more unusual breeds went about their daily business. His needs were simple and usually catered for by a ridge tent, a primus stove and quantities of fresh water freely available in the unpolluted streams in the area. There had been nothing to disturb the tranquillity of this existence until the year he saw a pair of Harris Hawks in the region of Snilesworth. This was an opportunity so rare that it was not to be missed, and was his for the taking before the rest of the 'twitcher' fraternity got wind of it.

Meanwhile 'back at the ranch' and completely unknown to Reggie, another chain of events was unfolding which was to intersect with his own in dramatic fashion. At home in Ripon, two of his former school friends had been planning their own futures at the expense of a local banking establishment. Peter Harrison and Colin Jones, whilst not officially classified as 'bad lads' in their younger days, had developed into two characters of questionable integrity and negotiable loyalty. In other words they could be a couple of buggers if they'd a mind to, and they had a mind to more often than not. They weren't hard cases as such, but if an opportunity presented itself without too much effort on their part, neither of them was averse to taking advantage.

It was when they combined their talents that they presented a challenge for the local police, and the inspector in charge had long made it his ambition to put the two of them behind bars. Of all Reggie's classmates at school these two had made it their aim to inflict as much misery upon him as possible. That they failed was due more to his resilience than their own abilities.

Their current enterprise was to stage a hit and run on one of the local high street banks, late on in the afternoon to minimise the risk of being caught. They reckoned that this would also be the time when the amount of cash on the premises would be at its maximum before the arrival of the daily security van collection. If they were quick, it could be a case of in and out in fifteen minutes with all the tills emptied, no members of the public to get in the way and a fast exit on a 'borrowed' motor bike parked in the alley at the side of the building. Appropriate disguises would ensure that they could not be identified, and restricting conversation to the minimum was bound to reduce the risk of their accents branding them as locals. The bike would be dumped at the local hypermarket where Peter's car, suitably re-sprayed and with false number plates, would take them away from the district for the foreseeable future. Their ill-gotten gains could be hidden somewhere up on the moors leaving them to continue on their way to whatever destination took their fancy. It was foolproof.

Dressed in black leathers on the fateful day, with the bike engine running and Peter waiting in the alley, Colin walked into the bank with a holdall and sawn-off shotgun. It wasn't loaded of course, but it looked the business, and with a helmet and visor obscuring his face the effect, for the tellers, was terrifying. As planned, there were no customers waiting and he barked out the instructions to the three staff present. In no time at all the bag was full, the tills were empty and he was riding pillion away from the building and down the back streets towards the hypermarket car park. Progress was at normal speed to avoid attracting unwelcome attention, and a smart walk across the parking bays had them inside the 'getaway' vehicle and off up the A61 towards the moors. The whole thing had taken less than twenty minutes, and although Peter spent a nervous half hour looking in the rear view mirror, there was no sign of any pursuing vehicle. They couldn't believe how easy it had been. Now to find a spot for hiding the bag, and they turned off the A61 to the A170 at Hambleton from where the route across the moors was by unclassified road.

As they approached Snilesworth, Peter pulled up and got out of the car. Taking a good look around he suggested to Colin that the place was sufficiently out of the way as not to attract the attention of any casual holiday makers. Setting to work some fifty or so yards away from the road they started to dig a trench deep enough to conceal the large bag of cash wrapped in polythene. The excavation had been progressing for around fifteen minutes when the ground beneath them suddenly gave way, pitching both fifty feet down into some forgotten pot hole entrance. The sides of the shaft were steep and slippery, and the sheer drop caused injuries to both of them. Colin suffered a break to his right leg and Peter's collar bone had fractured as he tried to cushion his fall. Both men were in considerable pain and completely incapable of climbing out of the pit. Notwithstanding their injuries, the seriousness of the situation was not lost on them – they were in need of urgent medical attention, and the isolated location made the possibility of any casual passer-by unlikely. However, today was their lucky day.

Reggie had packed up the tent and stowed it with the rest of his gear in the car boot prior to departure, and was out on one last excursion to locate the elusive Harris Hawks when he spotted Peter's car by the side of the road. He was some distance away, and scanned the area with his binoculars before stumbling into any unknown situation where his presence would be unwelcome. He could see no activity anywhere near the vehicle, and as he got closer could hear the faint sounds of cries for help. He knew from past visits to the moors that they were dotted with abandoned mine workings and other perils for the unwary walker, and having approached the car now, saw the holdall containing the proceeds of the bank robbery. Making his way carefully to the edge of the pit he peered inside.

"Pete, look! There's somebody up there, we're going to be alright. Hey you! We're trapped. We need an ambulance and someone to get us out of here."

"Be back in a minute."

Reggie smiled to himself. He couldn't be sure but he thought he recognised the voice and its arrogant, commanding tone. He looked inside the holdall and grinned again – now he was fairly certain who was at the bottom of the hole, but felt the need to be sure before he decided upon his next course of action. Getting the torch which he always carried out of his knapsack, he shone it down on the two hapless robbers and peered at them once more.

"What's the matter?" he asked, trying to disguise his voice. He needn't have bothered, the two of them had more to worry about than the identity of the rescuer.

"He's broke his leg, and my shoulder's busted. You've got to get someone and quick." barked Peter, his short temper fuelled by the pain he was going through.

Reggie told then to sit tight and he would phone for help. They clearly had no idea who he was, as his face was obscured against the backdrop of the bright blue sky and the torch beam. He returned to the holdall, put on a pair of gloves and opened it again. A quick estimate gave him a figure of around forty thousand pounds – not enough to risk getting involved in the crime, and closing the bag again he took out his mobile. Network coverage up on the moors could be patchy at best, but he must have been close enough to a mast – the signal strength was adequate. Summoning the emergency services to the precise grid reference, he was careful not to give any personal details, but told the operator that he believed the individuals concerned had been involved in some criminal activity.

He now had around half an hour to make himself scarce. Returning to the pit for the last time, he looked down once more.

"Police and ambulance will be here in about twenty minutes, and you might want to hold on to this."

He dropped the holdall with the robbery proceeds into the hole, and amid screams of abuse, left the scene with a broad grin on his face. He could have just walked away with the cash and no-one would have been any the wiser. If the amount had been greater he may well have done just that, but the satisfaction of gaining some revenge on these two for all the treatment they meted out to him at junior and secondary school far outweighed any financial benefit. Anyway, getting caught with the cash still in their possession would make any case against them pretty watertight. It was the correct decision.

A few weeks later, Reggie read a report of the arrest in the local Ripon newspaper, and followed the trial of Colin and Peter with interest. With the facts of the current case virtually guaranteeing a conviction, the police had obtained search warrants for the homes of both of them and had recovered evidence linking both Jones and Harrison to a number of unsolved cases in the North Yorkshire area. It would be some considerable time before they were free to resume their lives outside the confines of one of Her Majesty's establishments. Reggie had never been one to look a gift horse in the mouth, but when fate presented him with a couple of thoroughbreds he was quick to take advantage of the situation. Revenge had been a long time in coming but in the end that just made it all the sweeter.

MARKS ON THE WALL

*T*he plain clothes detective sat in the lounge and looked around the room. He knew that Samuel North had killed his wife Susan. Everything was there. He had motive, opportunity, the weapon and there were enough people who knew that the marriage was going through serious problems to put the man firmly in the frame. Despite all this, Marks had nothing concrete to place North at the scene during the period that the pathologist estimated to be the time of death. If they went to trial based on what evidence was currently available he may be acquitted – hell, the CPS may not even agree to go that far, and even if they did the Double Jeopardy law would rule out any retrial on the same charge. Susan North had been shot, her body wrapped in plastic sheeting and dumped at the side of an isolated country road. According to the post mortem report she had been dead for at least two weeks.

North had married into money, becoming an essential part of his father-in-law's business, and inheriting a share of the company when the old man died. His wife Susan obtained controlling interest when her mother passed away, and became the driving force with her sixty per cent share to his own forty. Their marriage, although happy enough at first, had never been one of undying love for each other, and when disputes over the future direction of the company became more prevalent, it descended into purely a business relationship.

This suited Susan, leaving her free to explore her own social life whilst still keeping the brakes upon Samuel's ambitions, but when he found out about her affair with the tennis coach at her country club, their relations soured irreparably. Susan's golfing partner, Abigail Marshall, reported her missing to the local police when she failed to appear for her regular twice-weekly round. Susan had always been meticulous in her contacts with friends, but when Abigail's follow-ups revealed little progress, her next call was to another friend - the wife of the Chief Superintendent.

Dennis Marks received instructions from his boss to take a personal interest in the case and keep him informed of all developments. It was always frustrating when workloads were disrupted by requests from on high, but sometimes you just had to get on with it, and this case had something about it which he just could not put his finger on. Based on forensic evidence leading back to North's gun, a search warrant was obtained for the family home, and Samuel North was arrested on suspicion of murder.

The police team had been all over the house with a fine toothed comb, but nothing else connecting the place with the murder had come to Marks' attention – there was a loose end here somewhere, and he hated them. He decided to go home and review the case file in the morning. Picking up his coat he looked around once more – it had been done here, in this room he was sure of it, and all he needed was the final piece of evidence to put North away.

He was in early the following morning and well into the case file when Peter Spencer made an appearance. The detective sergeant had been Marks' right hand man for a few years, and their ability to bounce ideas off each other had led to some successful prosecutions in difficult circumstances in the past. He fetched a coffee for them both and sat down opposite his boss.

"Anything new jump out at you?"

Marks leaned back in his chair and scratched the back of his head – it was a habit he had when the blindingly obvious seemed to be lurking just out of his reach.

"No, and I've been at this for over an hour now. As I see it we have a couple of suspects, the husband Samuel North and this tennis coach – what's his name?"

"Mark Collingwood – but he has an alibi. At the time the pathologist says Susan was killed, he was in France with another one of his 'pupils', and they were there for a fortnight for some coaching. I cross-checked with the hotel manager where they were staying, and he corroborates the story."

"Well that just leaves us with North. The problem is we can't tie him to the scene. We know from the autopsy report that Susan was killed by a bullet matching the type in his gun. The gun is licensed to him and is used at the local firing range, so evidence that it was recently discharged doesn't prove a thing, and his are the only fingerprints on it. Witnesses at the range place him there regularly during the period when she was killed, but we can't pin any of them down to a time, and no-one heard any shots coming from the home at the time of death. How long have we been holding North?"

"Forty-eight hours up to last night." said Spencer, "That gives us just one more day before we have to either charge or release him. What about bringing Collingwood in again? He may be able to tell us more about the Norths' domestic situation."

"We could do; he may be holding something back. Let's return to the North house first – there's something there that I'm missing and it's driving me up the wall."

The house was still sealed off from the press and public, with uniformed officers covering front and rear entrances. Marks and Spencer 'walked' the entire property for the third time during the case, and sat down in the lounge where the DI was convinced that the murder took place.

"There's something about this room that bothers me and I can't make out what it is." he said to Spencer. "Take another walk around and see what you think."

Spencer carried out his usual routine of starting at the door and walking the perimeter of the room before ending up in the middle. Every piece of furniture and each ornament were examined for evidence, and when he sat down opposite Marks his words grabbed the DI's attention.

"Well, I'd certainly sack the decorator."

"What?"

"The decorator, anyone with the North's money would be entitled to expect a better wallpapering job than that." and he nodded over to the other side of the room.

Marks was out of his chair in an instant and at the place indicated by his sergeant. He looked back at Spencer with a broad smile on his face. The first time that had happened during the entire case.

"Look at that Peter." He pointed to a join in the paper. "Decorators start in the middle of a wall and work outwards, not the other way around. Somebody's replaced this whole drop, but it's just too wide and there's an overlap. Get forensics back in here, I want that entire length removing in one piece – let's see what's behind it."

They both sat with bated breath whilst the forensic team painstakingly removed the eight foot strip of wallpaper. One of the team turned to Marks.

"There's something here you should see, sir."

The lack of spatter had bothered Marks from the start of the investigation and now he knew why. Had Susan North been shot in the middle of the room, there would have been blood everywhere, and it would have been almost impossible for her killer to clear up the mess.

"Peter. If I am pointing a gun at your head from about six feet away, where would you go?" He raised a finger to simulate the shot.

Spencer involuntarily took three steps backwards and as his boss approached, continued until his back came up against the wall.

"Now I've got you pinned, a shot from here would only stain the area immediately behind your head. Turn around."

There, on the bare plaster was the trace of a blood stain which had been covered by a fresh piece of paper, and in the middle of the mark was a patch of filler covering a hole. An attempt had been made to clear the area of spatter, and enough had been removed to ensure that there was nothing to soak through the fresh drop of wallpaper. Marks tapped on the wall and smiled once more.

"A studded wall. I reckon the bullet will be at the bottom of the partition." He turned to the forensic team. "Let's get this section of the wall removed."

The team cut the entire area of plasterboard away for testing, and on the floor in between the studding was a blood-stained bullet. Marks put on his gloves and removed it with a pair of tweezers. Holding it up to the light he pointed out the blood and traces of flesh to Peter Spencer.

"He knew exactly what he was doing. Forcing her back to the wall reduced the spray of blood to the area immediately behind her head. He could have worked out that he would have to replace only one strip of wallpaper, or at worst two. What he failed to account for was the fact that the bullet would be lost in the partition wall, but he must have thought that filling the hole and covering the area with a fresh drop of wallpaper would conceal the facts."

"Back to the lab then?" said Spencer.

"Yes, and if forensic tests show these traces to carry Susan's DNA, North will have a hard job explaining it together with a match to his gun. We've now got him at the scene. Put that together with both her affair with Collingwood and control over the company and that's motive for murder. Good job you spotted that wallpaper, Peter."

Samuel North's solicitor was at the station when the two detectives returned late that afternoon. He was on the point of demanding they release or charge his client when Marks raised his hand and ushered him into an interview room. North was brought in from the police cells and smiled when he saw his lawyer. That disappeared rapidly from his face when Marks dropped a small polythene bag on the table. In the bag was the bullet removed from the wall in North's lounge, and accompanying it were the forensic and ballistic reports matching it to his gun and Susan's DNA. Marks inserted two new cassette tapes into the interview recorder and switched it on.

"This interview is timed at 16.05 on Thursday the 14th of July. Present are DI Marks, DS Spencer, Mr Samuel North and Mr Paul Firth, his solicitor. Samuel North, I am charging you with the murder of Susan North. You have the right to remain silent; but it may harm your defence if you do not mention, when questioned, something that you later rely on in Court. Anything you do say may be given in evidence. Do you understand?"

Samuel North sat with his head in his hands and nodded very slowly – he knew that it would be a while before he tasted freedom again.

KILLING ME SOFTLY

*T*he rain was starting now. It had been fine all morning but just when it looked as though she would make it through the day without crying, it seemed as though someone up there was sending out a message that it was alright to grieve publicly. Jane's eyes filled up, and slowly the tears cascaded down both cheeks and dripped, almost apologetically, on to the midnight blue outfit which he liked so much. If she couldn't do it, she who had lost everything that was dear to her, then no-one else had the right to. She had been Gary's only close support through years of pain and suffering, and was the last but one to see him alive, if the condition into which he had descended and subsequently recovered from could actually be called a life. The rest of the group were beginning to drift away back to their normal routines. It had been a gathering of friends and relatives, and those friends were few in number now. There had not been many others, apart from herself, who had stuck with him through the past few years, and it had been hard work.

It had all been so different when they both left home in Bristol for university, she to Manchester and he to Liverpool. Out of the sight of parents they had both taken up smoking and drinking, habits frowned upon by both sets. University life however, imposed its own set of peer pressures, and social activities consisted of a regular round of discotheques and parties. With their campuses being 35 miles apart, the only time to get together was at the weekend, and looking back there were little signs of the trouble to come which she didn't pick up on. Gary's cigarettes had given way to more exotic types of tobacco, and his periods of what she believed to be inebriation seemed to last longer each time she saw him. When her aunty Jen died of lung cancer it was enough to make her quit smoking, and as her studies progressed, the drinking went along with it.

He began mixing with an odd crowd in the more dubious areas of Merseyside, and she felt so uncomfortable in their presence that the regular visits were now few and far between. When he pressed her about it she hid behind her studies as an excuse for not seeing him so much. This, together with warnings from his tutors for persistent late work submissions, seemed to snap him out of his lethargic academic attitude, and at the end of their first year things seemed to be back on track. They got married that summer and rented a flat in Warrington during term time, leaving them both a fifteen mile journey on the days when they had classes. It wasn't long however, before Gary's Liverpool crowd tracked them down and dragged him back into his old ways. It was then that she began to notice things going missing from the flat. Small items of jewellery and a DVD player, clearly sold in order to feed a growing habit. He didn't come home one evening and Jane didn't know what to do at first.

When he failed to return for two days she contacted the Liverpool police and was told that he had been arrested for possession of a Class "A" drug, namely Heroin. To say that she was shocked would have been the understatement of all time, and Jane wondered again whether there were signs in his behaviour which she had failed to pick up on. When she saw him at the police station Gary was a mess, hadn't washed or shaved for forty-eight hours, and stank of stale beer. That he was displaying the signs of withdrawal told her that he had become more than a casual user, and his arms were starting to show the evidence of a regular habit. He was bailed to appear at the local magistrate's court and she was allowed to take him home. As a first offender he escaped with a fine and a caution, but there was now the added problem of weaning him away from the habit which was taking up not only much of his time, but also a considerable amount of his money.

Their local university GP recommended a rehabilitation clinic, where Gary could get counselling and a Heroin substitute to release him from his dependency on the drug. At first he was all enthusiasm for the program and their life returned to something resembling normality. It was when Gary realised how far his studies had slipped, and the amount of work required to enable him to successfully complete his second year, that the old craving re-emerged. His willpower didn't last very long and this time Jane noticed the changes in his behaviour which betrayed the return to dependency. The GP had warned her of this possibility, and had told her what to watch out for, but when she tried to discuss it, Gary flew into a rage and stormed out of the flat – this time he went missing for three days.

Bearing in mind his previous brush with the law, Jane decided to wait this one out, and when he returned on the morning of the fourth day she was surprised at his condition. There were none of the tell-tale signs of drug use. His speech was clear, he had recovered his temper and he had money in his pocket – all contrary to what she might have expected. He had been back to the rehabilitation clinic of his own volition, surprising considering his behaviour the week before. She was delighted and told him so – he smiled at her for the first time for quite a while. Over the next six months and as a result of a combined effort, he got back on track with his studies and just managed to squeeze through the second year without failing any of his papers. When they returned home to Bristol for the summer break it was with light hearts and optimistic plans for the future.

That future, however, would require a supreme effort for Gary when he returned to Liverpool in the autumn. Not only would he have the pressure of finals during his third year, but there would be the added problem of shaking off the crowd who had tracked them down to Warrington during the previous semesters. These were a group of down and out 'no hopers' who had fed on his weak willpower and, driven by an aggressive dealer, sought to drag him into their circle. He knew that if he slipped back into their sphere of influence he would end up on the streets, probably dealing himself to finance the habit. The past six months had seen him shake off both the Heroin and the Methadone, but that had been under Jane's close supervision; it remained to be seen whether or not he could face his demons alone.

That was then. They had from May to September all to themselves, and it would seem like beginning their married life all over again – a life that had never really got going during his addiction. For the first time in years he felt clean, and the five months away from what had become a pit of despair had reduced that memory to a locked cupboard – all he had to do now was to throw away the key. This final stage in Gary's rehabilitation faded into the back of his mind, but his awareness of it resurfaced periodically when they came across Bristol's community of drunks and addicts. These were the times when his willpower was tested to the limit. There seemed to be no shortage of either derelicts begging for money or shady characters offering little bundles for sale on street corners, but their unfamiliarity strengthened his resolve. If he could maintain this in the face of known faces back at college he would be alright.

Jane suggested they take a holiday. She had always liked the South West, and they booked into a holiday flat in Paignton just off the main promenade and five minutes from the sea front. She had spent most of her childhood holiday years there and the place brought back happy memories. Gary had never been to Torbay, and she took great delight in showing him around the area from Torquay to Brixham and beyond. They spent an entire day on the River Dart from Totnes to Dartmouth with its historic castle, and returned to their flat via the Dart Valley Steam Railway. She had no idea that this newly reborn period in their lives could be in danger of ending so soon and so tragically.

They dined out at The Inn on the Green and followed the meal with a walk along the sea front. The weather had been closing in all day, and there was now a stiff onshore wind blowing. It was strong enough to hamper their progress as they passed the pier on the way to the harbour, and by the time they reached the Yatch Club at the western end it was nearly dark. Still, the lights around the inner harbour were on, so they walked all the way to the end of the left hand arm. They heard the faint cries for help through the now gusting wind, and could see the figure of a young boy in a wet suit waving from a distance of about a hundred yards. He was obviously in difficulties, and a surf board was crashing its way over the waves out to sea. He must have misjudged the tide, and was now slowly but surely following it out into the English Channel. Jane pulled out her mobile and was turning to the wall in an attempt to cut out the noise of the waves, when she saw Gary disappear over the edge of the harbour.

He had decided to go in after the youngster and was now striking out through the increasingly heavy sea in his direction. Jane could see the progress he was making with each wave swell and held her breath as the two of them met, the boy grabbing desperately at Gary for something to keep him afloat amidst the worsening conditions. The surf board that he could have used was now long gone, and with no way of knowing how soon the coastguard would arrive, time was against both of them in their struggle for survival. Jane's heart sank with each wave that covered them and then rose with the swell which brought them back into view. The emergency services had told her that help would be there as soon as possible, and she could now see the inshore lifeboat putting out to sea from just beyond the pier. Each passing minute seemed to be an hour, and hours were not what Gary and the boy had to spare.

The little craft bludgeoned its way through the roughening swell and after what felt like an eternity, reached the spot where she had last seen two heads bobbing about in the water. They pulled the boy on board and circled round several times looking for Gary, but in near pitch dark conditions no-one else was to be seen. Jane could hardly believe it when the craft turned and made its way back to shore. She raced along the wall, past the Harbour

Light Restaurant and back to the pier. The boy was cold but safe. The boatswain of the lifeboat told her that they were unable to locate anyone else with him, and that the rescue helicopter had been called out. She waited on the seafront with the rescue crew, but no-one else emerged from the waters that evening.

Gary's body was washed up on the beach with the next incoming tide the following morning. The area was completely sealed off until he was formally pronounced as dead, and removed to the local mortuary where Jane identified him. The next few days passed by like a surreal dream, and friends came from home to help her pack up and return to Bristol. The funeral had been a quiet ceremony despite all the press coverage in Torbay where Gary had been hailed as a hero. The boy, Jack his name was, and his family made the trip to the West Country to pay their respects and Jane was grateful for their concern. 'Killing Me Softly' was played at the church. They had both been fans of Roberta Flack, and after the events of the past three and a half years it seemed somehow apt.

Now standing there alone at the graveside, with the rain coming down in a steady, persistent stream, Jane felt as if the whole of her world had been taken away from her, turned upside down and given back for her to put together once more. It wasn't until she felt an arm around her shoulder and she emerged from her reverie that the cold, hard reality of the situation finally dawned upon her. Looking around and half expecting to see Gary's smiling face she collapsed on to the shoulder of one of her college friends and sobbed uncontrollably.

SECRET LIFE

The smell was almost overpowering and it hit them as soon as they had forced open the front door of the house. Detective Sergeant Marks recognised it immediately – the smell of death and decomposition. He had experienced body discovery before, but nothing as bad as this and they hadn't even located the corpse yet. Ten years ago, as a uniformed PC, he had been called to a house on the local council estate where neighbours had reported an unpleasant smell coming from a property at the end of their street. They had noticed rats going in and out of the place and hadn't seen the occupant, a single woman in her late fifties, for some time. It had been down to him as the local bobby to effect entry and assess the situation.

You never forget the smell of decomposing human flesh once you have encountered it, but the body hanging from the stairwell by a piece of curtain wire was something which he hadn't anticipated. He ran back outside and was violently sick, retching until the pain in his stomach was almost unbearable and its contents lay on the ground for all to see. He slumped against a wall as his legs gave way, having strength only to instruct one of the now gathering crowd of onlookers to call for an ambulance and police backup. When his colleagues arrived he could not hide his embarrassment at not being able to deal with the situation, but the sergeant just patted him on the back, told him to forget it and sent him home. Standing here on another doorstep, and what seemed like a lifetime away from that incident, he braced himself for what he suspected he was about to see. Covering his mouth and nose with a wet handkerchief, Marks proceeded methodically through the house until he reached an upstairs sitting room. There, slumped backwards in a chair and surrounded by piles of newspaper, empty beer cans and the remains of what must have been his last meal sat the occupant, but what grabbed Marks' attention was the single bullet hole in the centre of the man's forehead. With no apparent evidence of a suicide they were looking at a murder enquiry.

The arrival of the medical examiner, summoned following an update of the situation to CID, provided Marks with an approximate time of death of two to three weeks based on the state of decomposition of the body. Following completion of the preliminary examination and the removal of the body to the mortuary, the scene was sealed off in preparation for a more detailed forensic examination, and Marks' team commenced a room by room search. Initial evidence revealed the man's name to be Thomas Weston, aged eighty-eight and a retired bus driver. There was no information in the house relating to a Mrs Weston, and all contents of each room were labelled, bagged and tagged for transport back to HQ.

The clearance of the house took the rest of that day and all of the following morning, and a uniformed guard was placed on the property overnight. It wasn't until the afternoon of the second day that one of the DCs reported finding more property in the back corner of the loft. It had been overlooked in the first instance due to falling darkness and the fact that it was wrapped in black cloth. Once brought downstairs and unwrapped, the contents had the CID team scratching their heads in amazement. Individually wrapped in tissue paper, and each within its own box were a collection of medals the like of which Marks had never seen before. Apart from awards from a number of high profile campaigns since the start of the Second World War, there were individual honours including the Victoria Cross, the Military Cross, the Order of Merit, the Distinguished Conduct Medal, and the Military Medal.

This man had obviously been a highly decorated soldier during one of the most turbulent times in recent history, but it wasn't until Marks came to the bottom of the parcel and picked up the final item that all his senses went on to high alert. There, in a large plain envelope was a buff file stamped in faded red letters "TOP SECRET", together with several passports and sets of ID cards. He dropped it as if his fingers were on fire, cleared the room, sealed it and called in for DI Harris, his boss. Harris arrived thirty minutes later together with some anonymous guy who bore all the hallmarks of MI5. They asked him if he had read the file, and upon receiving a reply to the negative, told him to complete the examination of the house, secure the premises and resume normal duties.

That Thomas Weston had been murdered was beyond doubt, and when door to door enquiries had been completed, several neighbours had commented on the fact that although visitors to the property were rare, there had been a middle aged man who called some weeks prior to the discovery of the body. Descriptions were sketchy at best, and no-one could agree on the type of car he used, let alone the registration number. They were all certain of one fact however, he was smartly dressed and seemed completely out of place for the area. Marks frowned after reading the reports – he needed to get back to the ME's office to find out more about the body.

George Groves had been the area Chief Medical Examiner for over twenty years, and Marks knew him to be methodical and meticulous in his work, and honest and forthright in his opinions. They had always worked very well together. The cause of death, not surprisingly, was a single gunshot wound to the forehead from fairly close range. The bullet retrieved was a 9mm and tests showed it to be from a Beretta 92FS Parabellum pistol. Striations revealed the likely use of a silencer, which accounted for the fact that there had been no reports of gunfire or similar noises from the house where Weston had lived. This was an assassination, the killing of a man in his eighties, but for what? The file removed by MI5? And what about the other sets of documents? What was going on here?

A full report from the ME's office would be available during the next 48 hours, but for now there were simply more questions than answers, and Marks returned to base to find out more from the property removed by CID and uniformed officers. He was disappointed to find that, apart from piles of accumulated rubbish, there was very little to indicate any more than the facts they already knew. The man was Thomas Weston, he was 88, lived alone, had no apparent family and kept himself very much to himself. So why kill him? There had to be more to it than this. He had been a soldier so the Ministry of Defence should have a record of him, particularly bearing in mind the number of special awards amongst the collection of medals. His initial calls to the relevant department went unanswered, and it wasn't until he contacted a friend in the ministry that a series of events started to unfold.

Marks was told that the records relating to his enquiry were not available as they had been removed from the file, and when he pushed harder a senior official told him that he did not have the necessary security clearance for any further information. Marks' instincts told him that he was on to something way above his head, but he persisted and went back to see Groves. George was not available, and one of his junior staff told the DS that an urgent telephone call concerning a family illness had compelled the ME to take an unexpected leave of absence. When he asked about the body of Thomas Weston, the same junior informed him that two officers from Special Branch had removed it, together with all items relating to the case, and he was told that no further action would be required by his department.

So there was now no body, no forensics and no records at the Ministry of Defence. When he returned to the house where Weston's body had been found, all traces of police activity were gone and the place had been boarded up – neighbours seemed to know nothing about it. Sitting at his desk back at the station he sipped his coffee as the events of the past few days replayed in his mind. He detested loose ends, and this case was littered with them – apparently the same two guys from MI5 (he assumed) had confiscated all contemporaneous notes made by officers at the scene. As senior SOCO he had not taken any – he was left with no hard evidence at all. His telephone rang and a call from the PA to the Detective Superintendent requested his presence at a meeting upstairs in fifteen minutes.

He had been up there on occasions before, but this gathering was unlike any of the previous ones. Present were Detective Superintendent Johnson, Detective Inspector Harris and a 'suit' with a briefcase. It was the 'suit' who addressed him.

"Take a seat please, Detective Sergeant Marks. I would like you to read and sign this."

He placed a document headed 'Official Secrets Act 1989' before Marks, and indicated a space for him to append his signature. The DS frowned and looked up at him questioningly. The 'suit' turned to the other two detectives.

"If you gentlemen wouldn't mind, I would like a few moments in private with Detective Sergeant Marks please."

Johnson and Harris looked at each other and then made their way out of the office. After a suitable interval the man turned back to Marks and introduced himself.

"You may call me Michael Roberts. You will not find me on any official contact list, and you may not even believe that it is my name at all, but it is not the reason for your being here. You will be aware by now that all trace of the man you know as Thomas Weston has been removed from circulation. As far as you are concerned, he never existed and any other people with whom he has been in contact have been, shall we say, 'persuaded' likewise."

Marks signed the document and listened intently as Roberts explained the penalties for breach of the 1989 Act, and also the reasons necessitating his signature. The man, Thomas Weston, was indeed a highly decorated war hero, and his name had been mentioned in a number of despatches from a variety of front lines across the globe. This, however, was not his true identity and the additional documents which Marks had not had the opportunity to scrutinise painted a different picture. It was that of an undercover operative working secretly behind enemy lines in a variety of scenarios, none of which were relevant to the police investigation.

"I am telling you all of this, DS Marks, because the documents you retrieved from the house where the body was found could have had serious repercussions for Her Majesty's Government, and the security services which protect it, had they fallen into the wrong hands. We are very grateful to you for your professionalism and expediency in the matter. They have been returned to the appropriate authorities, and we have noted your application for promotion to Detective Inspector – this will be receiving suitable attention in the coming weeks."

Marks stood up and turned to leave the office, assuming that the meeting was at an end, but Roberts held up one hand to delay him a little longer.

"There is just one further thing, I can reveal to you, off the record of course, the identity of Weston. We are alone in this office and the information will be of no use to you outside of our conversation which, of course, never happened. His real name was Gordon Marks, and should you wish to check what family records are freely available to you as a member of the public, you will discover that he was in fact your grandfather. The dates of his birth and marriage are of no interest to us and his death, should you need to check, was recorded under the heading 'Killed in Action' during Montgomery's part in the Ardennes Offensive during January 1945 – there will be nothing to arouse suspicion amongst the general public. You may wish to hold on to these though."

Roberts handed a package to Marks. The DS opened it and smiled to himself. Beyond the fact that his grandfather had lived and died, his own father had told him very little, presumably at the insistence of whatever government agency the man was working for at the time. All the war and campaign medals, together with the original individual citations, were there in a black box along with a single black and white photograph of a middle-aged man in the army uniform of a Captain. Marks looked up at Roberts and thanked him for the gesture.

"Finally, Detective Sergeant, we must never meet again, and your two superiors outside have also appended their signatures to the Act, so no discussion of any of the material facts of this case will be permitted, is that understood?"

Marks nodded in agreement, and Roberts (if that was his name) closed his briefcase and left the office. The two returning officers shuffled their feet as parting pleasantries were exchanged, and shortly afterwards Marks and Harris returned to their normal duties. Six weeks later he was called once more to the office of the Detective Superintendent, but this time there were smiles on all their faces as congratulations were expressed on his promotion to Detective Inspector. There would, of course, be relocation to another area together with a significant increase in salary and all moving expenses. The new position would be head of homicide with his own team of detectives. He was never given the location of the remains of Thomas Weston, but felt sure that his detective skills would provide him with all that information in due course. Marks hated loose ends, but perhaps there would be opportunities for tying them up in the future.

IDENTIFYING MARKS

*D*ennis Marks closed the file and smiled. Another serious criminal removed from the streets of Britain and looking at a ten to fifteen year stretch in one of Her Majesty's maximum security establishments. Since his promotion from DS to DI eighteen months ago his job satisfaction index had risen by a factor of around four. He had his own team of detectives, a budget which was the envy of every other Inspector in the division and a clear up rate which made him the area's top man. This last case had been particularly challenging, involving a triple murder following on from a serious fraud. It had taken them five months to unravel the complicated sequence of events leading to the deaths, but a combination of dogged determination, dedicated police work, a few strokes of luck and access to George Groves (the best forensic examiner Marks had come across) had finally wrapped up the case. All that now remained was to send the file off to the Crown Prosecution Service and let them do their work.

He unlocked his top left hand drawer and pulled out a brown A4 envelope, emptying the contents out on to the desk in front of him. The case of Thomas Weston (aka Gordon Marks) was still niggling away at the back of his mind. He had been given a clear hint by the man calling himself Michael Roberts that any investigation into the circumstances of Weston's death would not be welcomed, but there had been no specific instruction not to proceed in that direction. He sat, elbows on the desk, drumming the tips of his fingers together whilst he stared out of the window into the fading light of a November afternoon. Looking down at the black and white photograph of his grandfather in army uniform, he knew that he would be unable to resist the temptation to dig deeper into the man's history. He was aroused from his reverie by a goodnight call from DC Wallace, and replying in similar fashion he put the contents back in the envelope and returned them to the drawer, locking it afterwards.

During a holiday the previous summer, Marks and his wife June had journeyed to Belgium and found themselves in the town of Roermond near the German border. In a corner of the town cemetery stood half a dozen war grave memorials, one of which bore the name of his grandfather. As he stood there, he wondered just whose body was six feet down in the coffin where history recorded that his ancestor lay. It would not have been too difficult in the heat of battle for someone working covertly to exchange dog tags with a fallen comrade and simply become that person. In the confusion of one of the most bitterly fought battles at the end of World War II, Gordon Marks became just one more of the 1,400 British casualties suffered in the Ardennes Offensive. None of this could be revealed to June of course, who merely believed this to be something which her husband felt he had to do.

That was then – back in the present, Marks put on his overcoat and, before departing, left a message on George Groves' mobile, ostensibly to set up a meeting finalising the case he had just closed. He had one more call to make, and pulling a scrap of paper from his pocket, dialled the number of eighty-four year old Walter Price, sergeant in the same regiment as his grandfather during the Battle of the Bulge in Belgium in 1945. He had obtained the information relating to Walter's whereabouts from the Royal British Legion, and after assuring the old man that he was trying to track down a relative, arranged to call on him on his way home. Marks' distrust of the facts given to him by Michael Roberts compelled him to check it out with an independent source, and who better than an eyewitness?

The old man, although sprightly, was living with his daughter on the other side of town and it took Marks half an hour to reach the place. He was made very welcome, and having shown his ID card, sat down to a welcoming hot drink with Walter and Susan, the aforementioned daughter. He came straight to the point, that he was trying to locate the resting place of his grandfather and believed he and Walter had served in the same regiment in the push against the Germans in late 1944 and early 1945. Marks said he was aware that Gordon had fallen during the fighting, but that the precise location of his grave was not known. Walter frowned at this information.

"That can't be right. He survived the battle and I know that for a fact, because I saw him after it was all over. There was a lot of confusion, with units becoming separated but I'm as sure as I can be that he was still alive when Montgomery announced the allied victory."

Marks tried to look suitably stunned at the news, and asked Walter if he had any information as to what happened to Gordon afterwards.

"No idea, son. I tried to find him but you must understand that it was the duty of all of us to report back to whatever remained of our companies. After I'd done that I tried again, but he seemed to have vanished into thin air."

"So you're absolutely sure that he wasn't killed then? What about dog tags, weren't they supposed to be collected from the dead to help with identification?"

"Dog tags! Listen, if you wanted to go missing for whatever reason, how difficult do you think it would be to swap with a corpse and take its identity? Things were pretty crude in those days."

Walter's daughter stepped in at this point, seeing her father becoming agitated at the memories, and informed Marks that she believed there was nothing more that her dad could tell him. Thanking them both for their time and hospitality, he left for home where he would undoubtedly have to come up with a good line in explanation for his lateness again. Just as he was getting into his car, a call from George Groves to his mobile voicemail stopped him in his tracks. He would not go into detail and his voice sounded edgy, but he needed to see Marks at his office first thing in the morning. It was on a matter of some urgency, but a return call revealed that Groves' mobile was now switched off. The mystery deepened when he arrived home to be told by his wife that an unnamed man had called at the house only thirty minutes previously. He left a telephone number which, he said, would be manned around the clock – Marks decided to speak to Groves in the morning before taking any further action.

George Groves was one of those men who never seemed to age, no matter how long it had been since Marks last saw him, but his expression the next morning was grave and careworn. He was at the station when the DI walked in and had been there for a good half hour. Marks looked at his watch.

"You're early George. What's the matter, can't sleep?"

"Not funny, Dennis. We can't talk here – come on, we'll take my car."

He ushered Marks back through the door and round to the car park at the rear of the building. They drove a couple of miles to the Common where Groves said they should take a walk to avoid being overheard. Marks was intrigued – he had never seen George so engrossed and concerned, and was impatient to learn of the forensic scientist's information.

"OK less of the melodramatics George, what's going on?"

"You are. It looks like you're getting too close to something or someone. I got a visit yesterday when the rest of my staff had gone home from two 'gentlemen' from MI5. It could have been them who removed the body and effects of Thomas Weston after I was called away from the lab. Don't be concerned for me, there was no threat of violence, but they made it plain that your activities are causing concern at a fairly high level. What exactly have you been doing?"

Marks told him of the visit to Belgium, the churchyard at Roermond and the subsequent trip to see Walter Price. Groves had also been making his own discreet enquiries concerning the whereabouts of the body of Thomas Weston after its removal eighteen months ago, and had been down several blind alleys until he received a Home Office memo concerning the man. He could only assume that he had been copied in to the e-mailed document in error, since it was marked up as 'Confidential'. The text of the note was brief, but led him to believe that there was more to Weston than had originally been divulged. Marks took a deep breath. He needed to trust George; after all, they had been colleagues for a number of years now. They sat down on a bench.

"Thomas Weston was my grandfather. His real name was Gordon Marks and he was some kind of special agent working undercover for the government. I've signed the Official Secrets Act, so telling you this could land me in trouble. Nevertheless, you seem to be involved now anyway, so one way or another that doesn't worry me at present. I need to find out where he's buried, and it's not in Belgium because one of his army buddies swears that he survived the war. I've already had a visit from what I believe was a 'spook', and no doubt I'll be contacted again. It's up to you whether you want to pursue the matter any further, but I'm damned if I'll let them get away with burying him in some unmarked grave somewhere."

Groves sat silently throughout Marks' revelations, and taking a small envelope from his inside pocket, passed a photograph over to him.

"Don't ask where I got that but the man in the middle is, I believe, Michael Roberts. He runs an independent 'agency' within the security services, and the two men with him are the same ones who removed Weston and his effects from my department. I suspect they are also the two who cleared up your crime scene for you."

Marks put the photograph into his wallet, thanked George for his help and they went their separate ways. He called in at home on his way back to the station and handed his wife a plain brown envelope from a locked drawer in the study. He told her to post it if he should fail to return home at the normal time that day. The address was that of the editor of one of the daily newspapers – a personal friend of his. June looked very anxious and asked him what it was about, but he explained that the less she knew at this stage the better it would be for both of them. Thirty minutes later he was back at his desk going through the next set of files which had landed in his department. There was no time for any detailed review however, as a call from the front desk informed him that there were some gentlemen to see him.

He was politely requested to accompany them to a meeting with Mr Roberts, but was left in no doubt that he could not refuse. Getting his coat he informed his sergeant, Pete Spencer, that he would be out for a while but that he was expecting to be back in the afternoon. The car was fitted with tinted windows, so that it was impossible to see where they were going, and there was a screen separating the rear from the front seats. One of the men sat in the back with him, but it was clear from the outset that conversation was not on the agenda. The car pulled up about half an hour later outside a house with a gravel drive, and Marks stepped out to be greeted by Michael Roberts himself.

"Good morning, Inspector Marks, it seems that our paths were always destined to cross again. Would you come with me, please?"

They walked up the steps of a large country house and into a drawing room furnished in late Edwardian style. Marks was invited to sit down and tea was poured by a butler.

"Thank you Jones, that will be all for now."

Roberts smiled as he walked over to the coffee table and picked up his cup. He looked across at Marks and shook his head slowly.

"I understand your motives for persisting in this search for Thomas Weston, but you must let go of the matter. There's more at stake here than merely a lost relative, and unless I can find some way of dissuading you in what has become a quest, there are matters of national security which could be seriously compromised."

He walked over to the large bow window and gazed out into the impressive grounds. Pausing only momentarily he turned back to Marks who was, by now, staring at him intently.

"What will it take for you to abandon this search? I have a certain amount of influence in a number of circles and I am sure that we can come to some sort of arrangement. I see from your records that you have become one of the force's most effective detectives, and it would be a shame for such a talent to be wasted."

Marks detected a thinly veiled threat in this statement, and the change in his demeanour was not lost on Roberts.

"We are prepared, if it is your wish, to divulge the location of the interment of Thomas Weston and no-one will prevent your visiting the site. However, nothing must be left at the grave which could possibly associate him with you or any member of your family – is that clear?"

Marks nodded, sensing that he could come out of this whole matter completely unscathed if he played his cards right. There did seem to be more to the package however, and he delayed his reply choosing instead to sit back in his chair and sip his tea. Roberts laughed and at last sat down.

"We have a lot in common, Inspector Marks, and I have been watching your career with some interest. In the eighteen months since our first meeting, you have become something of a star, and certain faces high up in the force would like to see you progress further so that your talents can be used more effectively. How would the position of Chief Inspector suit you?"

Marks tried hard to conceal his clear surprise at this statement, regarding Roberts with a deadpan stare before returning his cup to its saucer. He stood up, walked across the room to one of the book cases where he feigned interest briefly. Turning quickly around he addressed Roberts.

"Very nicely if you can pull it off. I will however, require the services of some of my existing staff and one or two of them are overdue for promotion themselves."

"That will not be a problem – simply provide me with a list of their names and we have an agreement. I must reiterate though that any thoughts of you continuing your extracurricular search must stop here and now."

Marks arrived back at his office early in the afternoon and immediately telephoned his wife - he would destroy the letter himself that evening. A call to George Groves set up a late lunch at one of the local pubs where Marks brought the curtain down on the Weston matter. Groves was himself curious as to the location of the remains, and they travelled to the cemetery indicated by Roberts. Marks placed a small pebble on the headstone of Thomas Weston's final resting place and George looked at him curiously.

"Something I picked up from a friend – it means that I was here. Roberts specifically said that nothing was to be done which could link Weston back to me, but you'd have a tough job interpreting a stone as a bunch of flowers. It would be better if neither of us were to discuss Weston in public again."

At a celebratory gathering four weeks later, Detective Chief Inspector Marks, Detective Inspector Spencer and Detective Sergeant Wallace, all newly promoted, took their leave of the remainder of the station staff before commencing duties in a neighbouring division heading up a new serious crime squad. Marks smiled and wondered who exactly it was watching over his career and its sudden climb into rarefied atmosphere.

FOOTSTEPS IN THE DARKNESS

*I*t had been two years now. Two years since the facts about Thomas Weston had finally been revealed to him by the man calling himself Michael Roberts. A shadowy figure operating in the background of the security services, Roberts exuded an air of menace with the subtle smile of the predator about to consume its prey. They had crossed paths on a couple of occasions, and each time Marks had come away from their encounters unscathed, but with the uneasy feeling that he was treading upon very thin ice. Their last conversation had revealed the location of the body of Weston who was, apparently, Marks' grandfather Gordon, and Roberts' parting remarks left him in no doubt that the case should now remain firmly closed. However, he was a detective and his natural instincts told him that the jigsaw puzzle was one piece short. He had no idea what shape it was or any clue as to its colour, but it was missing, a loose end — and he hated the damned things.

He had visited the graveside on a number of occasions, and each time had placed a pebble upon the memorial. Taking the tube of superglue from his pocket he fixed another alongside those already there – glued so that weathering would not remove them, and also so that a permanent record would be made of each visit. The wording on the headstone was simple and to the point:

Here Lies Thomas Weston
Born 14th January 1912
Died 2nd November 2000
Rest in Peace

Until Dennis Marks stood back, he didn't notice the additional inscriptions which had been appended at the bottom right hand corner of the headstone since his last visit. He couldn't read the text and moved closer to get a better look. It was not in English and although he had suffered a year of Latin at school, very little of it had sunk in. Nevertheless Latin it was, and taking his notebook out he wrote it down word for word. There was only one person he could trust with the information and that was George Groves, chief pathologist and known Latin scholar. A call to his office was enough to set up a private meeting that evening. It was 8.30 when he rang the door bell at Marks' home. June answered the door.

"Evening m'dear, is the old devil at home?"

"Yes, come in, George. Let me take your coat, he's in the front room."

Groves had built up a familiarity with the Markses over the past few years, and this had developed into an easy friendship with both of them, built on mutual trust and understanding. Dennis had been compelled by circumstances to put June in the picture regarding Thomas Weston, and knew that it would go no further. They sat down to dinner shortly after George's arrival and the talk moved almost immediately to the inscription on the headstone.

"I didn't notice it last time, so there's no telling when it was put there, but here it is."

Marks passed the sheet from his notebook bearing the transcription of the two phrases and Groves put on his glasses. He studied the note for a moment and then replaced the spectacles in his pocket.

"Well, what is it then?"

"Not very good Latin I'm afraid, but the first phrase, *'Peto quod vos vadum reperio'*, roughly translated means 'Seek and ye shall find'. The second is a little better – *'Non solus es'* comes out as 'You are not alone'."

"What the hell does that mean, and why in Latin?"

"No idea my friend, but it looks to me as if somebody is trying to tell you something. As for the Latin it's anybody's guess, but probably to prevent the casual observer from suspecting anything. Anyway, you're the detective and I'm the pathologist; it's over to you I'm afraid."

They passed the rest of the evening in more general and non work-related conversation, and when Groves' taxi arrived just after 11.30 the mood was considerably lighter. After they had tidied up for the night and gone to bed, June asked her husband what he intended to do about the subject of their earlier conversation. He had to admit to being confused but intrigued by the message, and hadn't a clue how to make contact with whoever had left the inscription. Despite a pleasant dinner in George Groves' company he spent a restless night tossing and turning, with those involved in the Weston affair flitting in and out of his mind. As it turned out he didn't have too long to wait for an answer to the riddle of the Latin message.

The team had been working on the case of a young woman found in a patch of woodland. She had been robbed and strangled, and the body had been left with no identification at all. Marks was in the office early to find documents from the forensic lab already on his desk, and after a visit to the coffee machine he commenced his usual scrutiny in search of anything to point them in the right direction. His gaze was drawn to the brown foolscap envelope protruding from the pile about half way down. It was almost as if it had been deliberately placed in such a way so as to attract his attention and he withdrew it, pushing the rest of the documents to one side. There was nothing on the back or front to indicate a destination, and it was completely out of place amongst the remainder of the paperwork which bore the meticulously presented style of George Groves' department.

Uncertain whether or not to treat the package as suspicious and summon the bomb squad, he nevertheless carefully examined it and, taking a deep breath, slit the top edge with his letter opener. It contained a single sheet of paper bearing a photocopied section of a street map. There was a red cross at the intersection of Ramsey Road and Norris Street, with a message which read 'Tonight, 10.30pm – come alone'. There was no-one else in the office at that time of the morning, and the desk sergeant downstairs had not seen anyone unfamiliar on the premises since the start of his shift. Marks rang George Groves.

"George, the forensics you sent over, anything odd about them?"

"Odd, I don't know what you mean. What's wrong?"

"I don't know. Can't talk now, but I'll see you later – same place as last time."

This was a coded message of the type to which Groves had become accustomed since the death of Thomas Weston, and he knew exactly where and when to meet. The park bench was empty, not surprisingly during the winter, and guaranteed them complete privacy. Marks showed him the envelope and its contents and asked for discreet tests to be carried out for possible DNA traces, with comparisons to staff in each other's departments. Someone had clearly intercepted the batch of documents between the lab and CID, and that someone must have known of Marks' connection to Weston. Groves bagged the envelope and its contents after ensuring that no-one else apart from themselves and the courier had touched it, and told Marks that he would have the results the following day.

Back at the office, the rest of the team had assembled and Pete Spencer was conducting the morning briefing on the current case. He stepped aside as Marks entered the room, making way for his boss to take over.

"No, it's OK Pete, you carry on; I've already been through the file."

He sat down, ostensibly re-reading the forensic reports delivered that morning whilst listening to Spencer's briefing, but his mind was focussed on the message in the envelope, and the day seemed to drag as time wound slowly around to the appointment that night. The crossroads of Ramsey and Norris was marked by the presence of a telephone kiosk, and as Marks approached on foot from his car three streets away, the phone was ringing. Picking up the receiver he was greeted by a distorted and impatient voice.

"I said 10.30, it's now 10.35. Where've you been?"

"Traffic." said Marks in a matter-of-fact manner. "Who are you, and what do you want?"

"Never mind that, just shut up and listen. There's a key taped underneath the shelf in front of you. It opens a locker at the railway station. Take the contents away with you and don't hang about. Roberts is not the man you think and the contents will prove that. You are in danger and this thing is bigger than you could possibly believe."

With that the line went dead, and in the distance Marks heard the sound of footsteps receding into the darkness. The person, whoever it was, had been watching from a distance and the detective was still no closer to getting to the bottom of the Weston matter than he had been eighteen months ago. No, that was not true; he now had a key, a key to who knows what information about Michael Roberts, and there was no telling where it would lead without the contents of the locker at the railway station. He decided that there was no time like the present. Retracing his steps back to the car he headed for the town centre and one of the NCP car parks.

The left luggage lockers were at the end of the entrance hall and to the left. It was now 11.15pm and the station appeared to be empty. Marks made his way casually to the unmanned locker room and inserted the key into one of the locks. He half expected that it would not work, and a sense of nervous anticipation ran through him as the door opened to his touch. Inside was a large, plain, unmarked white envelope and looking round like some schoolboy stealing an apple, he slipped it inside his coat and walked away, leaving the only evidence of his visit, the key, still in its slot ready for the next customer. He had, of course, wiped it clean. Trying to remain anonymous, and hoping not to bump into any colleagues, he returned to his car and drove home, arriving there shortly before midnight.

He had made no attempt to examine the contents of the envelope at the station, but now in the privacy of his lounge and behind closed curtains, he tore it open. The contents took him by surprise, for there before him was the very same file which had been recovered from Thomas Weston's house on the day they discovered his body. Marks was certain of that fact, as it still bore the small cross which he had put on the back cover before handing it over to Harris and the 'suit' that afternoon. The 'TOP SECRET' stamp stared defiantly out at him as it had done before, but this time he had no qualms about opening it; after all someone had taken the trouble and the risk to put it into his possession.

The contents were old, dating back to WWII, and it was a while before the names rang any bells with him. When they did, he sat down in amazement – 'Lidice', 'Heydrich', 'assassination' and 'Ravensbruck' all flew from the pages like thunderclaps. Reinhard Heydrich was one of Hitler's closest allies and Reichsprotektor of Bohemia and Moravia. He was assassinated by Czech patriots in May 1942. Retribution was swift and brutal – of the inhabitants of the village of Lidice, all the adult males were executed, the women were transported to the concentration camp at Ravensbruck and the children were taken away to be 'Germanised'. The village was then razed to the ground. Marks had seen pictures of the place some years ago, and the whole episode was a chilling reminder of the ability of the human race to stoop to the depths of depravity. The term 'ethnic cleansing' did not exist during WWII, but its acts certainly did. This was all pretty dreadful stuff, but what did it have to do with him?

He flipped through most of the detail and came to a slimmer file relating to one Kurt Daluege. This was the individual charged by the Nazis with extracting revenge for the killing of Heidrich, a task which he carried out with enthusiasm. Apart from a brief summary of the man's military career and family history, there was nothing to connect him to the present, but Marks' attention was then drawn to three pages of handwritten notes headed up 'Ranier Guttman', together with a black and white photograph of a man in the uniform of an SS officer. He had served as deputy to Daluege at the time of the Lidice massacre, and pages one and two gave a biography from his birth to his execution after the Nuremberg Trials at the end of the war. It was not until he turned to the third and final page that Marks let out a gasp of surprise.

Guttman had a son by the name of Mannfred, born in 1940, and amid all the confusion and movement of refugees at the end of the conflict, the boy and his mother disappeared. The notes claimed to have tracked them down to Oxfordshire in the 1960s where she had married one Maurice Roberts and the boy's name had been changed to Martin.

Martin had a son who had been educated at the local grammar school, and joined the civil service where he rose quickly in the hierarchy and ended up working in the Home Office early in 1987. Marks read and re-read the name before him – Michael Roberts, and attached to the top of the page was a colour photograph which, if there remained any, removed all doubt from his mind that he and Mannfred Guttmann were one and the same person.

The consequences were obvious. If this news were to become general knowledge, the career and life of Michael Roberts would be utterly destroyed – he would surely go to any lengths to conceal it. The final and clinching fact for Marks was the signature at the bottom of the report 'Thomas Weston'. Had Roberts therefore either killed or arranged the killing of Weston to protect his own identity?

The fact that he was now in possession of the file once again, indicated that someone else had more than a passing interest in Weston. Marks decided to conceal the documents in a place known only to himself and await any further contact from the mystery caller. Things were quiet for a couple of weeks as the department carried out its work on the latest homicide enquiry, but then a call out of the blue set him back on the track of Weston and Roberts. The voice was similar to that of the night at the phone box and Marks transferred it to his private office, closing the door behind him.

"Marks?" It was a familiar voice, obviously muffled and Marks could not say definitely whether it was male or female.

"Speaking."

"Get the file?"

"Yes. I've read it several times, but what has it got to do with me?"

"The links are there, you're a detective aren't you? How can the son of a war criminal be working for the British security services?"

"What I am supposed to do, take on the whole of MI5 and MI6 on my own?"

"Roberts will know by now that it's missing and the trail will lead to you. Weston got hold of the file and was blackmailing him, that's why he was killed."

"So you are putting me in the line of fire. Why can't you do it?"

"Too close to him, and I need to stay undercover until the matter's resolved. Look, when Roberts contacts you he'll want a meeting. Specify the place, insist that he comes alone and call me on this number. It's untraceable and I'll know it's you."

The line went dead and Marks' head was spinning. How the hell had he allowed himself to get involved in this? He was a copper not a spy, and was now dealing with shadowy figures playing by rules that he didn't even know existed. The fact that he now had the file again gave him no option but to play along with the caller's instructions. He was certainly on his own now, and there was no point to be gained by involving George Groves again.

When the call came from Michael Roberts, Marks noticed a definite change of manner. His voice was hard and clearly threatening, and he spoke with a clipped tone. Gone was the friendly dialogue of their previous meetings, and his question regarding the secure nature of the line revealed his concerns for secrecy.

"I want that file back, Marks." This was the tiger stalking its prey, and it was imperative that the detective remained calm.

"I'm not surprised, but did you have to kill Weston for it?" This was a gamble, but it paid off.

"The old fool thought he could blackmail me, but in the end he had no idea who he was dealing with. Hand it over before you get hurt."

"What if I do?"

"Then the whole thing goes away, the file gets destroyed and you return to your games of cops and robbers."

This nettled Marks and he could feel himself rising to the bait. Nevertheless he stayed in control and arranged a meeting for that evening at the intersection of Ramsey and Norris as before, and for the exact same time. The irony of it was lost on Roberts if he made the connection, and the call ended. Picking up the receiver again, Marks called the mobile number given to him earlier and the response was immediate.

"Marks?"

"Yes, Roberts has been in contact. The meeting is arranged at the same place and time as before. What now?"

"I'll be in touch."

Later that afternoon, a call from the Chief Superintendent's office had him hurrying to the top floor of the building. In the room were the CS himself and two other individuals. One of them he recognised as George Watkinson, a senior figure in government circles with whom he had co-operated in the case of Philippe and Danielle Moureau. The other was a young woman who took him completely by surprise.

"Wallace, what are you doing here?" The DS from Marks' department smiled at his reaction.

"Wallace works for me," said Watkinson "I'm sorry for the subterfuge, but it was vital in the circumstances. Look, we needed you to flush Roberts out after we discovered his secret. Weston had stolen the file and Roberts had him killed in an attempt to retrieve it. He must have thought Christmas had come when you handed it back. It was Wallace who returned it to you, and now we need your help to end the matter and rid ourselves of Roberts once and for all."

Much as he disliked all this cloak and dagger behaviour, Marks agreed to co-operate. He was wired with a listening device and instructed to goad Michael Roberts into a repeat of the admission made earlier. Special Branch officers would be positioned to ensure that no harm came to him, but they had 'shoot to kill' orders on Roberts if things got out of hand.

Aware that his movements may be under scrutiny, Marks made his way home and retrieved the file. He knew that Watkinson's men would be tailing him and that he could be intercepted at any moment, but he made the location at the exact time agreed. The street was deserted and it wasn't until a further fifteen minutes elapsed that he heard a distinctive 'click' of footsteps in the darkness as someone approached from his right. Roberts stopped ten feet short of Marks and pulled a pistol from the inside pocket of his coat – it was fitted with a silencer.

"Is that the one you used on my grandfather?" Marks steeled himself at this opening gambit.

"Weston was never your grandfather. That was a ploy to keep you from digging into the real truth of what you had stumbled across, but yes this is the gun. He was an easy target once he had been located. Now hand over the file."

Marks reached into his own inside pocket and froze briefly as Roberts levelled the gun barrel at him. Withdrawing the package he reached out to his former benefactor.

"Put it on the ground and step away."

Marks placed it carefully down and retreated a further ten feet, now wondering why Watkinson's people had not stepped in to arrest the man. He was alarmed to see Roberts raise the gun a little further so that it was pointing at his forehead.

"My report will show, Inspector, that you rang me to arrange this meeting and records will be arranged to support it. This gun has no serial number and in the struggle when I attempted to disarm you, the weapon went off killing you. The only fingerprints on it will be your own, and the whole matter will be quietly forgotten – just one more corrupt policeman in a force which the public no longer trusts."

The 'pop' which Marks heard to his right, left a single entry wound in the side of Roberts' head and he collapsed to the ground. Several black-clad figures emerged from the shadows, removed the body and all evidence of the encounter, and disappeared. Dennis Marks was left standing alone as the rain started to fall, when he heard the now familiar sound of footsteps in the darkness. George Watkinson appeared before him and waved his arm towards the black Mercedes which had pulled up silently at his side.

"If you wouldn't mind please, Inspector."

In a nondescript office somewhere in the city, they sat over coffee as George Watkinson revealed the full extent of the Michael Roberts story to the bemused detective.

"Thomas Weston was never your grandfather, and that is the only truthful thing which Roberts told you in the end. Gordon Marks was a highly decorated soldier killed in the line of duty, and really is buried in the churchyard at Roermond where you and your wife found him."

"OK", said Marks, "But what about Walter Price? He saw my grandfather and swore that he was still alive."

"Money will buy the most convincing information at times, and I am sure that Roberts paid him to say that. Sadly, I cannot prove that now, as Price died six months ago from a heart attack whilst his daughter was out. Odd isn't it?"

"What about Weston?"

"A sad but ambitious man, totally out of his depth, completely unaware of who he was dealing with and the danger into which he had placed himself. He was a minor operative who had stumbled across Roberts's identity in the aftermath of the war and routinely reported it along with other information which he had collected. He later saw an opportunity to cash in, as it were, and stole the file but the gamble cost him his life."

"So that's it?"

"I'm afraid so. You have been terribly helpful, but unfortunately none of this can be officially recognised. You may, of course, rest assured that you and your family are now completely safe from harm."

Watkinson stood up, put on his coat, shook hands with Marks and left the office, the now familiar footsteps in the darkness echoing along the corridor and down a set of stairs. As Marks prepared to leave, another figure stepped into the room. It was DS Wallace.

"I'll be leaving the department to return to MI5." she said, "Sorry for all the confusion, but it really was necessary."

Marks smiled and they left the building together for the last time.

In a churchyard across town, the casket of Captain Gordon Marks was lowered, with full military honours, into its final resting place before a small crowd of family and friends. Funds had been made available by an unnamed source to relocate the remains from Belgium, and the headstone now bore the details of the man's military career together with the honours he accumulated during its progression. As the sun broke through a grey blanket of cloud, a volley of rifle shots split the air in final salute to a fallen hero.

BY THE SAME AUTHOR

"A Ticket to Tewkesbury"

An innocent-sounding love letter, discovered 45 years after it was written but never posted, sets in motion a frantic chase for a set of documents so sensitive that their impact, in the wrong hands, could bring about the fall of democracy in modern Britain.

Julie Martin, an unlikely heroine, finds herself at the centre of a struggle between the forces of good and evil, as no quarter is spared in the fight for possession of the top secret files.

The story twists and turns through a succession of scenarios as you try breathlessly to keep up with the fast-moving plot. As the drama comes to its shattering climax on the platform of Nottingham's Midland Station, you are left to ponder the true outcome of the battle between the two opposing forces.

Lightning Source UK Ltd.
Milton Keynes UK
UKOW04f0830281217
314977UK00001B/42/P